WELCOME TO JESSIE'S

WELCOME TO JESSIE'S

*A vampire, a ghost,
and a fairy walk into
a bar…*

ELI RAINWATER

Eli Rainwater Books

Copyright

Welcome to Jessie's
Eli Rainwater
Copyright © 2022 by Eli Rainwater

This book is a work of fiction. Names, characters, places and incidents are the product of the author's imagination and are used fictitiously. Any resemblance to actual persons, living or dead, events, or locales is entirely coincidental— except for the cats.

Cover photography by Juliana Finch, https://bio.site/julianafinch

Taken at Arcana Bar and Lounge
331 West Main Street, Durham NC 27701
https://arcanadurham.com

ISBN 978-1-7923-9310-5 (ebook)
ISBN 979-8-218-05342-0 (paperback)
ISBN 979-8-218-05441-0 (hardback)

Eli Rainwater
www.elirainwaterbooks.com

Acknowledgments

For Chass, who wanted to be the first to read this. I know you read it over my shoulder the whole time.

This was a labor of love that desperately needed to come out into the open, and I couldn't have done it without my friends and support system. Well, I *could* have. It just would have been a lot harder.

Thank you Dave and Erin for all the editorial feedback, Alicia for keeping me caffeinated and fed and keeping the cats distracted so I could write, and thank you most of all to Brenda for being the most amazing person I know and for letting me shamelessly use you as inspiration for Jessie.

Contents

Fae & Cryptid Index

This list consists of fae and cryptids either mentioned or who appear in the story in order of appearance:

Vampire: Cryptids that were once human, they now survive off of blood for nourishment. Vampires are supernaturally strong, fast, can fly, and can shapeshift into different species of bats at night. By day they are weak and lose their powers of flight and shapeshifting. They are obsessed with wealth and prestige. They maintain a human facade, but their true form is almost batlike with gray, leathery skin, red eyes, large pointed ears, fangs, and talons.

Succubus: No one is sure whether the succubi are cryptids or fae. They are part demon and creatures of chaos but not necessarily evil. They are extremely attractive and are drawn to physical beauty as well as intelligence. They possess great powers of seduction which they use to attract lovers or stun and subdue prey and enemies.

Gargoyle: Gargoyles are stone during the day but appear human at night. Their skin and hair are dark gray like stone.

They are some of the oldest cryptids in existence and are the keepers of the balance of good and evil in the universe. No one knows where they originated or how old they are.

Ogre: Ogres were once Oberon's Honor Guard until they disappeared right before the first cabal uprising; it was believed that they were extinct. They are over six feet tall and close to 300-pounds with grayish-green skin, humanoid faces, and horns similar to a bull's. They rampage in battle, at which point they grow to over nine feet tall, their eyes turn red, and their skin becomes diamond hard.

Werewolf: Werewolves can be born or created through a bite by a shifted wolf. They are human/wolf hybrids with the ability to change at will. Their wolf forms retain their human intelligence and comprehension, and they are larger than wild wolves. They answer to a pack leader but don't necessarily travel or live as a pack in their every day lives.

Matagot: Matagot are spirit cryptids from France who typically prefer the forms of a cat, crow, or dog. They can sometimes appear human as well. They can bestow fortune and aid to those who treat them with respect or kindness, but they can also attack or ruin those who treat them unfairly or with disrespect.

White Lady: White ladies are spirit cryptids. They are essentially ghosts of women who died through some form of violence, usually at the hand of a jealous lover or husband.

They are considered harbingers of death or doom, known to lead people to their deaths.

Puck: Old English fae, the most famous Puck is Robin Goodfellow, who serves King Oberon. The puck is a household spirit, known for being both helpful when properly rewarded for their work and destructive and mischievous when they feel they are not properly compensated with bread or milk. Unlike brownies, pucks prefer solitude.

Centaur: Greek cryptids with the body of a horse and torso and head of a human, these creatures are renowned for their wisdom, medical advancements, and fighting prowess, particularly with a bow and arrow

Kalanaro: These spirit cryptids come from Madagascar and are characterized as being small and hairy with backwards facing legs and feet. They can be nasty and mischievous, but they are also protectors of children and will kidnap children if they feel the child is not cared for at home. They have the power to protect and heal humans and typically work with a "mosie", a Madagascar medium, to communicate.

Brownie: Brownies are Scottish and Irish fae and are classified as household spirits. They are known for cleaning and cooking in exchange for compensation (usually a bowl of cream, milk, or bread; no other gifts are considered acceptable).

Nain Rouge: The Nain Rouge are North American fae from

Detroit and are hybrids of French dwarves or goblins and Native American spirits. They are said to be omens, appearing before disasters and with the power to strip fortune or luck from humans when attacked or antagonized. They are the same shape and size as dwarves but with red eyes and a disheveled appearance.

Tuatha de Danann: Pronounced (tooth du dahnahn). The original rulers of Ireland, they are the predecessors of the Aos Sí. They are tall with red or blonde hair and blue or green eyes and worship the Goddess Danu. They were driven underground by humans where they lived in the fairy mounds known as the sídhe.

Naga: The Naga are Hindi and Buddhist cryptids that are part human, part cobra. They can work on the side of good or evil, depending on how they are treated. They live in an underworld realm and are very wise and usually considered to be benefactors.

Kitsune: Japanese fox spirits that originated in China as the huli jing, the Kitsune could be classified as fae. They can appear as beautiful women or men or as a fox, and they grow a new tail every hundred years until they have nine tails total. Their coats change from red to gold to white as they age. They possess magical abilities and great wisdom.

Banshee: Celtic fae, although there is speculation on whether they are actually cryptids, banshees are harbingers of death. They are always women who scream or wail to foretell the death of a member of an Irish family and are solitary creatures. Reports of their physical appearance vary.

Hobgoblin: Celtic household fae, they can be helpful when rewarded, but mischievous, spiteful, and destructive when they do not feel appreciated. They love playing pranks and are related to pucks and brownies as well as goblins.

Pixie: Small, winged fae with a tendency toward theft and mischief. They have pointed ears and teeth. They are flighty and easily distracted, but they can be helpful when treated with kindness.

Ghoul: Arabian fae who haunt battlefields and cemeteries, ghouls feed on the dead, especially those who die violently. If summoned, ghouls will single-mindedly hunt their prey, and if their prey escapes, they will devour those who summoned them.

Werepanther: Cryptids who can be created through birth or a bite from a fully shifted panther. Werepanthers travel in claws and have a leader, although they are not pack-like. They are great fighters, playful, and tend to keep to themselves.

Lamia: The original Lamia is a Greek cryptid who was one of Zeus' many victims. She was a beautiful Libyan queen, but after Zeus became enamored of her, Hera, in jealousy, forced Lamia to kill her own children. As Lamia went mad, she began to steal and eat other women's childrens until she became a monster, snakelike and bestial and living in shadows.

Leprechaun: Leprechauns are Irish fae, believed to be descended from the god Lugh, who was the god of the sun, arts, and crafting. Known to be skilled craftsmen, they tend to be solitary. They can be kind and helpful, but they are tricksters and can be malevolent. If captured, they can be forced or persuaded to grant three wishes.

Fir Darrig: The Fir Darrig (pronounced "fear dare-ig") are Celtic fae. They are characterized by a ratlike appearance, red coats and hats, and living like rats. They are generally looked down upon and considered to be malevolent, but they can provide aid and protection when treated with respect.

Nisse: A Norse fae similar to a brownie, the Nisse is a household spirit who takes the form of a small, old man and has one eye in the center of his forehead. They offer aid and assistance in return for payment.

Huldra: Norse fae in the troll family, the Huldra have the form of a beautiful, seductive woman with a cow's tail and sometimes hooves in place of feet. Her back can be covered in tree bark or hollowed out. They are forest spirits, but they can help humans when they so desire. They can also be malevolent and deadly when they choose. The males, or *huldrekall*, live underground.

Keiju: The Keiju are Norse fae. They are very small with beautiful wings, and they have the form of beautiful humanoids. They are shy by nature, but they will warm up to humans and dance around them.

Peikko: Peikko are Scandinavian fae who are related to trolls and ogres. There are two types of peikko, hill and field. The field peikko lives in forests and often appears as an ugly, human man wearing clothes made out of bark. They are very strong and can't be defeated alone, but they are willing to provide assistance in return for aid or favors.

I

"No one will ever love me again. I shall die alone with naught to mourn my passing."

Jessie MacCaverty stopped wiping down the bar top to raise an eyebrow at the chestnut curls belonging to the adorable and devastatingly handsome yet extremely annoying, melodramatic vampire who flounced through the door in a swirl of early autumn air and leaves before dramatically collapsing on a stool in front of her. Her bartender and apprentice Caroline rolled her blue eyes before going back to pouring beers for the amused regulars at the other end of the bar.

"Get your head off the bar. I just wiped that spot," Jessie tucked a long, silver-gray curl behind her ear, completely unsympathetic to her friend's plight, whatever it was *this* time.

Nicodemus shot up on the stool, outrage and wounded betrayal reflected in his honey gold almond shaped eyes. The younger of two vampiric siblings, he was as beautiful in death as he had been in life as a long dead king's military advisor and member of a noble family.

"You! You who are supposed to be the one I hold most

dear, the most treasured of my bosom companions, have you no mercy on my poor soul? My wounded heart?"

"Not when you start talking like the bastard child of a Hallmark card and Harlequin romance, I don't." Jessie was extremely unimpressed-- and unsympathetic.

"So be it," he huffed, slumping back down to prop his elbows on the oak bar top that had been lovingly polished over the decades until it gleamed forever. "Take away my poet's soul. See if I care."

Jessie beamed. "See, isn't that better? Now, do you want a drink while you calmly and sensibly tell me what's going on without all the histrionics?"

He scowled before relenting. "Fine. But none of those weird, fruity, sweet things the kids are drinking everywhere! Those colors should never have been put into anything consumable," he shuddered in disgust.

"Caroline, make him a Manhattan, will you?" Jessie called over her shoulder.

"Sure thing, boss," Caroline replied cheerfully, tossing her long, blonde, curly ponytail over her shoulder as she deftly flipped a martini glass over and grabbed the bottle of rye.

"You really lucked out with her," Nicky commented as Jessie poured a glass of sweet tea and came around the bar to grab the stool next to him. She had to agree.

Caroline was a brilliant and highly motivated young woman whose witching powers would probably rival Jessie's own. When she decided to seek Jessie out for training, she showed up at Jessie's bar every day for two weeks until Jessie relented.

Jessie is a witch. Not just any witch, mind you; she's the

strongest, oldest, and best known in the state of Georgia and one of the most talented in the world. It had been years since she took on an apprentice. She didn't have anything against it-- she just liked the semi-retirement of being able to run her little bar and stand in for matters involving the supernatural community when they arose while helping her neighbors when they needed help without any complications.

Caroline, and then Jared after her, had not been in her ten year plan, and now she wouldn't give them up for anything.

Nicky studied Jessie as she settled down next to him. She was tiny. Long gray curls framed a slightly oval shaped face, high cheekbones, and huge, piercing blue eyes. She lived for broken in jeans and obscure band or bar t-shirts that were so soft and well worn, they were one stitch away from falling apart. Like all witches, she stopped aging in her mid forties and was eternally in that stage of beauty when the laugh lines enhanced the late summer glow of youth.

"Now. What happened this time?" she asked, settling in for the long haul.

He heaved a melancholy sigh that sounded like it came from his toes. She resisted the urge to follow Caroline's eye-rolling example.

"I thought I met the one. He was so perfect. The gargoyle of my dreams!" Jessie choked on her tea.

"I'm sorry, the *what* of your dreams?"

He looked affronted. "Gargoyle! I told you about him last week!"

Jessie barely managed to hide a guilty look. To be fair, when he started on the love interest *du jour*, it could get a little... repetitive. It wasn't her fault if it was easier to tune him out and concentrate on inventory. Bits and pieces of his hours-long recitations of adoration started to come back to her.

"Oh, right! *That* gargoyle!"

Jared, Jessie's other apprentice and barback, a tall, young man with impeccable style and skin the color of dark chocolate and who had lined up a promising career in role playing game production, stopped with the ice bucket in midair to stare at Nicky.

"Dude! How does that even *work?*" He demanded, fascinated. Jessie heaved an internal sigh of relief because she really wondered the same thing and couldn't figure out how to ask without exposing herself as a confidante fraud.

"Well, if you *must* know," Nicky drew himself up haughtily, "Gargoyles are only stone by day when they revert to their... less attractive but more widely known visages."

"So, what, at night they're hot?" Sometimes talking to Jared was like talking to the blunt side of a hammer and about as subtle.

"If you must put it that way, yes, they can be. Are. Usually are." Nicky would have blushed if blood pumped through his veins. Jessie realized that he hadn't fed recently. He must really be enamored with this guy.

"Did he ghost you?" Caroline asked with a sympathetic glance. "No offense, Charlie!"

"None taken." Charlie was the bar's resident ghost. When Mary Jo Sutton, who was still the town's most beautiful and seductive succubus at the age of fifty, had propositioned him in the bathroom, he had neglected to mention that he had a heart condition. He swore the resulting heart attack was worth it. She still felt guilty about the whole thing.

"Ghost me? Ghost *me??*" Nicky was stunned, floored, flabbergasted that anyone could even consider such a thing. Jessie gave in to the urge to roll her eyes. Trying to hold back was exhausting.

"Focus!" she slapped her hand on the bar harder than she planned and instantly regretted it. "Where were you supposed to meet?"

"Well, here, tonight actually. I wanted him to meet you."

Jessie blinked at him.

"So you're telling me that you just waltzed in here and immediately went into hysterics without even bothering to see if he was here first? I mean, we're not exactly balls to the walls over here, but it's not like we're dead either! No offense, Charlie."

"None taken," Charlie replied with a burp. One of Jessie's neatest (in his opinion) little pieces of spellwork involved creating a mug that acted as a portal that gave whatever it contained the ability to exist on the spiritual plane. At the moment, that happened to be beer. No one was entirely sure if the belching was necessary, but not even Jared was willing to ruin Charlie's contentment by asking and possibly ruining the experience.

Nicky looked faintly abashed. "I don't see him though! That's understandable, right? I mean, I even came late on purpose!"

Jessie dropped her head in her hand and shook it with the long suffering patience of one who realized a long time ago that their friend genuinely did not have a clue how personal relationships should go.

Caroline stared at him, flipping her ponytail over her shoulder again with a scornful little toss of her head. "So you sent someone none of us know in here, and then you came late on purpose because, let me guess, you didn't want to look like a lost puppy checking out the door every five seconds, and it never occurred to you that maybe he got tired of waiting and left?" For such a perky blonde, Caroline could turn scathing at the drop of a hat.

Nicky squirmed on his stool.

"Well... it *seemed* like a good idea at the time. But he didn't stick around, so it doesn't matter! And besides, I was only about fifteen minutes late!"

Jared shook his head as he walked toward the back to put away the ice bucket.

"Man, even I know better than that, and I can't keep a girl around to save my life. No offense, Charlie."

"None taken," Charlie replied with equanimity. He had never realized how many turns of phrase involved life or death until he himself switched from one side to the other.

"Hey, Jared, check the bathroom for trash and toilet paper on your way back, please," Jessie called before turning back to the matter at hand.

"Admittedly, I don't really remember seeing a stranger hanging around tonight. What does he look like? And what's his name? Also, have you tried calling him or do you have a picture, she asks, knowing that of course you didn't, you just immediately broke down into hysterics and started talking like you came off the cover of the best selling romance novel of the decade?"

Now Nicky rolled his eyes. Jessie felt herself get twitchy as she resisted the urge to pop him on the arm.

"I do not talk like that," he protested.

"Well, no, not when you remember what year it is," Jessie replied. Nicky pulled out his phone.

"His name is Warsaw, and unfortunately, I can't take a picture. Gargoyles turn into stone in front of a camera," he showed her a picture of him kissing a stone... lion? dog? on the cheek while gazing coquettishly at what was obviously a phone camera perched at the end of a selfie stick.

"You carry a selfie stick? Of course you do. Why do I even ask?" She snorted in amusement.

Caroline snickered, grabbing the phone,"You're such an adorable couple! Do you think your kids would have your eyes or his density?"

"Ha ha!" Nicky glared as he snatched the phone out of her grasp. "You're so funny." He tried-- and failed-- to regain some control of the conversation. By this point, Caroline was giggling uncontrollably, and Charlie laughed himself through his stool.

"Okay, okay, let's calm down," Jessie grinned. "Try to call him. See what happens."

"Fine, if it will get you all to stop cackling like a pack of hyenas," Nicky huffed as he hit a button and held the phone to his ear.

"Wait, did you hear that?" Caroline switched from hilarity to alert in seconds. Jessie was way ahead of her.

She met Nicky's eyes with a growing sense of dread. Out

of nowhere, a phone had begun to ring, a muffled sound that could only come from behind a closed door.

At the same time, they heard Jared's scream and the thud as he fell over backwards, scrambling away from the bathroom. Inside was a lifeless body that once belonged to a shy, love struck creature who had, for one brief, shining moment, thought he could have everything his heart, which would never be stone, had ever longed for and found in the deep, deep love of a whimsical, sometimes overly dramatic, slightly narcissistic vampire.

2

It took the sheriff's department less than ten minutes to get there, but it felt like ten hours.

"Thank you, John. I'll have Cassie go over the security footage to see if she can get anything useful out of it," Jessie murmured to Sheriff John Rossford as he followed the shroud covered gurney out the door and to the waiting ambulance.

Nicky was in shock. For the first time in the centuries since his and Jessie's improbable friendship had formed, he was silent. He sat in the corner staring at the wall with empty eyes as if officers and techs weren't milling around marking, measuring, and painstakingly plucking unidentifiable things from the floor into small plastic bags sealed with caution tape.

Caroline came around the bar to Jessie, her blue eyes full of concern.

"What should we do? I'm worried about him," she whispered to Jessie. Jessie swallowed the urge to point out that whispering was pointless in front of a vampire since their senses were dialed up to fifteen.

"Keep an eye on him, will you? There are some blood bags

in the cooler. Maybe heat up an AB negative and see if he'll drink it. I'm going to make a phone call."

Caroline nodded and hurried away. Jessie sighed as she pulled out her phone and scrolled through the contacts.

"I just hope he picks up this time," she muttered under her breath as the line started to ring on the other end.

"Hello?"

Her relief at hearing the faintly accented, urbane voice was palpable.

"Hey, Mikael, it's Jessie. Do you have a minute?"

"Jessica! How delightful to hear from you! It's been too long. How is my rapscallion of a brother?"

"It's good to talk to you too. Nicky- I mean Nicodemus- is actually why I'm calling. Something happened, and I wanted to get your take on it"

Mikael chose to ignore the diminutive of his brother's name (honestly, why would anyone want to shorten such a fine, upstanding name like Nicodemus? It was baffling!) and instead replied,

"Of course! Anything for our favorite witch. What's going on?"

Jessie sighed.

"His lover turned up dead in my bathroom. He hasn't spoken a word to anyone in over an hour." She raised a questioning eyebrow at Caroline, who stood by Nicky, helplessly holding a steaming mug filled with red liquid. Caroline frowned and shook her head.

"He's even refusing to drink. I've never seen him like this."

The silence on the other end grew heavier before Mikael answered.

"I see. Yes, that is unlike him."

It's not that Nicky's lovers had a tendency to turn up dead, although when you fall for a vampire, there are some inherent risks. While he genuinely cared about and mourned every ended relationship, regardless of whether or not the other party was still alive-- or whatever passed for alive, he could shift through the phases of a broken heart with enviable speed. The standing pool around the bar put him between forty-eight and seventy-three hours of recovery time. But with those phases came a good amount of crying, moping, declarations that he simply could not go on; there was almost a script.

"Do you need me to come there?"

Jessie felt some tension go out of her shoulders at the idea that maybe she wouldn't have to circumnavigate this strange, new Nicky alone.

"If you have time. I know you're pretty busy with the FCWH alliance talks."

The Fae, Cryptid, Witch, and Human Alliance (or "fick-wah", as Jessie and Nicky liked to call it behind Mikael's back) was instrumental in creating the Cohabitation Act designed to ensure equal rights for all groups and outlaw hunting and persecution. As one of the oldest vampires in the world, Mikael took his responsibilities as ambassador very seriously and sought to help the emissaries from each group broker peace among the various races, species, and alignments that populated the continent.

Jessie, who was glad she and her best friend Greta had long ago shunted the roles of representative and head of the Witch Council for the witching community off on their close friend

Isabel, sometimes let the Alliance hold informal get-togethers at her bar whenever emissaries visited Atlanta. Usually only the fae and cryptid representatives showed up. The humans were trying, but it was hard to overcome centuries of distrust and persecution on all sides.

Before Mikael could reply, Jessie's phone beeped. She was surprised to see the sheriff's office on the caller ID.

"Hold on a sec. The sheriff is calling. I'll be right back," she didn't wait for a reply before switching over.

"Hey, what's up?" She asked, trying not to sound too worried. Maybe he just forgot something, but when the sheriff is a werewolf with a damn good nose and eye for detail, that's not likely.

"Hey, Jessie. I got something to run by you," he said, trying to sound nonchalant and failing miserably.

"Sure, what is it?"

"Well, I picked up a scent I couldn't place around the body, and it kept niggling at the back of my mind, so I rushed the prints when we got back to the station."

"Okay, and?" she asked.

"I just got them back."

Jessie waited while the silence grew and strongly resisted the urge to see if she had the power to come through a phone line and shake the person on the other end.

"Sheriff, what--"

"I don't know where Nicky found this kid, but this is big, Jessie. Your boy is the head secretary for the Western European cryptid representative, Madame Blanche."

Jessie sat down with a thud. Luckily she managed not to miss the bar stool and wind up on the floor.

"What did you smell?" she asked.

"What?" he sounded puzzled.

"You said you smelled something that made you rush his fingerprints. What was it?"

His voice turned grim. "Acid. Our tech is pretty sure it's either hydrochloric or nitric, but either way, they're both used to dissolve rock. I gotta do some more digging, but I can't imagine many other ways to kill a gargoyle."

"Okay, keep me posted if you find anything else. I'll take a look around and see if I can figure out what the killer might have used or when and where this happened."

"Thanks. We don't know a lot about gargoyles, so it's hard to tell if he was killed somewhere else and dumped there or if he was attacked in your building. And Jessie-- be careful," he warned. "Anything that can kill a stone is going to be extra lethal against flesh, no matter who or what you are."

"Understood. Thanks, John." Jessie switched back to Mikael who patiently waited on the other end.

"We have a problem. You need to come here now," she said without preamble.

"What is it?"

"Nicodemus' lover was Madame Blanche's head secretary."

She heard the sharp inhale of breath on the other end, her mind pausing to marvel that a creature that did not have to breathe could still make such a gesture.

Madame Blanche, an affectation to try to help people forget that she was the *de facto* ruler of the *Dames Blanches*, or the White Ladies native to France, had been the target of splinter cells among the cryptid community ever since she assumed her position among the Alliance and fought to bring cryptids into the open.

Not everyone was happy with the change. Humans were inherently distrustful of what they couldn't understand, a large number of cryptid and fae feared humans and witches and wanted to stay invisible, and the witches never forgot the not so long ago witch hunts. Jessie and Greta themselves had been leery of coming out of the shadows and never really stopped looking over their shoulders for the pitchfork and torch laden mobs.

"I'll be there within the hour," Mikael's tone was sharp. "Meanwhile, try to get Nicodemus to eat something. Call me if anything changes."

"You got it," Jessie replied before ending the call and absentmindedly shoving the phone in a pocket.

For a prominent cryptid leader's secretary– who was romantically involved with the brother of one of the leaders of the alliance– to wind up dead in a witch's bar that was frequented by local humans, the fae, and other cryptids was sure to raise a few eyebrows and point even more fingers, regardless of Jessie's reputation. She needed to get to the bottom of it and fast.

Jessie sighed, wincing as she tried to massage a knot out of her shoulders. It had been a long night. Mikael had finally convinced Nicky to go home with him, and she had started the arduous task of cleaning up behind the investigators and looking around on her own. The sheriff's CSI crew had been pretty thorough, including taking all of her trash and going over the entire bar with a fine tooth comb.

Her best efforts to scroll through social media turned up very little, probably due to the fact that gargoyles don't photograph well, so she had turned to news searches, which weren't much better.

Her own security cameras were no help. They showed Warsaw walking in the bar and going straight into the bathroom (the fact that gargoyles turn to stone on camera made for an interesting display) and then nothing until Jared passed down the hallway to get ice about twenty minutes later. So either someone had the power to turn invisible, or someone had tampered with her cameras. Unfortunately, either option was possible.

"Hello, hello!" a cheery voice called out along with tinkling from the bell over her front door.

"Oh, hey, Cassie," Jessie waved to the young human woman headed her way.

Best known for her sharp mind, Cassandra Rodriguez's skills with technology made her an invaluable asset. She had worked tirelessly to insulate and rewire cell phones, cameras, everything Jessie needed short of building an actual computer, hence the old fashioned cash register still in use behind the bar. Being able to work with technology without shorting out everything with an electromagnetic field was one of humanity's greatest advantages, and Cassie chose to use her talents to help the local magical community.

"So... anything new?" Cassie asked in what was probably the least subtle fishing attempt ever as she played with her long, thick, black braid. As if everyone in a town this small didn't already know that something bad went down last night. Jessie shot her an exasperated glance.

"Whatever would make you think there's anything new?" Jessie asked.

"Oh, come on! What happened? We saw the sheriff's department and ambulance lights. Did the succubus get someone else?"

Jessie took a deep breath to get her temper under control.

"That's enough, young lady!" Charlie popped up out of nowhere, a faint reddish tint coloring his normally translucent incorporeal form. "That was an accident, and you know it! Mary Jo didn't do anything I didn't ask for, and if you can't handle that then maybe this isn't the place you should be."

Jessie winced. On the one hand, it was great hearing

someone else say what she thought. On the other, business wasn't booming to the point that she could afford to pay some outside firm even more money to modify and maintain her equipment.

At the same time, Jessie felt a twinge of sympathy. It was no secret that Cassie had a thing for Jared. It also wasn't a secret that Jared and Mary Jo's daughter, Ruth Ann, had hooked up ever since Ruth Ann began to come into her own powers.

"Sorry, Charlie," Cassie said, abashed. "You're right. That was uncalled for."

"Hey, while you're here can you take a look at something for me?" Jessie asked, in a very obvious attempt to change the subject.

"I guess," Cassie's voice was subdued.

"You're right, something did happen last night. You'll find out eventually, so you might as well hear about it now. Someone was killed in the bathroom. The weird part is we can see the victim go into the bathroom but then there's nothing until Jared walks by about twenty minutes later. I can't tell if someone messed with the camera or not. Can you take a look?"

Cassie couldn't pass up the opportunity. Her insane curiosity was legendary.

"I suppose, since I'm already here," she said, trying to sound offhand, as she followed Jessie to the office.

"What am I looking at-- is that a moving *stone?*" her jaw dropped. Jessie sighed and pinched the bridge of her nose against the headache she felt coming on.

"Yeah, apparently Nicky's been dating a gargoyle, he sent

the poor guy in here alone to meet everyone and then showed up late on purpose so he wouldn't look– I don't know, I guess he didn't want to look like he was waiting for someone, but Warsaw-- that's the gargoyle-- tried to go into the bathroom, and the moving stone is what happens when a gargoyle is caught on camera."

Cassie stared.

"Okay, so skipping past whatever made Nicky decide *that* was a good idea, what happened next?"

"Well, nothing. Jared comes by a little later to grab ice, then I send him to make sure the bathroom's stocked, and that's when he found Warsaw who was already dead."

"Poor thing," Cassie murmured. "Let me see the rest of the footage between when he goes in the bathroom and when Jared finds him."

"Knock yourself out," Jessie replied, turning the mouse over to the other girl.

Charlie disappeared back to wherever he stayed these days, which was probably a good thing. He was still fond of Mary Jo, and what's a little death between friends with occasional benefits? Still, she made a mental note to see if he could detect any residual... something from Warsaw's death after Cassie left. It occurred to her that she had a golden opportunity to learn what ghosts could and could not do for posterity and had not taken advantage of it.

"Hey, Jessie! Take a look at this!"

"What'd you find?" Jessie turned back to the screen.

"Well, we can rule out someone messing with the camera," Cassie told her. "The pseudo magnetic field you generate as a witch guarantees that anyone who tried to mess with my work would have shorted everything out since it's all tuned to your magic signature. It could have been a shapeshifter, but even something as small as a bug would have triggered the motion sensor," she pointed to the green bar at the bottom of the screen that remained serenely still, showing no movement.

"So that leaves invisibility. But there's no such thing as true invisibility by disappearing. You become invisible by bending the light. So if I do this," she tweaked a dial, and the screen suddenly shifted into shades of white, orange, and red, "we have ourselves an infrared heat signature! Someone slipped into the bathroom ahead of Warsaw-- probably so he wouldn't suspect anything when he tried to shut the door-- and then came out again when Jared opened the door."

"Can you see what they did next?" Jessie asked.

"They walked to the front door and slipped out in all the commotion."

"Damn! So we can't see who it is at all."

"No, *you* can't," Cassie sounded smug.

Jessie raised an eyebrow and waited for Cassie to finish delighting in her own cleverness. Cassie caught the look on Jessie's face and cleared her throat before continuing.

"Sorry! You know the QuikTrip next door? I did their security system. George Dunn, the owner, comes in here all the time. I bet he'd let us look at his cameras and see if anyone shows up."

"Great, let's go!" Jessie took off down the hall, Cassie on her heels.

Unfortunately for their investigation, they were stopped short at the front door when a vampire came through followed by a fairy, a very pale woman, and a giant cat, and who, from their appearances and the looks on their faces, were clearly members of the supernatural community, very important, and very unhappy.

"Well, fuck," Jessie said, coming to a dead stop.

Jessie and Cassie were face to face with a strikingly handsome, gray eyed vampire whose long, raven black hair was pulled back in a top knot.

He hated the term man bun. Jessie and Nicky used it often.

Mikael was impeccably dressed in a slate gray bespoke suit over a royal blue button up shirt open at the neck that complimented his slim, athletic build. Everything he wore complimented his build. Vampires focused on the more materialistic aspects of life, but the brothers took it to a whole different level.

Next to him stood a tall, slender, extremely pale woman wearing a simple but elegant pale green sleeveless sheath dress, suitable for an afternoon at a place much nicer than Jessie's small town bar, and cream colored kitten heeled pumps with only a fire opal on a delicate gold chain around her slender throat for jewelry. Her long, silver blonde hair hung loose except for some intricate braiding at the temples.

Behind her was a fae puck who hovered slightly off the ground and dripped dust everywhere. He wore a wrinkled black suit with an untucked shirt and looked like he had rolled out of bed and into the first thing he could find on the floor.

A very large black cat, probably the size of a wolfhound, brought up the rear. He looked her up and down, clearly passed some sort of judgment on her faded t-shirt and ancient but perfectly broken-in jeans, and offered her an extravagant yawn that practically reeked of amusement.

"Um, Jess, I'm just gonna go do that thing we talked about," Cassie nervously edged past the group and flat out ran out the door, leaving Jessie to face them alone.

"Jessica! So wonderful to see you!" Mikael came forward and offered her his hands.

She plastered a very fake smile on her face as she met his eyes and glared daggers. He winced.

"Please accept my apologies for not calling ahead. We were in the neighborhood and decided to drop in for a quick drink."

Which was Mikael for "these are very important people, please don't start an international incident."

"No, no! What a simply *delightful* surprise! I'm thrilled! I can't *wait* to share my joy at this moment later!"

Mikael winced harder. The puck looked like he had just walked into the most disgusting pig sty ever created. The woman looked almost as amused as the cat. The cat jumped on the bar, found the sunspot coming from the old cut glass windows that lined the walls, and promptly passed out. Jessie swallowed a sigh and pulled away, walking to the bar to greet her guests.

"Welcome! It's a delight to host such esteemed guests. Please enjoy my hospitality freely under no obligation or compulsion."

The puck looked like he wanted to be anywhere but there.

"We'll see," he sniffed, his accent placing him somewhere around Wales.

"Jessica, this is Robin the Puck, Oberon's ambassador to

the United States," Mikael gestured with a slight bow. Jessie inclined her head. As a witch, particularly one as old and powerful as she was, she was not under any obligation to bow or otherwise indicate that she owed fealty to any member of the magical, cryptid, or human communities, but it didn't hurt to play nice.

"And this is Madame Blanche, emissary of the cryptid community to France," Mikael's tone took on a guarded note. Ah. So Madame Blanche must already know about Warsaw.

"*Merci pour votre hospitalité, mademoiselle*," Madame Blanche inclined her head in return. "I welcome the opportunity to speak with you further."

"And this," Mikael now sounded annoyed. He did not like things that didn't fit into neat, little packages. Sometimes Jessie wondered how he ever became such close friends with a pair of witches, arguably the messiest and least predictable of the magical tribes.

"Is Rupert, Madame Blanche's companion." He gestured to the cat who flopped over onto his back and dozed off while taking up half the bar for sunbathing.

Jessie stared, unable to keep the surprise out of her voice. "Forgive my curiosity, but is he a *Matagot*? I've never heard of them traveling outside of France or had the pleasure of meeting one."

A Matagot could probably be best described as chaotic neutral. Spirits that preferred the shape of a black cat, although they weren't opposed to being a raven, fox, dog, or whatever else struck their fancy, they could bring evil or good depending on how they were treated in return.

"Why, yes!" Madame Blanche sounded pleased. "He is very

helpful in my travels and is an excellent companion. I understand that you helped with the effort that saved them from near extinction."

Rupert twitched an ear in acknowledgement of the praise.

"Yes, I did along with our dear friend Greta," Jessie nodded to Mikael. "Okay then! Can I offer any of you some refreshment? Food and drink may be freely enjoyed in my establishment with no obligation, trickery, or attempt on your person or life be it physical or otherwise."

"I doubt that," Robin muttered, squinting at the nearest stool, running his finger along the seat, and squinting at it in disapproval.

Jessie chose to ignore the blatant rudeness. It was not normal, of that she was certain. The local faery population had its ups and downs, and some could be as snobbish as the next person, but an emissary representing the king of all Fairy was expected to behave with aplomb. That he chose not to verged on insupportable. To call him out without more information certainly would be. Madame Blanche did not share Jessie's reservations.

"Unlike others in my party, I accept your offer in all the grace with which it was given and am grateful for your undoubtedly delightful hospitality," she said before sliding onto a stool in front of Rupert. Rupert granted his approval by opening one eye and purring, a deep, rusty thing that made the bar vibrate. Robin scowled but didn't say anything. He dropped onto a different, presumably less offensive stool and glared.

"I don't suppose you have any decent white wine," he sniffed, clearly without any high expectations.

"Italian or French? There's a lovely Vernaccia I picked up in Tuscany which is delightful for a fall afternoon, and this White Bordeaux from the Pessac-Léognan region is a bit rich but quite nice."

Robin scowled. Mikael hid a smile, and Madame Blanche openly grinned.

"Robin, stop being such a little pest," she said before turning back to Jessie. "I would love the Bordeaux, *s'il vous plaît*. My rather grumpy companion will have the Vernaccia."

"My pleasure," Jessie replied, pouring the wine and passing the glasses over the bar. Robin, of course, inspected his glass minutely, looking for something wrong. She wondered how much longer she would have to put up with this.

Madame Blanche rolled her glass between her fingertips before taking a sip.

"Quite lovely, my dear," she approved. Robin scowled but didn't say anything before draining his glass in one swallow. Jessie stared at him blandly without offering a refill. She had fulfilled her obligations as host and wasn't going to cater to this little prick any longer than she had to. Picking up on her mood, Mikael (finally!) spoke up.

"Well, this has been lovely," he beamed as if they had met for a stroll through the park instead of the murder scene of one delegate's secretary while enduring the rotten attitude of the other.

"We still have many more fascinating people to meet. Robin, perhaps you would like to be introduced to the leader of the local fairy Court?"

"I highly doubt it," Robin muttered under his breath but stomped out the door anyway. Jessie let out a huffy breath.

Madame Blanche shook her head. "Honestly, I don't know what's going on with him. He's never been like this before. It's as if he's a completely different puck."

Jessie frowned. "Is that normal? I must admit I've never heard of pucks or any of the fae going through personality changes like that. I kind of wanted to hit him over the head with a bottle."

"You wouldn't be the first on this trip," said Rupert in a gravelly, rusty voice, making Jessie jump in surprise.

Madame Blanche chuckled and took another sip of wine before sobering.

"I apologize for our unexpected visit. You must know why it was necessary," she said, looking up at Jessie with grief-stricken eyes.

"I do, and I'm so sorry," Jessie replied. "All we know so far is that he came to meet Nicky- that's Nicodemus, Mikael's brother- and was... killed," she winced as she said the word, "in the bathroom. The sheriff, who is an excellent werewolf," here Rupert sniffed in disgust but didn't offer any comments after Madame Blanche shot a glare in his direction, "found traces of acid on the body. They sent them to a lab, but they're pretty sure it's either hydrochloric or nitric-- something used to dissolve rock."

She put Robin's glass in the sink and wiped down the bar, a gesture that came more from habit than necessity.

"We can't see anyone else in the hallway when he went into the bathroom on our cameras, but Cassie-- that's the girl who was with me when you came in and handles all of my tech support-- used a special setting on the camera to pick up a heat signature. I was about to go next door to see if their cameras had anything from the parking lot and then send it to the sheriff when you got here. That's all we know right now. I'm sorry."

Madame Blanche was silent for a moment.

"I see," she said as she reached for the fire opal pendant at her throat and rubbed it between her fingers as if the stone somehow gave her comfort. "And where is my dear Warsaw now?"

"At the coroner's office. I can take you to him if you like," Jessie offered.

"Yes, I would like that. Thank you for your hospitality. Rupert? Are you coming?"

It hadn't occurred to Jessie that the giant cat would just hang out and sleep on the bar.

"I suppose I must, to make sure nothing has been bungled," he yawned, showing off razor sharp teeth and a raspy pink tongue.

"You're too kind," Madame Blanche said dryly. "Shall we then?"

"After you," Jessie gestured toward the door, grabbing her phone and keys and hoping they would all fit in her little ancient Prelude.

4

If the sheriff was surprised to see a tall, pale, almost translucent woman followed by an enormous black cat come through his door, he didn't show it. He tipped his hat.

"Ma'am, Jessie, uh—"

"Rupert," Jessie piped up.

"Rupert. What can I do for you folks? I assume you're here about your friend? I'm sorry for your loss, by the way."

"My, how civilized for a... canine," Rupert muttered.

"Behave," Madame Blanche admonished him with a quick frown. Jessie considered pointing out that some Matagots preferred to appear as big, black dogs and then decided to let it drop. Rupert chose to ignore them all and groom a front paw.

"Sorry we didn't call ahead, John," Jessie said. "Madame Blanche wanted to see... him, and I have camera footage for you."

"No worries," the sheriff pushed himself up from the desk. Tall and stocky with a shock of sandy blonde hair, angular face softened by a neat if slightly unruly beard, and hazel eyes that turned liquid gold in his wolf form, he moved with a quiet, animal grace. He led the local pack, and Jessie had always counted him among her favorite people.

"Follow me," he headed out the door to the elevators leading down to the morgue.

Rupert yawned and stretched before following the rest of the group. As they entered the elevator, his mien of lazy indifference dropped, and he became as alert as if he were on the prowl. Sheriff Rossford shot the big cat a glance of approval.

"Glad y'all are here. Kind of stumped on this one. All we found so far are the trace hints of acid, but we haven't gotten the results back on what kind it was."

"Does it matter? We know that someone intended to kill my dear Warsaw for reasons we do not understand," Madame Blanche's voice was tight around the edges.

"Well ma'am, if we know what kind it was then maybe we can narrow down where it came from or who made it. Jess, what did you get on camera? I thought nothing showed up."

"Yeah, turns out Cassie has something called an infrared setting on my cameras? She made a copy for me to give you."

"What did she see?" he reached for the thumb drive Jessie pulled from her bag.

"The hall looks empty, but the infrared picked up a heat signature that ducked in the bathroom before Warsaw did and left when Jared opened the door to check on supplies. Then it slipped out the front door in all the confusion. Cassie's asking the owner at the QuikTrip next door if he'll let her see if his cameras got anything. They pick up part of my parking lot."

"Good. Do me a favor and tell her to get in touch with

me as soon as she's done. You can give her my cell phone number."

"Yes, sir!" Jessie snapped a salute and ignored his eye roll to send Cassie a quick text. "I told her to send you the recordings."

"Thank you. Greatly appreciate it."

The doors opened to a blast of cold air and the heavy smell of chemicals and decay, something Jessie always thought about whenever she came across the phrase, "smelled like death". She took a deep breath and noticed Madame Blanche do the same. Interesting. Did white ladies, who were essentially part of the ghost world, need to breathe? Then Jessie noticed the tightening around the emissary's mouth and realized Madame Blanche was trying to keep herself under control.

A wave of sympathy washed over Jessie. By all accounts, Madame Blanche was kind and attentive to everyone who worked for her. She took personal interest in her employees' lives and believed that if they were happy and fulfilled at home, then they would bring that same energy to their work. It would be so easy for someone in her position to abuse power, but she never had.

"Right this way," the sheriff gestured toward a table at the back of the morgue. Jessie could see the misshapen form under the sheet.

"I need to warn you, this will not be pretty. Gargoyles revert to their stone form once rigor mortis sets in, and the acid did its job well. If we hadn't gotten to him as early as we did in time to get fingerprints and photos of the crime scene, we wouldn't have been able to make a positive ID."

Jessie felt Madame Blanche tense next to her. "It'll be okay," she murmured, gently touching the other woman's shoulder.

Madame Blanche grimaced.

"If you say so," she replied. "Let's, how you say, 'do this thing'."

Whatever Jessie thought she was expecting, nothing prepared her for what she saw when the sheriff unceremoniously pulled the sheet off the table. If she hadn't seen Warsaw's body firsthand, she never would have known that he was the same creature as the misshapen, twisted, corroded lump of stone on the table. If she squinted just right, she could see where there *might* have been a face and maybe some arms.

Madame Blanche couldn't hide her gasp of dismay.

"No! Oh, my poor Warsaw! What have they done to you?"

"Sheriff, I don't understand. If he was hit with enough acid to cause this much damage, why did he look... well, normal when we found him?"

"The corrosion didn't spread from the outside, Jessie," the sheriff grimly replied, hoping she got his meaning so he didn't have to say the awful truth out loud. She stared at him in horror, realization setting in.

"Oh Goddess, no," she covered her mouth with her hand.

"Yeah. 'Fraid so," he shook his head. If the corrosion didn't start from the outside, then that only meant one thing. Warsaw's murderer had forced him to drink enough acid to eat through solid stone all the way to the surface of his body.

The silence was broken by a thud as Madame Blanche hit the floor in a dead faint.

5

The atmosphere at the bar was subdued. Jessie stared at the water rings on the bartop as she absentmindedly spun a glass of sweet tea around her fingers while Rupert watched with a narrow eyed gaze. Madame Blanche had returned to her hotel to recover from her shock.

"So tell me about this Nicodemus," he said in his raspy voice.

"Hmm? Oh," Jessie shook herself out of her reverie. The horror she felt at learning how horribly Warsaw died had not abated. Who would do something so unspeakably cruel? From all accounts he had been a sweet, quiet, intelligent young gargoyle who never hurt anyone.

"Well, he's one of my oldest and best friends. I love him dearly, but he can be a bit... flighty. Warsaw was the first time in a very long time he truly fell for someone. This hit him hard," she said, feeling a rush of guilt as she realized she hadn't checked on him since Mikael took him home.

"I see," Rupert's voice, though even, still somehow managed to sound threatening. Jessie stared at him.

"Wait. Do you think he's responsible for this?" she demanded.

"I'm simply covering all the bases, *ma cherie*," Rupert began grooming his tail. Jessie swallowed her anger and frustration and tried to remind herself that the French contingency didn't know Nicky like she did.

"How long had they known each other?" he asked, pointedly ignoring her irritation. She squinted, trying to remember all of Nicky's love-stricken ramblings.

"A few months. Nicky's an artist, and he had a gallery opening in New York. That's where they met. Apparently Warsaw hates-- hated-- Nicky's favorite piece, and they argued over coffee and wine for hours before ending up in France at the Louvre for two weeks so Nicky could make some artistic point or other. Nicky fell hard. Like, really hard. Believe what you want, but he would never resort to something this cruel or underhanded to get rid of a lover. The term 'ghosting' was made with him in mind."

"Well then," Rupert stretched and yawned, pink tongue curling between his fangs. "It seems we must look elsewhere for the culprit."

He was interrupted when Cassie burst through the door.

"I got George to let me take a look at the footage--" she came to a dead stop at the sight of a black cat the size of a large dog on the bar. "Is that a *Matagot?*" she exclaimed in disbelief, forgetting that Rupert had been there when she and Jessie ran into the delegates earlier.

"Rupert, this is Cassie. Cassie, Rupert. Rupert is Madame Blanche's associate, and Cassie is my technological guru."

"Nice to meet you," Cassie sketched a little bobbing curtsy.

"*Enchanté, mademoiselle*," Rupert regally inclined his head.

"You were saying about George?" Jessie nudged Cassie back on track.

"Oh, right! So yeah, he let me look at the camera. I got something, but I don't know how much it will help. I could see the door open, and then at the edge of the parking lot a guy suddenly showed up. He was all dressed in black, and I couldn't see his face. Here, I recorded it for you."

The three of them huddled around Cassie's phone and watched as a man in a black hoodie and black pants with his head down appeared out of nowhere, holding his wrist and shaking violently before vomiting in the grass. Jessie frowned. Rupert looked at her.

"Interesting reaction. Perhaps an aftermath of adrenaline?" he suggested.

"Maybe, but that's also what it looks like when a human comes out of a witch's spell, especially anything transformative. The stronger the spell, the stronger the reaction," she explained. "See how he's holding his wrist? He may have had some kind of talisman that let him stay invisible as long as he needed to be– probably that bracelet he's wearing. Unlike a spell that's directly cast on a person, talisman spells don't have a time limit. They last until all of the power stored in them is used up. We need to get this to the sheriff."

"You do it," Cassie said. "I'm going to go back over your cameras and see if anyone matching his general build has been around here lately."

"Good idea," Jessie shot the girl a quick, grateful smile.

Rupert jumped off the bar, somehow making no sound whatsoever despite his size. "I believe I shall accompany *mademoiselle* Cassie. I might be able to help our young friend here identify our mystery caller. Should my companion feel up to leaving her hotel room, please be so kind as to let me know."

"Of course. Yell if you find anything."

"'K, see ya!" Cassie was already halfway down the hall, Rupert padding along behind.

Jessie shook her head as she grabbed her phone and dialed the sheriff's number from memory while mentally kicking herself for shrugging off Mikael's painstaking attempts to school her in politics.

The factions that made up the world's population existed in kind of an uneasy truce. Because none of them were stronger than another, a balance had to be maintained, much like the cardinal corners and elements. Within each group were races, species, and creeds who all had unique specializations and skills. Some were nocturnal, some diurnal, some crepuscular, some were stronger in summer or fall, others in winter or spring, and all had strengths and weaknesses.

Fae were pure magic and had the strongest illusions. Most had humanoid forms with otherworldly features, sharply planed bone structures, cat eyes, and delicately pointed ears, and they all possessed the ability to manipulate and mold the perceptions of others, a skill known as glamour. Iron burned them, and they were technologically inept.

Witches were creatures of nature. They drew on leylines for power, and each witch was attuned to an element that was the base of their power. They were technological disasters; their natural magnetic fields wiped out pretty much everything they came in contact with that wasn't witch-proofed.

Cryptids were by far the most complicated of the factions. Made up of an enormous plethora of creatures from around the world, they could exist in day, night, any time of the year and had more strengths and weaknesses than one could count. The many species that made up the cryptid family were still being cataloged, and Jessie felt that it was an undertaking that could go on forever. As far as anyone knew, their one uniform weakness was metal, especially silver, followed by iron, and they could not perform magic beyond the instinctive magic that fueled their transformations and defenses.

And humans were hardly at the bottom of the totem pole. Capable of advancing technology at lightning speed, humans were more innovative, inventive, and ruthless than the rest of the factions. Their ability to handle all metals also gave them an advantage.

Mikael had been instrumental in forming the alliance, but its hold was tenuous at best. Despite the seeming peace that encompassed the world, there were factions within factions who believed that they shouldn't be part of any world order. Some, especially among the more shy and lesser known cryptids and fae, wanted to be left alone to live out their lives in peaceful obscurity, but dangerous others among the witches, cryptids, fae, and humans alike felt that maybe they were the superior species after all. It was pretty obvious to Jessie that the attack on Warsaw was political, which made tracking down the guilty party even harder.

The sheriff's voice broke through her musing. "Hey, Jessie, what's up?"

"Hey, John, I'm about to send you the footage Cassie got from George at the QuikTrip. She found something. It's not much to work with, but we might have our killer. We can't see his face, just his back and a hoodie. It's all circumstantial," she sighed in frustration. "We're checking the rest of my camera footage to see if anyone who looks like him from the back could have been at the bar lately."

"Gotcha. Can you put it on the thumb drive you gave me earlier for me? I just grabbed lunch, so I can be there in a second."

"Sure thing," Jessie said, glad that Cassie was still there.

"Great, see you in a little bit," he hung up without waiting for a response.

"Well, that was a waste of time," Cassie remarked as she walked back in the bar with Rupert on her heels. The big cat jumped back onto the bar and started grooming himself.

"Apparently Nicky has a goth fan club. Our killer could be any one of about twenty guys, although based on height, I think I have it narrowed down to three. We need a way to narrow it down further."

"Well, let's think," Jessie said, staring thoughtfully at the bar. "We know they're probably human. Any fae or witch can cast their own illusions or transformation magic, and cryptids are immune to transformative magic."

"I didn't know that," Cassie was surprised. "Even if it was something that cloaked them without changing them?"

"Yes. Because cryptids have their own instinctive magic, any outside magic just bounces right off with the exception of Fae glamour."

"Why aren't they immune to Fae glamour?" Cassie asked curiously.

"Because Fae glamour is defensive," Jessie explained. "It's

part of the checks and balances of the magical world. We all have ways to defend ourselves through either immunity or defense. Cryptids also don't usually have that kind of reaction when they shapeshift. But one possibility is a magical force field that doesn't directly cloak them. Hey, Rupert, can I borrow you for a minute?"

Rupert glared at her out of emerald green eyes. "If anyone else had been killed, I would scratch you to bits for even suggesting such a thing. I will allow it just this once."

"Aw, thanks. Just for that I'll buy you the best tuna I can find."

"I will accept nothing less than sushi grade. What must I do?"

"Just hold still and let me see if this works."

Jessie moved behind the bar and dug around until she came up with a piece of string. She gathered her magic as she drew on the love and energy imbued in the old wooden bar as she walked past. She whispered the suggestion that the string would like to provide a field of invisibility to its wearer and clinched her fist around it to seal the spell.

"What are you doing?" Cassie asked, leaning forward to watch more closely.

"I'm drawing on the power in the bar to fuel the spell. See, all objects have some kind of energy, and the more an object is around the living and used by the living, the more power it holds. The fae use the ether and universe as the source of their magic, but witches use the elements and objects on earth," Jessie explained. "I use the energy from the bar all the time when I do small things around the place. The building itself is a wealth of energy, and there's a leyline beneath the property. Greta gifted the bartop itself to me when we were finally able to openly be witches. She had the wood cured and treated with fire to enhance my fire magic."

"What's her element?"

"Earth. It's great for healing, creation, and defense, and fire is usually used for attacks, purification, and energy," Jessie replied. "Fun fact, I actually don't drink alcohol. Neither does Greta. It dulls our magic, but Greta still used to bartend as a front so we could sell our herbal compounds, potions, and elixirs. Now I keep the bar going, she does research for the Witch Council, and this is our home base."

"I wish humans could do something special," Cassie sighed, leaning her head on her hand.

"Don't sell yourself short," Jessie told her. "Humans are far more innovative and inventive than the rest of us. Plus, you can handle things like iron and silver pretty easily, and you can use and develop technology in a way that we can't. Do you think I could keep this place running as well as I do without you? A witch who can use a cell phone and look at security cameras is practically unheard of."

She carefully tied the string around Rupert's paw and tapped it three times to release the spell. Nothing happened.

"Do you feel anything?" she asked.

"I itch," he snapped, ears going back. She pulled the string off his paw.

"I suspected that might be the case. The magics must be conflicting with each other. Well, at least now we know that the killer is almost definitely human. Of course we can't rule out deception, like a witch who didn't want me to pick up on his magic signature."

"What are we not ruling out?" Sheriff Rossford asked, removing his hat as he walked through the door.

"We're pretty sure the killer is human and probably one of the kids hanging around looking for Nicky. He tends to generate his own fan club, even when he's in the middle of nowhere. Oh, Cassie, can you get the QuikTrip footage onto the thumb drive for the sheriff?"

"Way ahead of you," Cassie held out a new one. John carefully tucked it away in a pocket. "Here, I already have it up on my phone if you want to take a look."

"I'd appreciate that," he replied. He watched in silence, frowning. "Not much to go on. The jacket looks generic. The bracelet could be something, maybe the source of the spell?"

"That's what I thought too," Jessie agreed. "It looks like he's pretty tall based on the cars he's standing by. Hard to get a feel for body shape though. Half the kids who come in here looking for vampires wear black jeans, black boots or shoes, and black hoodies like that."

"Can you show this to Nicky and see if he has any ideas?" John asked. Nicky's flightiness was legendary, but Jessie knew that was a carefully cultivated persona. In reality, Nicky saw every detail and heard every snippet of conversation and filed it all away in the infinite vaults of his eternal mind to use as he saw fit.

"I plan to tonight. If anything, he might recognize the bracelet. It's the only unique thing we have to go on," Jessie said.

"Well, at least it's something. I'm going to get this back to the office and see if any of my techs can pick up any more details. Thanks, Cass. Good work," he tipped his hat to Cassie as he headed for the door.

She beamed, "Oh, it was nothing."

Jessie smiled. "He's right, you know. I didn't even think about the QuikTrip. Do you think there's anywhere else around here with a camera we can take a look at?"

"I don't know, but I'm going to find out. I love Nicky too. Not as much as you, obviously, but he's my friend, and I'm gonna help him," Cassie set her chin with stubborn determination as she swung her bag over her shoulder, scratched Rupert behind the ears-- something Jessie never would have dared to try-- and headed out the door.

"Don't say a word," he warned as he closed his eyes and dozed off again.

"I wouldn't dream of it," she grinned, grabbing her phone to call Mikael and Nicky and wondering what Caroline and Jared were going to say when they showed up for their shifts in half an hour to find a giant black cat stretched out over half the bar.

6

The sun had been down for about an hour when Mikael and Nicky walked in the bar. Nicky looked... flat. His normal vivacity and spark were gone. Jessie's heart twisted for her friend as she made a mental vow to make sure whoever hurt him and Warsaw this much would pay. From the looks on the faces around the bar, she wasn't the only one. He came straight to her, and she folded him into her arms.

"I'm sorry, sweetheart," she murmured, stroking his shoulder-length curls. He clung to her fiercely, never saying a word. She met Mikael's worried eyes over Nicky's head. He shook his head and turned away, but not before she saw the same flash of rage streak across his face.

Nicky pulled away. "What do you want me to see?" he asked. She hadn't told them a lot over the phone.

"We got footage at the edge of the parking lot of someone who looks like he's shaking off an invisibility spell. He's probably human. Do you think you're up for taking a look? See if it's someone you know?"

"Sure," he absently ran his hands through his hair. She realized that he was disheveled-- emerald green silk shirt partially untucked over tailored jeans but no belt and no jewelry, nothing like the carefully made up and costumed playboy persona he usually wore. For some reason, that made her rage flare again. This time he saw it in her eyes and reached for her hands with a sad, little smile.

"It'll be okay, Jess. I'll get over it. Promise."

She gave him a helpless glance, wanting to sit down and cry. Instead she pulled her phone out of her pocket and pulled up the footage from the parking lot before she handed it over to him. His brow furrowed as he watched.

"The walk and height are familiar," he said, handing the phone back to her. "A new kid who started trying to talk to me about a week ago. I never got his name."

"Did anything else ring a bell? The bracelet maybe?"

"No," he shook his head. "I'm sorry."

Jessie sighed and hugged him to her again.

"Grab a drink. There's someone at the bar who wants to meet you if you're up for it."

"Yes, Mikael told me. I guess I might as well get this over with." He squared his shoulders as he turned to the bar where Rupert and Madame Blanche waited, not trying to hide their curiosity and impatience.

Madame Blanche had changed into a black linen pants suit over a crimson chemise that created a stark contrast to her pale skin and hair, which she had twisted into an elegant knot. The fire opal and a pair of onyx and gold stud earrings were her only jewelry.

Robin had graced them with his presence too, bellying up to the bar and cutting ahead of several customers to loudly demand a bottle of wine, which he then chugged. His suit looked worse for the wear. His behavior baffled Jessie. The fae were renowned for their exquisite manners and grace. Robin was something out of left field, and she didn't like it.

She looked over the bar. In one corner, Charlie and Mary Jo Sutton cozied up despite his lack of a corporeal body. Mary Jo, like all succubi, found intelligence as stimulating and sexy as anything physical, and her interest in Charlie did not end with his death. Jessie suspected that was why he still hung around.

Meanwhile, her daughter, Ruth Ann, flirted outrageously with Jared, whose handsome face and athletic build kept him at the center of attention for quite a few of Jessie's regulars. Cassie glowered at the two of them from a few seats down, nursing something a vile shade of pink that Caroline had put in front of her sympathetically.

Caroline had never said anything, but Jessie had been around long enough to see that her apprentice had her own unrequited crush going too. Men may swoon day and night over Caroline's homecoming queen good looks, but she only had eyes for Cassie.

Tug, the ogre, stood impassively at the door. He was an enigma. Jared had just walked in one day with fire in his dark brown eyes, torn clothing, a cut on one arm, and Tug in tow and informed Jessie that Tug would be working for her and was interested in renting out the small apartment over the bar. Jessie, who knew Jared well enough to know that there had to be a damn good reason and he would tell her when he was ready, decided to trust his judgment. Tug had proven to be a very neat and respectful tenant and employee.

The funny thing was that ogres were supposed to be extinct. She planned to get to the bottom of that later.

At the far end of the bar, not far from where Mikael and Nicky talked to Madame Blanche in low voices, were the vampire groupies who inevitably showed up wherever vampires were known to frequent. Jessie and Caroline called them the vampies. Mikael and Nicky didn't find it as funny as they did.

Dressed all in black with pale skin and hair dyed everything from cotton candy pink to jet black, they desperately wanted to be turned or loved by the creatures of the night. Most vampires just ignored them until the attention became too intrusive or obnoxious. Then the vampires would give the kids a reason to run away-- usually screaming. Mikael pointedly ignored them. Nicky had a tendency to lead them on until he became bored, much to Jessie's and Mikael's annoyance.

This was the group she paid the most attention to, looking for anyone who seemed overly attentive to Nicky. Unfortunately, that included more than half of the kids who were there that night. Cassie gave up trying to glare Ruth Ann to death and came over to where Jessie stood.

"What do you think? I figure at least four of them could be our guy."

"Yeah, I know. I need to go be a good hostess. Is there any way you can be on goth camera patrol? Maybe if we can get him-- or her-- walking away or can pick up jewelry, like bracelets, then we can find out who did it."

"Goth camera patrol?" Cassie asked, amused. "Sure, I'll do it over here from my phone."

"Thanks, Cass. I appreciate it," Jessie paused. "Wait, your phone? You can do that? Can I do that?"

"I mean, yeah, if you want."

"Well, yeah, if it's going to help, then it would be smart, right? I might as well learn how to make technology work to my advantage."

"Okay, I'll set it up for you. Now go schmooze, or whatever it is you do."

Jessie rolled her eyes at her friend before moving toward the bar.

"Ah, Jessie. It is quite delightful to see you again, *ma cherie*," Madame Blanche smiled. "Darling Nicodemus has been quite obliging. It means so much to me to hear another speak so of dear Warsaw. *Merci beaucoup*."

Nicky inclined his head and raised his glass in a toast, but not before Jessie saw pain shadow his eyes.

"*C'est mon plaisir*," he replied.

Robin belched. "How sweet. I may vomit. How much longer do we have to stay here?"

Mikael scowled. Jessie kicked his ankle. The last thing she needed was an incident in her bar because Mikael's strong sense of propriety was disturbed. He shot her a wounded look.

"I have business I must attend to in the city, so I will take you back to your hotel," his tone left no room for argument. Robin wasn't interested in arguing anyway.

"About time," he muttered as he slid off his stool and pushed his way through the openly staring crowd and out the door, pausing only to look up at Tug with a puzzled face. Tug calmly returned the stare. He was used to it.

"Is that an--"

"Ogre, yes. We were leaving?" Mikael pushed Robin out the door.

Jessie didn't bother hiding her sigh of relief as she watched them leave. Madame Blanche followed Jessie's gaze.

"Yes, that one is a puzzle, *non*? I have never had dealings with a fae like that except for once when we came up against the Nain Rouge," she sipped her wine.

"Nain Rouge. Aren't they native to Michigan?"

"Detroit, to be specific. They're said to be born of both my land and yours. Or rather, those who lived on your land before the Europeans settled here."

"So I've heard. They're supposed to be pretty nasty characters."

"They are *tres mal*. They are prone to trickery and delight in causing conflicts and, how do you say, scenes?"

"Interesting," Jessie stared at the door. Something to ponder later, she decided, as she watched one of the more anemically attractive vampire groupies– one who was tall and wore a black hoodie– peel himself away from the rest of the group and approach Nicky.

"Nicky," she warned with a lift of her chin toward the young man who moved closer, his eyes gleaming with an unnatural light of obsession that made alarm bells go off in Jessie's head.

"Hey, Nicky, we're all sorry to hear about Warwick," he shuffled from one foot to another.

"Warsaw," Nicky corrected him without turning around. Jessie caught Tug's eye and started moving toward the kid, trailing her fingertips along the bar to gather energy.

"Whatever, hey--" was as far as he got before Nicky wheeled around, baring a mouth of fangs that didn't seem to have room in his mouth.

Jessie had seen her share of vampiric transformations in her day, but they never got easier to look at. His once beautiful face elongated, mouth widening around bristling fangs as his skin turned grayish black and his ears became bat-like. His eyes flared red as blood as she threw up a barrier between him and the kid. The poor boy's eyes widened in shock, and he fell backwards over a stool and into Tug's grasp.

"Come on, time to go," Tug's voice, which Jessie was sure probably registered on a Richter scale, rumbled through the shocked silence.

"But... but.. He was going to *attack* me! Me! After everything I did for him!" the kid squealed, his voice climbing in outrage.

Jessie groaned and dropped her face in her hands. Obviously this was one of Nicky's little conquests he collected when he was bored. How could she not have foreseen this happening? He was notorious for using his vampiric glamour to lure people to him and then getting tired of them just as quickly. Hell, that was who made up probably half of the ever present vampire groupies.

Nicky was already turning back to his human form and looked at Jessie with guilt in his eyes.

"I'm sorry. I didn't mean to. Warsaw is-- was-- more than a 'whatever'. I'm sorry, Jess. I didn't mean to."

"I know. Why don't you go hang out in the office for a little bit, okay?"

"Okay," he hung his head and shuffled off, looking more

defeated and dejected than Jessie had ever seen him before. She sighed and turned back to the group of kids, who stared at Nicky's retreating back, stunned.

"He attacked Morticent!" one girl shrieked in a high, unsteady voice.

"No, he didn't. And maybe Morticent-- wait, is that really his name?" Jessie stopped, blinking in surprise. She knew the names these guys came up with were ridiculous, but *Morticent*?

"Yes, he's an artist, and he's going to be famous!" the girl's shrillness wasn't going down as she drew herself up while trying -- and failing-- to look imperious.

"Uh huh. Well, he's not going to be much of anything if he doesn't stop trying to piss off vampires. If he's that important, then you should go after him and leave Nicodemus alone."

The girl sneered in derision at this... *witch* who dared talk to them in that tone when they were all obviously meant for better things and started to sit back down. Her attitude really got on Jessie's nerves.

"That wasn't a suggestion," Jessie's voice was ice cold. So cold, that the air seemed to freeze in a direct line between her and the girl. When looking at Jessie's tiny frame and delicate features, it was easy to forget how much power she actually had. All of a sudden, she was the biggest thing in the room, and the vampies couldn't get out of there fast enough.

"Well! That was... bracing. I think I need more wine-- or perhaps something a bit stronger," Madame Blanche remarked. Rupert's tail was twice its normal size (which was impressive), and every hair on his body stood on end. His growl rivaled Tug's voice for who could make the deepest rumble. Jessie thought she could see the glassware move on the bar.

"You're telling me!" drawled a peaches and cream voice from behind them. Jessie glanced over her shoulder at Ruth Ann. As alluring as her mother, Ruth Ann was as down to earth as she was devastatingly beautiful with creamy skin dusted with a smattering of freckles, leaf green eyes, and flaming red hair that fell past her waist.

"Did you know Warsaw, Ruth Ann?" Jessie asked more out of curiosity than anything else. The Suttons pretty much made it their business to know every eligible adult around. And some who weren't quite so eligible, truth be told.

"Yeah, I tried to crack that one-- no pun intended, so no offense-- but he was too much in love. That's the only way a being can really be immune to someone like me, you know? Do me a favor, Miss Jessie, if you don't mind, and let Nicky know how much Warsaw loved him for me."

"That's really sweet, Ruth Ann. I'll tell him," Jessie smiled.

Ruth Ann smiled back as she headed out the door, making sure to put an extra swing in her sashay for Jared's benefit. Jessie sighed as she walked down the hall toward Nicodemus and a much needed stash of chamomile tea.

7

"Hey, how are you holding up? Want some tea?" Jessie slipped past Nicky, who, for someone who wasn't much bigger than she was, took up an awful lot of room when he moped. He had good reason to be mopey, but still.

"No, I want to rip that asshole's head off."

"Nicky! No! Bad! Bad vampire! No beheadings!" she scolded, shaking a finger and at least getting a little tug at the corners of his mouth.

"I'm sorry, Jess. Really I am. I didn't mean to lose control like that."

"I know, sweetie, and nothing happened anyway" she settled down in an ancient chair behind an ancient desk. Both were held together mostly with duct tape and spell work, and both were so comfortable that she frequently threatened to turn the many people who tried to talk her into replacing them into toads.

"When's the last time you ate?" she fixed him with a piercing stare.

He blinked at her.

"Ate?"

"Yes, that thing you do when you put blood in your system and start to function like a normal... well... whatever normal is for you."

"I *know* what eating is," he sounded peevish. Nicky really wasn't a fan of people poking fun at him, which, in Jessie's opinion, made it even more gratifying.

"Great!" she beamed at him. "Then when's the last time you did it?"

He looked away, a flash of guilt in his eyes. It was imperative that vampires kept their hunger at bay to avoid losing control. Luckily, Jessie had connections with both a centaur who ran the local Red Cross and a kalanaro who had moved from Madagascar to study at Emory and was now the director at the medical center. They both passed along any blood that couldn't be used.

One of the advantages to being undead was that you couldn't get sick if something was contaminated. She had a strict no feeding on the patrons rule at her bar, so she always tried to keep some blood on hand for visiting vampires-- but mostly Nicky. Mikael would never be caught dead(er) slumming it with a bag of blood at a bar.

Jessie wheeled her chair over to the little refrigerator in the corner. She ran her index finger across the edge and, whispering the words to release the spell she cast over it to stop anyone from helping themselves to its contents, pulled out a bag. She let her natural fire magic heat it up before tossing it to Nicky.

"Drink," she ordered.

He drank in silence, huddled up in a little ball of misery on the sofa.

"I really loved him," he finally whispered.

"I know. He loved you too. Ruth Ann wanted me to make sure to tell you that."

He looked at her, wide eyed.

"She did? How did she know?"

Jessie sighed, coming around the desk to curl up next to him and hug him to her.

"He wasn't interested when she came on to him. The only way someone can be immune to succubi is to be in love."

"I haven't been in love with someone like that in centuries. Not the real thing. I don't want to live without him."

"Well, we would really rather help you grieve and learn how to move on."

"I know. Thanks, Jessie. I don't know what I would do without you."

"I know," she said more flippantly this time. He gave a small chuckle. "Do you want to stay here tonight or go home?"

"Home. I don't want to be around people, and if Mikael can't make sure I'm okay, he's just going to pace holes through the floor and blow up our phones," he said with a wry twist to his lips.

"Okay, I'll get Jared to drive you."

"No, I'll fly. I need to do something for myself."

"Okay, but let me know when you're home," she gave him one last hard hug before letting go.

"Yes, ma'am," he snapped a mock salute before shifting into a large fruit bat. She scratched him behind the ears and opened the window so he could get out.

Jessie sat for a minute thinking about how amazing it was that such a flighty creature could have found true love and that whoever decided to take that love away needed to suffer very, very badly.

Nicodemus and Mikael were roughly seven or eight hundred years older than her. They met by chance at the court of King Louis XV when Jessie and Greta were in search of the Madame de Pompadour's aid to help persuade the king to sign a clandestine treaty granting trade rights to witches for their herbal compounds and services, and the four of them quickly became inseparable. Even now with Greta flitting all over Europe working as a historian and researcher for the Witch Council and Mikael's hands full with politics, their little band somehow always managed to come together at Jessie's bar, their cozy home away from home.

In the two hundred plus years since she had known Nicky, he had fallen in and out of love more than she knew was possible, but she had only ever seen this deep, true love a very small handful of times. Even though he wore the facade of empty-headed flirtation, promiscuity, and shallow romance like a badge, in reality he was a well versed scholar, brilliant tactician and strategist, and deeply loyal to his loved ones. To Jessie, he was truly one of the best men she had ever known.

"Hey, Jessie, you in here?" Charlie's head poked through the door. The first time he had done that when he realized, to his dismay, knocking was somewhat off the table for him now, he had scared the living daylights out of her. Now she thought it was funny. He did not.

"Yeah, Charlie. Come on in," she replied, swallowing her smile.

"How's our boy holding up?" he drifted to the battered sofa and carefully perched next to her, being careful not to get too close. She had accidentally walked through him once. It felt like being stuck in a foggy, cold, slimy pool. Neither of them were anxious to repeat the experience.

"Hanging in there. He just flew home. This hit him hard."

"Did Ruth Anne talk to you?"

"Yeah, I think that helped. She's a good girl," Jessie said with a small smile.

"Yep, takes after her mama, that one. It'd be nice if other people recognized that too," he said, making it clear with his tone who the "other people" were in that scenario. Jessie sighed.

"I'll talk to Cassie," she said, rubbing her temples. "Hey, speaking of, do you have any kind of ghostly powers?"

He blinked at her in confusion, trying to make the jump from Cassie's dislike of Ruth Anne to his current physical condition.

"Sorry, she picked up something infrared on my camera footage. That's how we know someone was in the bathroom with Warsaw. I wondered if maybe you can see something I can't or feel something different or if maybe you can pick up something from Warsaw's death."

"Well, gosh Jessie, I don't know. I mean, I can always take a look, but I don't know what I'm looking for. But I will say this, right before that kid started mouthing off to Nicky out there, I felt something weird. It was like something pushed through me, like wind."

Jessie frowned. "I didn't know you could feel anything like that," she said.

"I can't. Or at least I thought I couldn't," he shrugged his transparent shoulders.

Her frown deepened. "That may be something we should look into. If you're okay with it, I'd like to run some tests on you. Nothing bad, I promise! You don't have to do it if you don't want to."

"Of course! Anything for our Nicky, you know that," he beamed. Charlie, who while living had been one of those people who hated the concept of "downtime" and was never happy unless he was working on a project, struggled more and more with boredom in the afterlife. Jessie figured he would probably jump at the chance to liven things up. No pun intended.

"Hey, Jessie, you got a minute?"

Jessie looked up to see Jared at the door with Cassie and, surprisingly, Tug right behind them. "Yeah, what's up?" she asked as her small office suddenly became very cramped.

"You gotta see this," Cassie pushed past Jared. "Remember that footage from QT's parking lot?"

"How could I forget?" Jessie remarked, earning an eye roll and huff from Cassie.

"Well, I showed it around to the regulars. I figured, you know, it wouldn't hurt, right?"

"Right," Jessie cautiously agreed.

"I know that kid," Tug rumbled.

"Wait, what?" Jessie stared at him startled.

"Yeah, I saw that bracelet he's wearing. That kid we threw out tonight? Morti-whatever? That's him," Tug shrugged his massive shoulders as Cassie held out her phone with the footage pulled up.

"Let me see," Jessie reached for the phone.

"Jessie, that looks like him from behind," Charlie said from over her shoulder.

"Tug, you're positive? I'm calling Sheriff Rossford right now if you are," Jessie grabbed her phone and looked at the ogre, already knowing it was a stupid question. He missed nothing and never spoke about anything unless he was absolutely certain that it was fact. But human-cryptid relations were still delicate, and falsely accusing a human of killing a cryptid, even if that human was a vampie, could go badly.

"Yes," Tug was an ogre of few words.

"Okay," Jessie started dialing. The sheriff answered on the third ring.

"Jessie, hey. What's up?"

"Hey, John. We got something. There was a disturbance earlier tonight. A kid tried to talk to Nicky, and we had to throw him out."

"Wait, you had to throw someone out for trying to talk to Nicky or you had to throw Nicky out?" John sounded confused. Poor guy. He probably had a perpetual headache trying to keep the peace between the communities and sorting out all the weird entanglements.

"The kid! It's a long story, but it turns out this kid is really obsessed with Nicky. Like under a spell. His eyes when he tried talking--" Jessie broke off with a shudder remembering the gleam that bordered on insanity in Morticent's eyes. The pieces were starting to come together.

"Anyway, Tug recognized the bracelet he wore from the footage Cassie picked up from the QT. I think he's our murderer, and I think that someone used him to do the job and picked him because of his infatuation with Nicky. And I think he's under a love spell to make sure he got the job done."

John was quiet for a minute.

"Are you sure? That's a lot of thinking and not a lot of evidence other than the bracelet."

"I know," Jessie sighed in frustration. "But the thing is there are no true love spells. They are designed to create a compulsion and obsession. You can't make someone fall in love, but you can make them become obsessed. And John, I know what a compulsion love spell looks like, and I'm telling you, he's under one. I promise someone hand picked him because of his interest in Nicky, spelled him, and gave him the bracelet."

"But why? I mean, if someone wanted to attack Madame Blanche, wouldn't they do something more public? Bespelling a lovesick kid and turning him into a murderer against her aide seems... I don't know. It seems too complicated for just a political agenda."

"I know. Unless Madame Blanche isn't the only target," Jessie's mind raced. "What if this is supposed to be a distraction? I mean, think about it. Nicodemus, the brother of one of the most influential and powerful vampires in the world, discovers that his lover, who happens to be the aide to Madame Blanche, the most powerful and influential incorporeal being in Europe, is killed. Then a few days later, our most viable murder suspect approaches Nicky while under the influence of an obsession-compulsion spell that could only be cast by a witch, and he does it in the bar of one of the oldest and most powerful witches in North America, and he can't keep his stupid mouth shut and makes Nicky turn."

"Wait, you didn't say anything about Nicky turning!" John sharply cut her off.

Maintaining the illusion of humanity helped to dampen a vampire's thirst because the persona needed to be true to the bone, including providing a built in moral compass. Once vampires turned though, all bets were off. Turning was considered a precursor to an attack because once a vampire shifted into their true form, they were no longer held back by the instinctive sense of self-preservation the moral compass provided that stopped them from going on a feeding/murder spree, pissing off humanity, and starting an outright war.

While a vampire as old as Nicky could shift to his true form and still control the urge to rip out a victim's throat, making the public believe it was possible was a hard sell.

"Yeah. Nothing happened, but you know as well as I do, it doesn't look good."

"Jesus, Jess..." John's voice trailed off, and she could had a mental image of him sitting at his desk, rubbing his temples, wondering why he ever thought this job would be great in any capacity.

"Well, we have a name for the kid. Kind of."

"How do you 'kind of' have a name?"

Jessie sighed and made a mental note to buy him a couple of beers for this.

"Morticent."

"I'm sorry, what?"

"Yeah. Sorry, John. We'll try to find a credit card slip or something with his real name on it."

"Well, you're not going to believe this, but you may not have to," he sounded smug.

"Why?" Jessie was taken aback.

"A few years ago a vampire in Atlanta was involved with one of those groupies who kept bugging her to turn him. She didn't want to, so she thought it would be funny to compel him to think she had to make him shut up. Only she forgot to turn off the compulsion."

Jessie groaned. "And the groupie attacked someone because he thought he was a vampire and needed to feed because of course compelling him to think he was a vampire instead of compelling him to stop *wanting* to be a vampire made perfect sense."

"Got it in one. She is not the smartest vampire around by a long shot. So the Georgia Bureau of Investigation started an unofficial database for these kids. Let me see if I can find him."

"Can you actually share all of that with me? I mean, isn't this an official investigation?" Jessie asked, her many nights spent watching crime TV coming back to her.

"The investigation is. The database is not. Now hush and let me look this up."

Jessie grinned. The attraction between the two of them was undeniable, and only her reluctance at getting involved with anyone while trying to juggle all of her responsibilities held her back from pursuing it. He had been up front about wanting to take their relationship to another level, and he was willing to wait for her, no matter how long it took. Meanwhile, she enjoyed the banter and took solace in his company whenever she could. He had become a port in the storm of her life.

Nicky constantly pestered her to get over herself and just

go for it, while Greta thought she should wait. To be fair, Greta didn't believe anyone was good enough for Jessie, so her opinion was a little circumspect. Not that Nicky's was exactly the most trustworthy either.

"Got him. Marshall Woodford, address is in Athens though. Supposed to be a student at UGA. How long has he been coming to the bar?"

"I have no idea," Jessie ignored the disapproving tut on the other end of the line.

"They all look the same," she said defensively. "Nicky said this Marshall kid started trying to talk to him about a week ago though. I mean, if you think about it, picking one of the groupies was a stroke of genius. They look the same, act the same, they're virtually interchangeable. Not to mention once you take the hair and make up into account, none of us are even sure what they look like in their mundane lives."

She thought for a moment.

"If anyone would know for sure how long he's been coming here though, it would be Caroline. She remembers almost everyone. I'll ask Tug too. He recognized the bracelet, so maybe that jogged something else, although he's a lot better at remembering the trouble makers than the regular customers."

"Yeah, ask them. Hey, can I ask you a question?"

"Is it about Tug? Because he's still off limits."

Silence.

"What if it's important to this investigation?" his tone was mild, knowing that he was close to pushing a button. If there was anything he knew about Jessie, it was that she was loyal to a fault. You did not come for her staff and friends without preparing for a long, dirty fight. She refused to open up about where Tug came from and steadfastly maintained that he had never broken the law, he had valid forms of ID (which John suspected came more from her magic than the DMV), and his background was no one's business.

"Get a subpoena," she snapped, her goodwill evaporating fast.

"Hey, I'm just trying to figure out what happened! As long as I don't have a reason to look at him, I won't. Truce?"

"Fine," she said, clearly not fine at all. "I've got to get back to the bar. I'll call you if I find anything else."

"Okay, thanks, Jessie. Bye" he said to an already empty line. Maybe he should stop asking, but it was important to the protection of the community to know why an ogre suddenly popped up out of nowhere. And, if he was being honest with himself, he was curious as all hell.

Jessie stomped back to the bar. Madame Blanche was gone but Rupert, oddly, since he was supposed to be her companion, was still there, by the door where he sat like a sentinel opposite Tug. She laughed despite herself. If anyone came in trying to cause trouble, they were in for a big surprise with those two on her door.

Mikael waited at the end of the bar, trying to look casual and failing. Cassie sat next to him glued to her phone and sipping something that was an odd shade of yellow. They looked up as she approached.

"You okay?" Cassie asked, reading Jessie's face.

"Yeah. So this is where we're at," she filled them in on the call with the sheriff.

Mikael frowned, the soft light from the candles on the bar reflecting off the amber wood into his gray eyes. Jessie welcomed almost everything modern with open arms, but she would always be a sucker for candles.

"You're right, that is too convoluted to just be a political message against one emissary," he agreed. "This seems more sinister, especially since we're all affected now-- almost like a declaration of war. And we're still no closer to knowing who this young man is?"

Jessie shook her head.

"We have a name, but he's not from around here. Remember when he mentioned everything he had done for Nicky? I thought he meant all the stuff these kids do to try to please vampires, but what if he was talking about killing Warsaw? What if someone convinced him that by killing Warsaw, he was doing Nicky a favor?"

"What kind of favor could that possibly be?" Cassie was baffled.

"I don't know," Jessie said. "We need to figure out who this kid is and find out what he meant and what he knows. Hey, Caroline, did that guy we threw out look familiar?"

"Yeah, he started coming in about a week ago with the rest of them and always asked about Nicky," the tall blonde shrugged as she deftly flipped a mixing tin over and strained the contents into a glass. "He didn't really stand out though. Every vampire has at least one of those in here. Even you, Mikael," she grinned with a little wink.

"Lovely," he grimaced. Mikael had never been one for the

whole entourage and adoration thing. Unlike most vampires, he found all the fawning repulsive, probably because he identified as asexual.

Jessie hid her smile. "What about that girl he was with? Do you think she knows him pretty well?"

"Probably," Caroline said with another shrug, tossing the tin in the sink with a clatter of ice. "They always came in together, but she's been coming here a lot longer than he has. She goes by Belladonna, but her real name is Jennifer. Before you ask, he always paid with cash, but more often than not, someone else paid for his drinks."

"Really? He didn't look like he was broke." Jessie's brow furrowed.

"Yeah, I didn't think so either. I don't think he asked. I think everyone just did it. I think when the rumors that Nicky was in love started to go around, they all assumed it was with him."

Jessie snorted. "Well, you know what they say about assume..."

Caroline laughed. "Seriously. Cassie, ready for another?"

Cassie perked up. "Yes, please! Only make it blue."

Jessie and Mikael shuddered in unison.

"To think, this is what centuries of careful study into the methods of distillation and spirituous creations has led to," he said mournfully.

"Preaching to the choir," she agreed.

"What on earth is she drinking?" Charlie drifted next to her, staring at Cassie's drink with a mix of revulsion and awe.

"I have no clue where Caroline comes up with these drinks," Jessie shook her head. "Do you have a minute? I want to see if you pick up anything from the bathroom. I also want to test some things on you."

"Sure, let's go," he gestured down the hall.

As they walked into the bathroom together, Jessie felt a shiver go down her spine. Violent deaths always left a ripple in the ether, whether they resulted in a haunting or not. Charlie gleamed a faint ice blue.

"Interesting. Do you know what makes you change color?" she asked.

"What do you mean?" he stared at her, puzzled.

Jessie blinked at him.

"You didn't realize you changed colors?" she asked, surprised.

"Wait, I do? When?" he was clearly as surprised as she was.

"Earlier when Cassie started in on the Suttons you turned reddish, and when we walked in here, you became a kind of icy blue."

"Huh. I had no idea. I wonder what it means," he mused.

"My guess is that it's how you show emotion. We should explore this more!" she brightened, the prospect of experimentation and discovery briefly chasing away her gloom.

"Now what color am I?" he asked, staring at her levelly.

"Pink! Cool! So we know what happens when you're annoyed!"

"Pink?!" Charlie was outraged.

"Hey, pink is a perfectly respectable color!" Jessie retorted before reining in the banter in light of the more somber task before them.

"Whatever. So glad I get to spend my afterlife as a lab rat," Charlie grumbled.

"Anyway, what did you feel when we came in? I wonder what would turn you that shade of blue," she asked more seriously.

"Dread. But you know what's weird? I didn't feel anything in the hall, but the minute we crossed the threshold, it slapped me in the face."

"What did?" she asked.

"Fear and despair. Longing. Pain. I can feel what *he* felt when he was dying," he said sadly.

"Whoever cast the invisibility spell did something to the bathroom so we couldn't tell what was happening until it was over, or we all would have known something was going on. Can you pick up on what went down in here?"

"I don't know. I never tried to feel death like this before. I didn't know I could, to be honest with you. I haven't been able to leave the bar since I died, and it's not like this place sees a lot of action," he admitted.

"If we could recreate the scene, it would help a lot. Morticent is tall, but he's not really that big. I know technically Warsaw wasn't either in stature, but he's a gargoyle. They're one of the strongest things on the planet. Even if Morticent caught him by surprise, how was he able to force Warsaw to drink enough acid to corrode him from the inside out?"

"Jesus, Jessie!" Charlie stared at her in horror. "You didn't tell me *that* part!"

"On the bright side, we know that when something really disturbs you, you turn dingy yellow like Atlanta smog," she remarked. "Sorry. Yeah. It was pretty horrible to look at. I hope I never have to see anything like that again."

Considering how old she was, that statement carried a lot

of weight with Charlie, who sort of rested his insubstantial hand on her shoulder.

"Well, let's see what I can do here. If I can help that poor kid, you know I will."

"I know," she smiled. "Want to siphon some energy off me? Maybe it will help."

"Yeah, worth a try."

His square cut jaw hardened with resolve, and Jessie found herself studying him as he closed his eyes and concentrated, slowly pulling on the dusky, bruised purple line of energy she fed him. He had been a good looking man with even features and a close cut beard, stocky in build from years of hard labor on his farm and starting to soften around the middle from years of bellying up to her bar.

He was by no means the first ghost she had ever encountered or even befriended before or after death. She hadn't known any other ghosts who were willing to let her study or experiment on them though. Very little was known about ghosts in general, and most either resented the living for getting to live or were desperate to get to their final destination. Charlie was the first she had met who faced his situation with equanimity and seemed as curious about it as the witches were. Greta was going to love this.

As he focused, she realized that the bathroom was changing. Where it should have been just a toilet, sink, trash can, and dispensers surrounded by warm tile and an antique mirror reflecting their pale faces back at them, now two hazy figures appeared, slowly snapping into crystal clear focus. She realized that for the first time, she was seeing Warsaw in his human form. She understood immediately why Nicky had been so in love.

His stone dark features were beautiful, delicate but strong at the same time like a Greek god. Even in the midst of the attack, determination still showed through the fear. His slate gray hair was almost as curly as Nicky's, and she felt a pang knowing she would never get to see them together, curls intertwining as they bent over some piece of art or debated a point. All of a sudden she was filled with blinding rage at the senseless loss and pain.

"Jessie!" Charlie yelped, breaking the connection. She blinked up at him flustered, the black that had filled her eyes from edge to edge bleeding out. As creatures of nature, witches were neutral, and they were slaves to the chaos of anger and hatred as much as the calm of love and peace.

"I'm sorry, Charlie. I didn't mean to lose it like that. I just saw him and how perfect he is, and I thought about Nicky, and I don't know," her voice trailed off.

Charlie reached for her again, his form tinged with red.

"I know. I saw it too. You just really lit me up there for a minute. I get it though. He was a sweet kid, and this is unforgivable. When I find out who's behind this, there'll be hell to pay."

Jessie didn't ask how a ghost was going to rain down hellfire and brimstone on a wannabe vampire kid. She just channeled a stream of her energy again, this time carefully building a shield between her emotions and the thoughts that kept her considerable power in check.

The scene rose before them again, and they watched in silence as Warsaw stiffened in shock and went rigid. He spun and grabbed at an invisible shape, and a large needle spun out of thin air and landed on the floor where it rolled to a stop at Jessie's feet. She stared at the cylinder, runes glowing on its side, and committed them to memory, a trick she learned centuries ago when cell phone cameras were not a thing, and lugging around quills and grimoires was tedious-- and dangerous.

Warsaw's movements became more sluggish. Whatever was in the syringe was clearly doing its job as he finally collapsed on the floor. She heard a soft scrape, like a lid coming off a jar, and sure enough, it gently appeared on the floor next to the prone gargoyle. Indentations appeared around Warsaw's mouth as it popped open, and a stream of clear liquid poured into his open mouth. Then the thrashing began and Warsaw's flailing limbs knocked the jar out of his attacker's hands where it rolled under the sink. Jessie cut the connection.

"I can't look anymore," she said, unaware that tears were streaming down her cheeks. Charlie was a veritable murky rainbow, shifting from blood red to ice blue to an ugly orange-yellow stain.

"I know. Too bad we didn't see the kid's face. You think the jar's still here?"

"He had time to pick it up, so I doubt it," she knelt down, hoping for a miracle.

Unfortunately, that kind of miracle only happened on TV. Either Morticent or his mysterious cohort had already thought ahead to make sure nothing was left behind. Considering the sheriff's office came up empty on the trash from the bathroom and all they had to go on was a bracelet and witch's intuition, which was not admissible in a court of law, Jessie felt like they were back at square one.

"Well, that was a bust," she said dejectedly, rising up from the floor and dusting her hands off on the thighs of her jeans.

"Yeah. Sorry, Jess. But hey, now we know I can do something to help out," Charlie shrugged.

"Hopefully we don't need to use that particular power very often, but yeah, it's certainly useful. Let's go tell the others. I want to try to figure out why you felt something like wind too. That's definitely odd," she said over her shoulder as she led the way out of the bathroom.

"Do you want to figure out what kind of whammy is on the bathroom though? I mean, it's kind of strange that I felt something on one side of the door but not on the other."

Jessie paused, considering.

"No, leave it. Whoever cast it doesn't know that I know it's there yet, and I can take a look when we're closed tomorrow to see if I can figure out the spell's origins. It has to be something that was physically done to the room, and I don't want to risk hurting any of the patrons or staff if I try to take it apart tonight and it's booby trapped. If it was on Morticent, and he *really* needs to come up with a better name; that one's ridiculous, then it would have ended when he left the room."

She led the way down the small hallway lined with golden oak panels that radiated comfort and warmth like the rest of the building.

"Anything?" Caroline asked, looking up from washing bar tools and glassware as they walked up to the bar.

"Nope, but someone did something to the bathroom so

anyone who's sensitive can't feel the energy from the murder in the hallway," Jessie replied, perching on a bar stool.

"You think it was Morticent?" Cassie asked over something that looked and smelled purple but was definitely not a color or taste found in nature.

"I doubt it. If he was a witch who was strong enough to cast a cloaking spell, he would be able to render himself invisible without a talisman. Besides, he's clearly under an obsession spell, so unless he's a very weak witch, he's not our guy."

"So what now?" Mikael asked.

"I need to figure out some stuff. I want to try something though while you're here. Can you cast a compulsion without a target?"

"I don't know, I never tried," Mikael looked surprised.

"I just don't want to compel anyone, but I want to see if Charlie can feel it when it goes through him to get to someone else."

"Would you care to enlighten us as to this particular request?" Mikael raised an eyebrow.

"He felt something like the wind. It's probably supernatural. He's been around me doing magic a million times, so I doubt it's anything a witch here would have done. But the vampires who come here aren't allowed to use compulsion. It's a house rule," she explained.

"But there weren't any other vampires here," Jared pointed out as he brought a towering stack of dirty glasses to the sink.

"I know, but it's always important to rule out everything. If Charlie can feel a vampiric compulsion, then maybe that could help us narrow down the field to other cryptids that have similar powers."

"Ah. Charlie, please stand-- er, float-- there," Mikael gestured toward an empty space. Charlie obligingly got into position and waited. Mikael's eyes glassed over and then turned pure silver. Even though she wasn't in the line of fire, so to speak, Jessie felt the intensity and was glad for the millionth time that she had a built in resistance to mind control and compulsion.

Charlie made a seesaw motion with his transparent hand.

"I felt that, but I wouldn't call it wind. More like a very gentle push. I knew you were doing something, but it was external, you know?"

"Yeah, thanks Charlie. I'll talk to Greta and see if she can think of anything. Caroline, you got this if I go do some digging?"

"Sure thing," Caroline waved Jessie off.

"I think I should leave and check on Nicodemus," Mikael said, pushing back from the bar and coming to his feet.

"Good idea," Jessie agreed. "I'll let you know if we find anything. Meet back here tomorrow?"

"Of course," he said with a simple bow.

"Great. Call me if you need me, Caroline" Jessie said over her shoulder, heading back to her office while the others stared at her retreating back.

8

All witches need a place of study, and as they grow older, learn more, and collect more books and artifacts, they often find themselves in need of a place to store their wealth of knowledge.

Jessie and Greta had joined the legions of witches who, once they reached their first century or two, decided to solve the issue by tapping into another plane to create their own Library. Jessie's and Greta's was only accessible through a series of complex keys and wards they had created together. If something happened to one of them, the Library would only open for the other– a failsafe put in place to protect each other and their impressive vault of knowledge and dangerous artifacts.

Jessie walked to a piece of oak paneling behind her desk and whispered a spell as she pushed against the knothole in the wood. The tiny flower tattoo on her ankle glowed in response to the spell. She and Greta both had one, each drawn by the other, that signified their bond and connected their minds and emotions. What one felt, the other knew.

The panel slid aside showing a cozy room behind a

shimmering veil. She stepped through, swallowing against the instant spin of vertigo and nausea that always hit witches when they crossed worlds and portals.

The room was lined on one side with tall windows that let in soft moonlight reflecting off snow capped mountains. A huge fire burned merrily at one end of the room in a cavernous stone fireplace flanked by mismatched and overstuffed armchairs and sturdy end tables.

An equally worn, comfortable, and patched sofa, draped with chenille and alpaca wool blankets and pillows all colors of the rainbow faced the fireplace along with an ancient coffee table covered in Jessie's crochet patterns and Greta's notebooks. They had an unspoken agreement that once they found furniture that worked, they would go to the ends of the earth and beyond to keep it standing.

Every available inch of wall space was lined with floor to ceiling shelves that groaned under the weight of books, scrolls, and boxes full of artifacts. Greta's slightly dented cherry red tea kettle stood on a table in a corner next to her french press, a stack of coffee mugs (also mismatched), and tins of coffee and boxes of tea she picked up around the world.

A purple Persian rug Jessie had found in her travels covered the flagstone floor, and sconces set among the shelves joined their golden light to the lamps the witches had scavenged and scattered on various tables and in the corners. All in all it was charmingly eclectic and cozy and absolutely their own perfect space.

Of course it wouldn't be complete without the cats, five in all. Aleister Meowley, the jet black cat who disdained all laps until the girls were trying to do something constructive,

Lemur, the sweet and shy gray tabby, Spot, the tortoiseshell who felt that all laps belonged to her, Lucy, the tiny calico, who was the smallest of the five with the biggest personality and bossiness, and Sunny, a sixteen pound orange and white tom who spent every waking minute convinced that he was dying of starvation.

Jessie stood in the center of the room perusing the shelves trying to figure out where to start first. At some point it would probably be a good idea to get some kind of cataloging system in place, but then again, it was also fun opening random boxes trying to find one thing and discovering something else entirely she forgot they had.

She was the more organized out of the two of them though. One day she would win the seemingly endless war between Greta's weird system that made sense one day and baffled them both the next and Jessie's own more organized style. As she fought down a wave of annoyance, another panel of shelves slid away and Greta stepped through.

"I figured you would come here at some point for answers. How's Nicky? Did you find anything out yet?"

Jessie regarded her best friend. Taller than Jessie by several inches, something that rankled Jessie to no end, Greta had one of those faces that somehow managed to be bookishly pretty and interesting even though her mouth was a little too wide, her nose a little too quirky, and one eye was shaped ever so slightly differently than the other. Her hazel eyes and oval face were framed by a silver pixie haircut.

"No. This whole thing is so weird, and some of it really doesn't make sense."

Greta scooped Lucy out of her favorite chair and deposited

the grumbling cat in her lap while she curled her long legs under her. Lucy immediately went back to sleep. Jessie grabbed a blanket from the sofa and stretched out under it. Aleister claimed her feet.

"Like what?"

"Well, for starters, there's the Puck."

Greta frowned, recalling information Jessie had already shared through their mental bond.

"Yeah, what's up with that? I thought it was against the fae's nature to be outspokenly rude and boorish, especially the ones from Oberon's court."

"Me too. He's such an ass though! I want to smack him!"

"Did you ask the local court what they thought?" Greta asked, scratching Lucy under the chin.

"Not yet," Jessie replied as Spot settled on her chest. "The full moon starts tomorrow night, and they usually swing by after they Ride. As Oberon's representative, he should be with them. It will at least give me a chance to see what he's like among his own kind."

"What about the kid you think killed Warsaw?"

"Did you ever meet Warsaw?" Jessie asked, suddenly curious for more information on the shy but sweet gargoyle who had captured Nicky's heart.

"Once. There was a benefit for cryptid-human relations in Paris, and they asked some of the witches and fae to attend just to balance it out."

"Lucky," Jessie grinned. She hated having to perform for the aristocracy. Greta was infinitely better suited to playing diplomat, even if it put her teeth on edge. Greta rolled her eyes.

"Yeah. Rolling in good fortune over here. Anyway, he was really nice. Very down to earth, very intelligent. He was a good match for Nicky. It broke my heart to hear what happened."

"What did you think about Madame Blanche?" Jessie asked, absently scratching Spot behind the ears and on her cheeks.

Greta pondered for a moment before answering slowly, "I don't really have an opinion about her one way or the other. She was nice and very gracious, but she didn't really get cozy with anyone. Apparently in life she was originally Charlotte de Valois, the illegitimate daughter of King Charles, who was married off to Jacques de Brézé, the Duke who inhabited the Chateau de Brissac in the fifteenth century. He killed her when he allegedly found her in bed with her lover. I was honestly surprised that she's the cryptid emissary for the Alliance. My understanding was the White Ladies have always been held at arm's length, even by the cryptid community. I mean, when you think about what they are, it's not all that surprising."

White Ladies were usually the ghosts of women who suffered a violent death, frequently as a result of the betrayal or jealousy of a husband or lover. They had long been viewed as harbingers of death, and Jessie had often wondered how one had been chosen to represent the French cryptid community. A *Dame Blanche* with royal lineage from the 1400's would probably do it though.

"You said she was aloof? Interesting," Jessie frowned.

"How so?"

"Well, the one I met is very friendly. In fact, she put Robin in his place a few times. She travels with a Matagot named Rupert too. I don't suppose you met him, did you?"

Greta laughed, "Ah, Rupert. Sadly I didn't get to actually meet him, but I remember him well. Not gonna lie, he was probably the best part of that whole event. Nothing throws off a bunch of nobility like a giant, black, possibly demon cat who refuses to stay off the furniture and eats all the fish."

Jessie giggled at the mental image.

"I can see that," she said before sobering.

"What else happened?" Greta asked, eyes narrowing. She knew all of that was information Jessie could have asked for without a face to face meeting.

"Charlie," Jessie replied, reaching around to get Lemur under the chin as he perched on her shoulder.

"The succubus' ghost?" Greta grinned.

"Yeah. Earlier tonight a bunch of the vampire groupies showed up, and one of them tried to get to Nicky. We actually think that he's the one in the video Cassie recovered from the QT's security footage."

"Do you think he's a witch?" Greta asked, craning to reach Sunny who wanted pets but refused to leave the warmth of the hearth.

"No, but we think that there is a witch behind this who gave him a talisman of invisibility," Jessie said, squirming under the cats to pull up the camera footage on her phone before tossing it to Greta, who, being athletically challenged, barely managed to miss hitting herself in the nose trying to catch it. Jessie snorted. Greta shot her an injured look before playing the video.

"That looks like a talisman all right. What about Charlie?"

"Tonight the kid got kind of crazy with Nicky and actually provoked Nicky to the point where he started to turn. Charlie said he felt like a gust of wind blew through him right before it happened. He's never felt anything like that when I do magic around him, so we got Mikael to try to compel him. He said he felt something like a mild push, but it wasn't as strong."

"That's because it came from a necromancer," Greta said grimly, scratching Lucy harder until the little cat growled in protest and jumped off Greta's lap to stalk away and clean her tail in disapproval.

Jessie looked at her friend expectantly. After the two of them ran into trouble against a group of necromancers created by a cabal of witches set on world domination, Greta had spent a significant amount of time in the seventeenth century studying some of the lesser known forms of magic, which largely included those relating to death. Jessie suspected that Greta probably had some insight the rest of them didn't.

Greta sighed.

"You already know that necromancers aren't naturally born witches. They're made from a creature of death, either a ghost or a cryptid or faery that's a harbinger of death, and the ritual to make them into a necromancer is very dangerous and difficult. Most don't survive the transformation. Any witch can perform the ritual, but because it's considered a defilement of nature, the witch who performs the ritual loses their connection with their spirit element until the balance of karma has been restored. Ones performed by the *völva* or shamans are stronger than what you or I could accomplish."

Jessie shuddered in horror at the thought of never being

able to touch the undercurrent of fire that ran through her consciousness like a river.

"That's terrible," she said, hugging her knees to her chest which caused multiple cries of protest from Spot and Aleister. She straightened her legs out, and they went back to sleep, slightly mollified. Lucy continued to pointedly ignore Greta.

"Yeah. The witch basically has to stockpile energy in artifacts for use after the spell wears off or siphon from people, which, as you know, is dangerous."

Jessie nodded. Siphoning from people was tricky. Like vampires, a witch couldn't drain a person completely without being drawn into their death.

"How long does it take to restore the balance?" she asked. Greta shrugged, the corner of her mouth quirking upward in thought.

"It depends. The transformation isn't permanent, but the balance can't start to be restored until the creature reverts to their natural state. If the necromancer was just a natural creature of death like a cryptid or faery that acts as a harbinger and neither the creature nor witch has ill intent, then it's only a few months, a year at the most depending on how many good deeds they perform in the interim. But if the witch wants to use the necromancer for evil or the necromancer is an agent of evil or chaos, then it can take decades if not centuries for the witch to regain her power after the creature reverts."

"How easy is it to find the ritual?"

"It's pretty damn scary how easy it is if you know what you're looking for. I can guarantee we have it in at least three of the books here. The other scary part is the karmic balance is more of a fine print thing. If you're a creature of death who finds an impressionable young witch to do the ritual or vice versa, you can get away with pulling it off before they ever find out what it cost them."

"And you're sure that's what we're dealing with?" Jessie asked, leaning forward despite Spot's protests.

"Yep. A ghost can only feel a necromancer's spell that strongly. Necromancers are actually the only magical beings that can directly affect the dead as far as we know."

Jessie stared off deep in thought.

"Can you make someone a necromancer without their knowledge?" she asked. Greta shook her head.

"No. There are certain things they have to do and bring to the ritual in order for it to work. Even if you tricked them into providing the materials, they have to recite their part with full knowledge and consent. And the karmic repercussions for a witch who tries to trick someone into becoming a necromancer are so bad that the witch may never come back from it. It's one thing to create an abomination of nature, but to do so without consent is a gross abuse of power that is unforgivable to the universe."

"How much of that is intent? Like if I wanted to turn a creature of death and didn't want to risk the karmic repercussions, could I talk another witch into doing it for me?"

"Unfortunately, yes. Whoever casts the spell deals with the penalty. Plus while the necromancer is active, the witch must turn all of their power over to it."

"That's pretty shitty," Jessie scowled.

"Yeah. But remember, we don't know what scenario we're dealing with here."

They sat in silence for a moment turning over the possibilities in their heads. Finally Jessie spoke, staring into the fire.

"Do you think that maybe Madame Blanche is the necromancer?"

"No," Greta said emphatically.

"Why?"

"Because she is too proud of her cryptid status and believes in the use of politics and diplomacy to move forward. She also fought too hard for cryptids to be recognized in their own right, and the most surefire way to undermine her efforts is to resort to witchcraft. It implies that cryptids aren't strong enough to stand up on their own. No, I think it's someone or something else."

"Okay, can a necromancer change their appearance?"

"Sure, but it takes effort like it does for any other witch. They would need a steady power source."

"What do they use as power?" Jessie asked, her curiosity starting to overtake her sense of urgency at solving the mystery. Greta leaned forward in her seat, warming to her subject.

"They don't have a natural power source, so they have to rely on artifacts. When the witch who performs the ritual finishes, as much of their power as possible is stored in artifacts or talismans that go to and can be used by the necromancer.

"If the ritual was done in good faith, as weird as that sounds, then the talismans are returned to the witch once the spell is finished and the necromancer reverts to their original state. The witch can access the power left in the talismans, but once it's used up, they're shit out of luck until the balance is restored. But if it was not done in good faith, then after the necromancer reverts, the power is locked in the talismans and can't be used again until the balance is restored."

"Trying to keep track of that makes my head hurt. What's to stop the necromancer from using up all the power?" Jessie asked.

Greta shrugged.

"Nothing. There's no failsafe to stop it from happening. It would be stupid to do it before the spell is up though. Plus then you have a really pissed off witch who will eventually be able to get revenge on you. When the karmic balance is restored, the witch will know because they'll feel their element within them again, but their magic reserves will be depleted. After all, the idea is to use whatever is left in the talismans to start filling those reserves. Think of it like having the power of regeneration. If you cut off a finger and still have the finger, it can be sewn back on, and you can use it again almost immediately. If you don't still have it, you'll grow it back, but you have to wait to use it."

"So it's stupid to do unless you really need it for one big thing, and also you come up with the strangest analogies" Jessie raised an eyebrow at her best friend.

"True."

"What if the necromancer kills the witch?"

"It doesn't change the basic underliers of the spell. The necromancer won't stay a witch forever, and any power that would have reverted to the witch would go back to the universe. Plus there's the question of karmic balance. Someone has to restore it, and if the witch is gone, then my guess would be the creature gets stuck with it all."

Jessie spoke slowly as her mind worked out a thought,

"Okay, here's a scenario. We know that if a witch puts her power in a talisman, then she's the only one who can trigger it so that it can be activated, right? Our magic is as unique to us as our DNA."

"Right," Greta nodded.

"But if the necromancer is using the witch's power, then would the talismans recognize the necromancer after they revert to their natural form? Does the necromancer get that same... magical DNA imprint?"

Greta stared thoughtfully into the fire.

"It should only work while the necromancer is active. Once they revert, they shouldn't be able to access the magic anymore. I can't think of a way to test that though without trying it ourselves."

Jessie shuddered at the thought of having to give up her magic for months on end to test a hypothesis.

"How about we add that to the list of things for you to look into?"

Greta shivered.

"Deal. I'd really rather not experiment with that right now— or ever."

"Okay, let's think. We have a White Lady who acts differently around me than she did around you, but that also could be due to my bar being a more casual and intimate environment," Jessie stood and started to pace around the room. Aleister and Spot were understandably disgusted. Sunny followed in hopes that her pacing would lead her to the cat food and second dinner. Greta leaned back in her chair and chewed her thumbnail.

"You also have a puck who is definitely behaving in a very uncharacteristic manner," she pointed out.

"True, but if the necromancer has strong enough magic or is funneling a lot of it at once, then he could be under a spell," Jessie replied.

"Right. And none of us really know anything about the Matagot. There's virtually no literature on them."

"Yeah, other than being chaotic neutral."

"Yes. Chaotic neutral," Greta snorted. "Anything else?"

"The attacker used a syringe on Warsaw. I saw it when Charlie recreated the scene of the attack. It had runes that glowed on the side, and I need to see if you can translate them."

Greta stared at Jessie.

"I'm sorry, when Charlie did what exactly?"

"Oh yeah, so ghosts can recreate the scene of a death if the energy is still there. And whoever did this put a spell on the bathroom to trap the energy from the murder inside so we wouldn't feel it when it happened, so that gave Charlie a lot to work with," Jessie said, secretly loving the look of surprise on Greta's face.

"When were you going to tell me this? What else can he do? How did you even think to try that? Because he felt the wind?"

"Now, we don't know yet, and yep. I figured if he could feel something like that, then maybe he could feel death energy. I mean, it's not that far-fetched of an idea. I just never had another ghost willing to try it out. They're usually too traumatized if they're not just over it all."

"That's brilliant," Greta marveled as she unwound herself

from the chair. Lucy immediately jumped up to claim the warm spot. "What were the runes? I might be able to help if they're Germanic or Nordic."

"That's what I was counting on," Jessie grabbed one of Greta's notebooks and sketched out the runes she had seen on the syringe.

Greta frowned as she took the paper.

"These are really old. Definitely Old Norse. I know someone who can probably translate them. I'll get an answer to you as soon as I can. Meanwhile talk to the members of the Ride tomorrow night and see what they have to say. Maybe you and your sheriff can set up a sting operation for the vampire groupies. Our old vampire buddy Renard is in New York. He would probably fly down to help."

"He's not my sheriff, and I'm already on that. I have a recipe for truth serum and a database of vampie aliases and real names to start with."

"Uh huh. Of course he's not," Greta grinned as Jessie's face turned red.

"*Anyway*," Jessie continued, pointedly ignoring her friend, "I'll let you know what I find out. Meanwhile I need you to hit up your contacts in Oberon's court and find out what you can about Robin. Check into covens and witch activity around France, Scotland, and Wales, too. See if anyone's suddenly gone inactive or disappeared. Maybe discreetly dig around on Madame Blanche."

"Got it. Meet back tomorrow night and compare notes?" Greta asked as they hugged each other.

"Yeah. See you then. Lubs you."

"Lubs you too," Greta said over her shoulder. Jessie caught

a glimpse of green hills, and then the panel closed behind her friend. Jessie sighed and headed for her own portal home, rubbing away the start of another headache. It felt like it had been two months instead of a day since Warsaw had turned up dead in her bathroom, and the end wasn't anywhere in sight. But at least she had something to work with now.

The next day Jessie ran errands before getting to the pub early. A good person may have died, sending turmoil and political intrigue rippling through her circle and the community, but the liquor order still needed to be placed, Matagots placated, bills paid, a wannabe vampire drugged, and a spell on her bathroom investigated.

She let herself in, her wards on the door dissolving into the late September morning air. Only the brownies she hired to keep the bar clean could get past her wards as long as her magical energy was undepleted.

She paused, not really sure why she was surprised to see Rupert sprawled out on his back on the bar in the sun, fluffy tummy turned up invitingly even though she would probably lose a hand and significant amount of blood if she even considered touching it.

"Did you stay here all night?" she asked, switching on the lights over the bar. He flipped over and yawned.

"*Mais naturement,*" he replied as he began to groom his whiskers. "It seemed to me that if one was able to cast a spell on your bathroom, then it was also possible the caster would attempt to undo the spell before you could investigate further. Indeed, it is a miracle in our favor that the caster did not already do so."

"That's the truth. We need a break in this. By the way, I believe I promised you sushi grade tuna, and I always deliver on my promises," Jessie paused to rummage in a bag before pulling out the fresh fish wrapped in butcher's paper. Rupert's whiskers twitched.

"Would you like a plate?"

He paused, trying to tell if she was making fun of him. Deciding that she was serious (she was), he jumped off the bar and stretched.

"No, *merci*," he reached for the tuna and began tearing through the paper.

"I could have unwrapped it for you," Jessie pointed out. He ignored her and started eating.

She headed down the hall to her office, wondering why she trusted him. After all, she had no more reason to trust him than anyone else in the group, but for some reason she couldn't pinpoint, he didn't seem to be the one they were after.

"It is because I am, as you say, 'chaotic neutral'," he said from behind her, making her yelp as she nearly jumped out of her skin.

"Rupert! Don't sneak up on me like that! And how did you know what I was thinking? Did you already finish the tuna?"

"I did, and it was quite satisfactory. I am very pleased," he said, sauntering into her office and jumping on the sofa. Well, more like stepping onto it since he was so big.

"As to your question, it was only a matter of time before

that occurred to you. The Matagot have a... sixth sense for lack of a better term that lets us translate body language more easily than most.

"As it is, I am aware that you have some reservations about my companion and the Puck. As much as it pains me to admit it, you have good reason to suspect both. However, I have no reason to wish to inflict any matter of political intrigue upon the world. It does not serve the purpose of the Matagot. If anything, increasing the distrust of the cryptid community among the other factions endangers those of us who have difficulty masquerading as human and are the least understood."

"Can you appear human?" Jessie asked, curious about this creature very few knew anything about.

"Yes, for brief periods of time, and it is quite taxing. To sustain the form longer than roughly five minutes, I need to draw upon the power of a witch. I'm sure you understand why this is not desirable."

Any type of siphon doubled as an energy exchange. When a creature drew upon a witch's power, the witch gained knowledge and insight into that creature's mind. Someone like Rupert, who held his cards so closely to his chest, wouldn't benefit from the experience, whereas Charlie really didn't have anything to hide from her when she allowed him to siphon from her to recreate the murder.

"Yes, and I would never ask that of you, you know."

"Yes, I do."

"Well, want to check out the spell on the bathroom with me?" Jessie asked as she put the rest of her bags down on the desk. He regarded her with his emerald green eyes.

"You are a very curious witch, Jessica. It is unusual to meet one such as you who is so accepting and respectful of boundaries."

Jessie sighed sadly.

"Yes, I know. I wish Greta and I weren't two of a kind and I could say there are a lot more out there like us, but there aren't."

"*Oui.* I would like to get to know this Greta of yours."

Jessie grinned, pulling the old leather satchel containing her tools and crystals out from a desk drawer.

"Oh, trust me. That can *definitely* be arranged."

They walked together back down the hall, the big cat padding silently next to her, looking for all the world like a Maine Coon on steroids.

"How long have you known Robin and Madame Blanche?" Jessie asked, trying to sound nonchalant. When questioning a creature with razor sharp claws that were easily three or four inches long, one had to be careful. He chuffed in amusement, clearly not fooled.

"Robin, not long at all. Before this trip I had seen him once or twice, but I never had the rather dubious pleasure of his company."

"There's pleasure to be had in his company?" Jessie's voice dripped with sarcasm.

"I wouldn't know," Rupert replied with a low growl.

"Madame Blanche I have known for quite a long time. She rescued me from hunters who had me cornered on the cliffs of Normandy. I owe her my life. And despite the Matagot's desire to remain neutral and chaotic," he continued with a sly sidelong glance at Jessie who smirked, "Warsaw was a good being. The gargoyles are the guardians of the balance of the world, you know. They are some of the oldest and noblest creatures in existence, and they are exceedingly rare. To end one, especially in such a manner, deserves nothing less than absolute and swift justice."

"I'm starting to think you might be chaotic good," Jessie remarked, pushing open the bathroom door.

"Perish the thought!" Rupert said with a gravelly chuckle.

She grinned and led the way inside. The remnants of the spell still lingered; it had been a strong one. She wondered how much of the stolen magic the necromancer had left and how strong the witch had been who gave it up.

Rupert gave her the all knowing gaze characteristic of cats everywhere. "You know something," he said.

"I do," she replied. "Before I tell you, I have to ask this, so please don't take offense. Do you think Madame Blanche is the same person she was before coming here?"

He became as still as a statue and stared at her impassively, only the lashing tip of his tail giving away his agitation. Matagots weren't the only ones who could read body language. Jessie sighed.

"Great. We have a puck and a white lady who are not who they seem, a necromancer, and–" she was interrupted by Rupert's sudden hiss.

"A necromancer! Here? No!"

"That's what Greta said it is. She said that's the only creature who can cast a spell that a ghost can feel, and last night before that Morticent kid came up to Nicky, Charlie felt something blow through him like the wind."

"*Merde!* To what end would a necromancer be involved?"

he snarled, his coat doubling in size. Jessie held out her hands, palms up.

"We don't know."

"Well, what do you know?" he demanded.

"A necromancer is most likely involved, I suspect to discredit Madame Blanche, myself, and Robin, which means there's another witch involved because you have to have a witch to make a necromancer," she said.

Rupert snarled and began pacing. Jessie began laying out her spell tools as she talked.

"I also know that Warsaw's death was needlessly brutal, which sends a statement and threat, because whoever subdued him used something in a syringe labeled with old Nordic runes to paralyze him before pouring a jar of acid down his throat. They also needed to make sure that the body was found at exactly the right time, so now we need to work on figuring out the spell that was placed on the bathroom before it deteriorates any further," she tried to keep her impatience and frustration under control. She never asked for a Matagot as an assistant, and frankly, she was getting tired of having nothing but questions and no answers.

"Sheriff Rossford has a database they use for the vampire groupies that I plan to use to stage a sting tonight so we can try to get more information on this Morticent kid, and I plan to talk to the Faerie Riders when they come in after the Full Moon Ride," she continued. "Now can we please get to work?"

He looked away.

"This is, how do you say, out of my wheelhouse," he admitted. "I was born before the Normans even came to what is now France, and yet I had never left my home before now. I know what a necromancer is though. It wasn't all that long ago when a group of witches decided to profit from the pelts of those of us who wore fur. Garments made from the coats of a Matagot were highly sought after. They created necromancers and promised them salvation from the life, such as it was, of a harbinger of death or ghost or whatever unfortunate lot had been bestowed upon these sad creatures."

"Oh, I remember. Nicky and Mikael asked that Greta and I be part of the party that hunted the cabal down," Jessie said grimly. It had been a bad time. The Matagot massacre was just the tip of the iceberg. "I'm sorry. It was horrible."

"Yes," he regarded her with his emerald eyes. "I was unaware of Nicodemus and Mikael's involvement in our salvation. I truly am sorry for the pain that Nicodemus feels at this moment. Well, shall we begin?"

"I thought you'd never ask," she smiled, sitting down cross legged on the floor and pulling a tiger's eye out of her bag.

"Crystals?" he asked, amused.

"A prison in case we unleash anything nasty. Now let me work. Also, we're going to be in a circle. I'll be in it with you. If you feel uncomfortable with that, tell me now because once we start, we can't stop until the ritual is over."

"You may continue," he began grooming his front paws. She rolled her eyes as she set the stone on the ground a few feet away and reached for the leyline beneath the bar with her mind. She threw up a protective circle around them that stopped just short of the crystal. Rupert growled softly as the circle went up. In light of his history she felt a twinge of guilt, but it couldn't be helped. After all, he had insisted on being there.

"What do you know about the Nain Rouge?" she asked as she settled into the spell. He looked at her in annoyance.

"Should you not concentrate on your spell work, witch?" he demanded.

"I can multitask. What do you know about them?"

"Very little. They are nasty little things that are distant cousins to the pucks and dwarves, created as a merging of sorts between creatures of fairy who existed in my land and this one. Why do you ask?"

"Because Madame Blanche said that the last time she met a creature who acted like Robin, it was a Nain Rouge."

"I see. Very interesting," he remarked thoughtfully.

"How so?" she asked, curiosity rising.

"Infiltration by the Nain Rouge could certainly explain the Puck's behavior, but they're too clannish and not organized enough to pull off something like that on their own. One also could not be your necromancer."

"No, but a necromancer with enough purloined power could disguise one as the Puck," she glanced at him, trying to gauge his reaction. He regarded her with a piercing gaze.

"Are you implying that this is the act of more than one entity? That perhaps neither of my companions are who they seem?"

Jessie shrugged.

"Anything is possible at this point," she said.

"Are you done yet? I would like to get out of here some time today," he complained.

"Working on it," she said, and settled down to concentrate.

She closed her eyes and pictured the bathroom as a grid. Casting her mind across each segment of the grid, she looked for what didn't belong in the ether. It didn't take long to find the spell.

She was glad she had the foresight to cast a circle of protection. All it took was one gentle probe to break it open and trigger the psychic backlash boobytrap designed to knock out whoever found it and probably give them a nasty headache for hours. Holding the circle in her mind, she came to her feet, gestured to Rupert to stay by her side, and walked carefully to the sink where a small sticker, the same color as the counter, was hidden from view.

"This is the spell?" Rupert asked, doubt coloring his voice.

"It's the carrier. I need to study it more closely, but at first guess, it was tuned to Morticent so that when he entered the room, the spell was triggered. Whoever cast it is not a natural witch. It was too strong for what it was meant to do."

"What do you mean?"

"Well, if I wanted to create a containment spell that stopped something bad from leaving a room and alerting others to what was happening, I wouldn't make it strong enough to last this long after the event. I would make it just strong enough to last during the event, and then it would release at the earliest convenient time."

"Like when first responders are at the scene, the bar is in turmoil, and everyone is already upset and panicked," he finished her thought.

"Exactly. I never would have known this was here if it hadn't lasted longer than it needed to. But because it was still active, Charlie and I felt its presence last night."

"Do you not use these facilities?" Rupert asked rather primly.

"Ew, no. I have my own bathroom in the office. Do you know what it's like using the same bathroom as drunk men and women? I mean, haven't you heard how Charlie died? That alone is reason enough to stay away!"

"Humans and humanlike creatures are disgusting," Rupert said in disdain.

"Preaching to the choir."

"Are you certain that was not intentional though?" Rupert asked.

Jessie paused.

"You think someone wanted us to find it?" she asked.

"We know this child who is obsessed with the vampires is not a witch, nor is he the necromancer. Until last night we were not completely certain that he had not purchased the talisman which rendered him invisible on his own," Rupert pointed out, choosing to ignore the fact that no one had actually reached that conclusion, which, Jessie realized, was as logical as anything else they had come up with.

"However, he could not have obtained a spell of this nature without the necromancer who assisted him being completely aware of the plan," Rupert continued. "That knowledge was imperative for the spell to work. But your strength and experience are well known. No witch would have created a spell that permitted the violent death of one who held a claim to your hospitality and protection and left it for you to find unless they're sending you a message."

"True, but a necromancer isn't a witch– they just use a witch's power, and they wouldn't have the skills to be able to subtly pull this off. That takes decades of training. It's like giving a child a hammer and telling them to make filigree jewelry." Greta wasn't the only one who could come up with strange analogies.

"There were enough other messages sent that I don't think this was one of them. It doesn't feel right."

"If you say so," he said doubtfully.

"I just really hate bullshit, and I hate murder, and I hate it when people hurt my friends. I need to call Mikael and John, set a trap for this Morticent kid, and then later tonight you and I can sit down with Greta and talk."

"Excellent. Now can you please drop this thrice damned circle before my coat comes off from the itching?"

"Yes, your majesty," she said, carefully inverting the circle so it wrapped around the crystal and the bespelled sticker. She forced the backlash into the tiger's eye and, pulling on a glove embroidered with protection runes, cautiously picked it up and put it in a matching velvet bag. Rupert watched.

"You may continue to address me as 'your majesty'," he loftily informed her. She rolled her eyes.

"I'll get right on that. Let's go make some phone calls," she said and led the way back to her office where Charlie greeted them from behind her desk with the worst attempt at nonchalance she had ever seen.

"Jessie! Rupert! How's it going?" he beamed jovially.

"Hi, Charlie. It's great! How are you?" Jessie was all innocence.

"Great! Great. So... how's things?"

"You asked that," Jessie pointed out.

"Oh, right! I did."

Jessie grinned. "Still want to pretend like you weren't spying on us in the bathroom? You're lucky you were in the circle, by the way. That thing was nasty."

Rupert stared in surprise.

"You knew he was there the whole time?"

"He wasn't there the whole time. He showed up right before I cast the circle. Don't worry, I wouldn't have let him eavesdrop on our conversation," Jessie reassured him.

"Fine. Let's get on with it," he was clearly miffed.

"Scoot over, Charlie. I need my desk," Jessie said, making a shooing motion with her hand.

"Aw, I just want to help," he protested, turning a faint shade of navy blue, something that was not lost on Rupert.

"I know, but you can't make phone calls for me. You can get the liquor order together though if you want."

"Fine," Charlie drifted out of the room muttering to himself.

"A ghost who purchases spirits," Rupert snickered. Jessie groaned.

"It's too early for bad puns," she complained. "Stop distracting me."

"As you wish," he smirked, curling into a ball on the sofa and pretending to go to sleep.

Jessie sighed as she pulled out her phone and made a mental note to ask Cassie what she needed to do to look at her cameras with it. Despite her natural tendency to disrupt anything technological, she had always been fascinated by computers, software, and anything that could be defined as a gadget. At the moment she had more important things to do, so she started with the sheriff.

"Hey, Jess. A little early isn't it?" He sounded as tired as she felt.

"Yeah, but you know how it is. Liquor and crime never sleep," she said and was rewarded with a wry chuckle.

"No kidding. What did you find out?"

"A lot more questions than answers. What do you know about necromancers?"

There was a long pause before he replied, "Nothing good. Are you kidding me right now? Fuck, Jessie. What the hell's going on?"

"Apparently that's what we're up against. Greta's digging around some more. We ran up against them a couple of centuries ago."

"But why? I mean what's the point? And how are a gargoyle and some kid out of his mind over Nicky involved?"

"Remember the part where I said I found more questions than answers?" Jessie sighed, wishing she had stopped to pick up coffee first.

"Great. So now what?"

"Do you have someone named Belladonna on your database of vampies?" Jessie asked, absentmindedly doodling on her desk.

"Vampies?"

"I'm tired of vampire groupies. It takes too long to say," she said as she scratched out the doodle and started over. Rupert cracked an eye open to watch her.

"Fine. Hang on... yeah. She's on here. Jennifer Wilcox, age twenty-three. She's been on this list for a while too."

"Apparently she's the one who's all up Morticent's– sorry, Marshall's ass."

"And you have a plan that involves her," it was a statement rather than a question.

"Sure do. Morticent has to be staying somewhere around here, but we don't know where. I'm going to get Mikael to fly our friend Renard the Fox, down here and send out the word that a new vampire is in town. If Morticent doesn't take the bait, then we know she definitely will. She can't resist any new vampire."

"You're bringing the Fox into my jurisdiction? And you think he can get the information out of her with his vampiric wiles," he sounded annoyed and amused at the same time.

"It won't be anything illegal. I just want more information about our dear friend, Morticent."

John sighed. "And I guess you need a way to let her know about said new vampire. How are you planning to control him, by the way?"

"He won't do anything to put Mikael or Nicky in jeopardy. But letting her know is a brilliant idea! If only I had her information," Jessie said brightly.

"I hate you."

"No, you don't, which is why you're going to text it to me since it's already something that's off the record."

"Fine, but keep me in the loop, Jess. I mean it!"

"Yes, sir!" Jessie said. Rupert muttered something about being surrounded by infants and closed his eye again. She ignored him as she dialed Mikael's number.

"Jessica, I adore you with every fiber of my being, but please tell me why you are calling me at this godforsaken hour."

"Sorry, Mikael. I need a favor. We're going to set a trap, and I need bait."

"And...?"

"Renard is in New York. I need you to fly him here by midnight."

There was a very long pause. Jessie thought maybe he had hung up on her before he said in the tone of one speaking to a very young child, "Jessica, you are aware that it is daylight, are you not?"

"Yes."

"And vampires cannot fly in daylight."

"Yes, but there are these things called planes that will get you there while it's daylight, and then you can fly back once the sun goes down."

"And why am I doing this?"

"Because I need to get to Morticent, but no one knows where he is, so I need to lure him here with bait."

"Bait. I cannot wait to tell Renard that he is to be bait."

"It's for a good cause. You know he loves intrigues."

Mikael sighed, a very long suffering sigh.

"And if Morticent," he said with the same distaste that Jessie felt, "does not take the bait?"

"I put a truth serum in his bestie's drink and get his whereabouts out of her."

"Well, I can't argue with the urgency of this plan. Fine. We shall be there."

"Thank you. Did Nicodemus make it home?"

"He did, right before I arrived. He spent the rest of the night in his studio. Hopefully there won't be any unpleasant repercussions from the events of the evening, but it is good that he is creating again."

"I agree. I hope it helps. See you at midnight, and thanks again, Mikael."

"You're welcome. Now good day, Jessica!"

She laughed as he hung up and turned back to her bags.

"What now," Rupert asked.

"Now we make up a little truth serum for tonight while we wait for the sheriff to get back to us," she replied as she pulled vials and sachets out of the bag. "Then we set a trap."

"Excellent. I am going to go partake of your bar's delightful access to the sun. Please fetch me once you are ready to leave."

"Of course," she replied absently as she started on her work.

10

One hour and a lot of swearing later, she successfully produced a tiny vial full of a clear liquid. John sent her a text with Belladonna's real name, address, and day job as a barista at a Starbucks off of I-75. She grabbed her phone and started down the hall toward the bar, dialing his number as she went. He answered on the first ring.

"Let me guess. This is where you need me to go with you because you don't know anyone else who is awake and functioning right now."

"I'm buying," she said, tossing her bag on the bar and ignoring Rupert's protest at being woken up for the second time that morning.

"Be there in five."

Jessie hung up and looked at Charlie, whose bottom half stuck out of the liquor cabinet.

"Hey, Charlie, I need to go out for a bit. I'm going to set the wards and alarm just in case, okay?"

"Sure thing, Jess."

"Rupert, you coming?" she raised an eyebrow at the

Matagot, knowing what the answer would be. He sniffed in disdain.

"As if I would be left behind. After you, *mademoiselle*."

"Actually, after the Sheriff. We're riding with him."

"I will *not* be behind bars in the back seat like some common criminal!" Rupert huffed in outrage.

Jessie laughed despite herself.

"No, you won't. He has a nice Jeep he uses for stuff like this. We'll be fine."

Ushering the slightly placated beast out the door, she paused to key in the alarm code on the panel and then set her wards for good measure.

"Doesn't that seem like a bit of overkill?" Rupert asked curiously.

"Maybe, but with everything going on, I'd rather be safe than sorry," she shrugged as John's old, beat up red Jeep pulled into her parking lot. Rupert gave her a level stare.

"One day you and I must discuss your interpretation of the word 'nice'," he remarked.

John didn't say anything about the addition of a giant black cat in his car. He just handed her a sheet of paper as they pulled onto the street.

"What's this?" she asked, starting to read.

"Everything we have on Jennifer Wilcox. That's Bella-donna's real name," he added for Rupert's benefit.

Jessie read in silence for a moment.

"Not a lot to go on," she commented as she pushed back a wave of disappointment.

"Yeah, she doesn't have a record. She just graduated from

Georgia State, she works, and she chases after vampires. That's about it."

"Well, it's more than we have on Marshall," Jessie sighed.

"True," he said as he focused on the road.

"How are the kids?" she asked into the companionable silence.

"Great. They're at their grandmother's this week. Probably going to be rotten by the time I get them back."

"Well, of course. That's her job," Jessie pointed out.

"Do you have children?" Rupert asked her.

"No, they were never really part of my life plan, and I like being Aunt Jessie to dozens of kids I can just send home at the end of the night. I love kids, but I just never found someone to try to have them with," she replied, settling back in her seat.

"I am embarrassed to admit that I do not know the nature of how a witch reproduces," Rupert said ruefully.

"Well, male witches are sterile. So until artificial insemination was a thing, the only way a witch could reproduce was by sex with human men. But relationships and marriage with humans weren't really options. Witches can live to be thousands of years old. No matter how much a mortal partner swears they love a witch, very few can accept that not only will their partner never grow old with them, but she has powers they can't even fathom."

"And that's if she can tell him who and what she really is. Because that wasn't even possible until recently, right?" John asked, glancing at her.

"Not really," she said as Rupert interrupted.

"Shouldn't you pay attention to the road?" he protested, clearly on edge in the car.

"I got this," John replied, glancing at the big cat in the mirror.

They didn't have far to go. The Starbucks was only two exits away off I-75 in front of a strip mall. Jessie, who hated the encroachment of the concrete jungle on her world, had never been to it. Like the rest of the local supernatural community, she preferred to get her coffee from the little cafe owned by a very nice Naga family a block down from the bar and leave the corporate coffee chains to humans.

"Do we have a plan, or are we just going to go in guns blazing?" John asked.

"Oh, you know, I figured we'd wing it," Jessie shrugged.

"Of course," he sighed.

She pulled out her phone and called him. He looked at her baffled.

"Um, Jess, I know you're old and all, but I'm right here."

She gave him a withering glare.

"I know, dumbass. Rupert can't go inside, and I want him to hear what we say. So I'm going to leave my phone in the car. Now answer me and put it on speaker."

"Right," he said.

"I would prefer to accompany you," Rupert growled.

"Sorry, but unless you can stand to be human, it's a health code violation."

Leaving Rupert to mutter to himself about fur-bearing cryptid discrimination, injustice, and plans to get revenge by destroying the seat ("everything had better be the way we left it when I get back," was the sheriff's input at that point), Jessie and John headed for the door.

"So now I have to deal with this stupid quarterly inventory audit, Nicky's hurt feelings, and to top it off, a new vamp is coming into town tonight and wants to use the bar for some meet and greet or something like that," Jessie complained as they pushed through the door and headed for the counter, casting a spell that projected their conversation to Jennifer Wilcox's aka Belladonna's waiting ears.

She was a pretty girl with brown eyes, a full figure, a septum piercing, and pale skin that probably hadn't voluntarily seen sunlight in the last five years. Her green uniform was incongruous with her candy apple red hair and black eyeliner. Jessie blandly made eye contact without a trace of recognition.

"Hi, vanilla latte please. Whatever the largest size is. I'm sorry, I never remember what they're called. John? You want anything?"

"Just plain coffee for me, thanks. Small. One of us needs to not bounce out of the car."

Jessie chose to ignore that, handing cash to Belladonna, who watched them with poorly concealed curiosity. Jessie had seen the recognition on the girl's face when they walked in the door. Now to finish setting the trap.

She pulled the loose change she had turned three times in her fingers out of her coat pocket and dropped it in the tip jar. John had suggested that she bespell the coins with an eavesdropping spell that would be triggered by Belladonna's voice. They moved a few feet from the counter, and Jessie could practically feel Belladonna's eyes burning holes in the back of her head.

"So who's the new vamp?" John asked, pitching his voice suitably low. The beauty of Jessie's spell was that the compulsion made sure that Belladonna wouldn't question why she could hear what was obviously a private conversation.

"An old friend of Mikael's. Renard."

"As in the Fox?" John asked, feigning surprise.

"Shh! Keep it down! He's only in town for the night on a stopover, but it's supposed to be on the downlow," she hissed, suppressing a smile as she heard Belladonna's gasp.

"Your drinks are ready," the other barista piped up with an artificial, sunny smile.

"Oh, thanks, have a nice day," Jessie turned back to the counter and grabbed the cups.

They got back in the car, and Jessie poured half of her latte in a travel mug before putting the cup with the rest in the back seat cup holder for Rupert.

"An offering of appeasement," she said.

"I accept," Rupert sniffed. "Now what?"

"Now we go back to the bar, see if the enchanted coins pick up anything, get ready for Renard, and wait," she replied, then swore as she burned her mouth on the coffee. John watched, not bothering to hide his grin.

"You're how old again?" He asked.

"Shut up," she glared.

"I just wondered if maybe they didn't have fire in the olden days, because, you know, hot drinks are usually hot."

"Just drive," she snapped.

"It's not like you can do something witchy like cool it down," he continued as he pulled out of the parking lot.

"There's about to be a bad accident involving this coffee and your crotch if you don't shut up and drive," she retorted.

He laughed. She reached into the backseat and grabbed her phone.

"Rupert, you heard all of that?" She asked.

"Oh, yes. Do you think it is wise to include the Fox? His reputation for leaving 'vampies' as you call them in gutters drained nearly to the point of death is well known."

"Mikael and Nicky came to his aid when he was still a human Visigoth named Hathus fighting off the Romans who tried to conquer his village. It could be another thousand years from now, and he would still consider himself in their debt. Plus, he can't resist a good scheme. He may be mischievous, but he's also extremely loyal. Really the only problem is he views humans as basically livestock, even though they're responsible for at least two thirds of the luxuries he swears he can't live without," Jessie replied.

"You know, your life is fascinating. You talk about ancient history the way someone else would say, 'yeah, I did laundry today'," John remarked.

"I don't mean it like that," Jessie started to protest.

"No, Jess, I know. It's not a criticism. You actually lived or are close to people who lived the things the rest of us are barely aware of, and you have this crazy, amazing wealth of knowledge. It's second nature to you. I admire that and am a little envious at the same time."

"You're not that young though," she pointed out.

"Yeah, but only by about three centuries. That's nothing.

Unless you want a detailed history of the Revolutionary War, and then I got you covered," he added.

"Rupert, how old do the Matagot live to be, if you don't mind me asking?" She asked, twisting around in her seat to look at the big cat.

"I actually am uncertain. I don't believe I have ever known one of my kind to perish naturally. We also don't measure time as you do. I have seen many nations rise and fall, but the concept of time as something that needs to be measured is as alien to me as your long life is to our sheriff here," he explained while grooming his whiskers.

"Not that I plan to try to murder you or anything, but how do you die?" John asked.

"Specialized hunters," Rupert replied sadly. "We have been hunted for our coats. They are virtually indestructible, you see, but there is a means to subdue and kill us. You'll forgive me if I don't share that knowledge. I have the utmost respect for you, wolf, but I do not know you well enough to trust you with my life."

"That's fair," John said, turning off the interstate. They rode in silence the rest of the way to the bar.

"Thanks for going with us, John," Jessie said, grabbing the remnants of the latte and climbing out of the Jeep. Rupert jumped down when she opened the back door and stretched with a yawn that revealed gleaming white fangs.

"No problem. Let me know if you get anything. Do you want me here tonight?" He asked. She thought for a moment.

"Stay close by. I don't want to give anything away," she said.

He gave her a cocky little wink and pulled away. She

turned back to Rupert, who regarded her with emerald eyes, looking like a four foot tall version of Tournée's *Le Chat Noir*.

"You should check on Madame Blanche. I still need to get ready for tonight. If I get anything from the coins we left for Belladonna, I'll find a way to reach you. Just do me a favor—don't share too much, okay? Just until we know what we're dealing with. Where are you staying, by the way?" It occurred to her that she had never bothered to find out.

"The Waldorf, *naturement*," he replied with a condescending sniff that made her eyes narrow dangerously. He ignored her.

"How are you traveling between Atlanta and here?" She asked, crossing her arms across her chest.

"While I may not be able to hold the form of a man, other creatures come quite easily," said the enormous crow that had been a cat a second ago. He cawed raucous laughter at the startled look on her face before lifting himself high into the sky and fading out of sight.

"Damn cats," she swore under her breath before stomping through the door and letting it slam shut behind her.

"Find anything interesting?" Charlie floated through the wall into the main room as Jessie tossed her bag and keys on the bar.

"I just cleaned that, you know," a tiny voice that carried the burr of a Scottish accent piped up from beneath the bar, followed by an irritated brownie. Jessie snatched up her bag guiltily.

"Sorry, Annie! I forgot you were coming today."

"That's fine, lass. Memory loss is the first thing to go, you know."

Charlie laughed.

"She got you there, Jess," he snickered.

"Ha ha. Very funny," Jessie rolled her eyes. "Keep laughing. I might forget that I agreed not to send you on your way."

"Nah, you wouldn't do that," Charlie beamed. Sometimes Jessie felt like her goodwill was seriously taken advantage of.

"Hey, Annie, can I ask you something?" She leaned over the bar to look down at the little brownie who industriously scrubbed the corners under the drink rail. Annie wore a kerchief over her nut brown curls and a tidy checkered apron over a neat, blue dress that was tied up around her knees.

Annie paused to rock back on her heels and squint up at Jessie, her little upturned nose wrinkling in mock annoyance.

"I suppose, since it seems you don't want me to finish," she said.

"Did you ever meet Robin the Puck?"

"Aye, many times. Not that my Ian and I are much for the Courts, but you can't be part of Faerie and not put in an appearance to Oberon and his queens every now and again, and Robin is often sent among the lesser courts on Oberon's behalf. Robin looks out for us little ones, you know. Always makes sure we are taken care of. Such a dear fellow. Loves a good joke and a spot of mischief, but his heart is made of gold, of that you can be certain."

Charlie stared at her.

"Are you sure we're talking about the same Puck?" he asked in disbelief.

"Seriously, I was about to say that," Jessie agreed.

Annie bristled and threw her rag into her bucket as she came to her feet.

"Now I never thought either of you would have an ill word to say about the Fair Folk, and you had better have a good reason for questioning my word, or you'll have to answer to me and the Duchess!"

"No, I didn't mean it like that! I mean, we didn't," Jessie hastily interrupted, spreading out her hands in a placating gesture. "The Robin who's been here this week is either leading up to the world's biggest joke, or something's wrong because there's nothing nice about him at all. That's why I asked."

Annie looked baffled.

"I don't understand. You say the Puck is here?"

Now Jessie looked confused.

"Yes. You mean you didn't know? Mikael took him to be presented to the Duchess at court yesterday."

Annie shook her head and bent down to retrieve her rag.

"Nay, lass. None came to the Court, and the Puck would have gone there before ever stepping foot in this place, of that I can promise you."

Jessie and Charlie exchanged looks.

"If I showed you a video could you tell me if it's him?" Jessie asked.

"Absolutely," Annie said.

"Okay, come with me," Jessie pushed off from the bar and started down the hall to the office, Annie on her heels, and Charlie floating along behind them. Once they got in the office, Jessie pulled up the security camera footage while Annie looked around in disapproval.

"One day you need to let me clean this room," she wrinkled her nose again.

"Maybe," Jessie grinned. Her office was off limits due to the number of spells, charms, and protections strewn about. "I'm just not sure how I feel about trying to explain to the Duchess that her favorite brownie cleaning service is now run by a porcupine."

Annie quickly pulled her hands back from a dust bunny under the desk and stuck them in her pockets.

"Here we go. Can you see?" Jessie asked.

"Aye, I'm not much shorter than you, you know," Annie scoffed, earning another snort of laughter from Charlie.

"Keep laughing," Jessie shot him a dirty look before hitting play on the footage she had pulled up of the night before.

They watched and listened in silence. Despite all of the background noise, the conversation was clear enough to hear Robin's diatribe against Jessie's establishment and how insufferable it was to be stuck there. Madame Blanche fingered her opal in silence, compressing her lips in an obvious attempt to hold her tongue. Jessie cut the footage before Morticent's outburst.

Annie was stunned.

"That certainly looks like the Puck, but if that's really Robin, then I'm a hobgoblin."

"Could he be under a spell?" Charlie asked.

"Perhaps, but I only know a handful of witches strong enough to bespell the Puck, or any of the Fair Folk. Our Jessie maybe, but not many more else."

"What do you know about the Nain Rouge?" Jessie asked.

"Not much to be honest. The few I met were on the ill tempered side, and they certainly play their share of tricks, but they're content to be left alone. What do they have to do with our Puck?"

"I don't know. Madame Blanche mentioned them, and I'm trying to rule out whether or not they could be involved. Can they shapeshift?"

Annie shook her head.

"No, that's not in their bag of tricks. Sounds to me like someone's trying to lead you astray. But we have one at court. I can arrange a meeting."

"That would help a lot," Jessie smiled gratefully.

Annie beamed. Brownies weren't overly self-important,

but they had a very strong and well placed sense of self value, and they enjoyed being recognized for their contributions--something that didn't happen as often as it should in Jessie's opinion.

"Well, since you won't let me do my magic in this place, I need to get back to what I can clean. Now if you're done wasting my time," Annie pointedly ignored Jessie's protest as she popped out of sight. A moment later the sound of an old Scotch folk song drifted down the hallway.

Charlie laughed again. Jessie glared, and he grinned back.

"You have to admit she got you," he pointed out.

"Whatever."

"Now what?" he asked, settling over the sofa.

"Now we place the liquor and beer orders."

"I meant about the case."

"The case? What, are we PIs now?" she asked, pulling out her desk chair and bending to throw away the dust bunny that had so offended Annie.

"Yes. What's next?" he asked, eyebrow raised. He had never been able to raise just one eyebrow when he was alive and now used every opportunity to do so. The first week he was dead he looked like he was perpetually waiting for an answer to a question none of the rest of them knew had been asked.

"Well, we need to find out when Annie can set up the meeting with the Nain Rouge at Court--"

"This evening at six sharp," Annie said, making Jessie fall out of the chair in surprise.

"Why, Charlie! I didn't know you could be such a lovely shade of orange!" Annie remarked to the ghost who would have cried with laughter if he was capable of producing tears.

She turned back to Jessie who picked herself up from the floor and glared daggers at Charlie who tried unsuccessfully to get himself back under control.

"The court will be up and moving around by then, and he has agreed to meet you."

"Thank you for setting that up," Jessie tried to reclaim some of her dignity.

"My pleasure. If something is amiss among the fae, then we all should work together to find out what, don't you agree?"

"Yes," Jessie nodded. She was secretly relieved to have another ally, especially since Annie was a brownie. The fae were the most mysterious and misunderstood of the factions. She had no idea how she would navigate the mystery of Robin if they closed ranks.

"Good," Annie nodded in satisfaction and disappeared again.

Jessie sighed. Charlie giggled. She squinted at him.

"You did turn orange. How did we never notice this before?"

"Well, to be honest, after I, you know, passed or whatever this is, I never had a reason to be emotional until now. I mean, I feel good when I'm around Mary Jo, but that's usually in a dark corner somewhere," he shrugged.

"Huh," Jessie regarded him with a thoughtful gaze. "After we solve this thing, I want to see what else you can do."

"Fine," he gave a long-suffering sigh. "Just poke at me like some kind of experiment."

"Consider it rent!" she beamed. "Now come on. We need to get these orders finished so I can make myself look half decent for court."

Charlie shook his head and drifted out of the office behind her while muttering something about spectral abuse, which she ignored.

Several hours later after a hot shower, a successful attempt to tame her mane of curls, expertly applied make up, tasteful jewelry and flats, and a dark gray worsted pant suit over a soft lavender blouse (contrary to popular belief, Jessie did, in fact, own nice clothes and could look as put together and polished as Mikael when she had to), Jessie was on her way to the local Court.

Located in an old cathedral outside of town, the property was surrounded by ancient oaks, sycamores, and holly interspersed with sprawling herb gardens. Jessie was pretty sure ninety percent of the plants on the property were extinct in the rest of the world.

She parked in a small, neat parking lot off to the side. Way off to the side. Iron burned the fae, and she made sure to be as respectful of that fact as she could.

A Tuatha de Danann page with ocean blue eyes and hair the color of wheat, wearing a doublet in the ducal colors of sky blue and new grass green, stood at attention waiting for her as she started up the flagstone path to the entrance. He made a deep bow as she approached.

"The Duchess offers you greetings this eve, Madame Witch, and wishes it be known that you are her guest in this establishment and under the boon of her hospitality."

In other words, no one could mess with her while she was there. For anyone else there would be some thinly veiled threat that the boon only lasted while they behaved themselves, but

Jessie's and the Duchess' long friendship and mutual respect made that stipulation unnecessary centuries ago.

She inclined her head in acknowledgment.

"It is a pleasure to receive a greeting from one who is so schooled in the art of making one feel welcome," she said, pretending not to notice the way his chest puffed out a little more, his shoulders squared a touch higher, and his face let a little smile of pride slip through.

The page was very young and green by fae standards, and a little encouragement never hurt. Sending out one so inexperienced to greet Jessie was not an insult. Her vast knowledge made such things a teaching experience for the young, and she was always happy to oblige.

He led her down a hall lined with ornate sconces that cast pools of golden light on walls covered with interlacing wood and stone murals that depicted scenes from the Court's history– scenes that were ever changing thanks to the local nymphs' abilities to coax the wood into new shapes.

The carpet under Jessie's feet was a deep, rich pile colored the same grass green and trimmed with blue. As they approached the reception hall, Jessie could hear the sounds of court– laughter, voices rising and falling in conversation, and, most of all, the ethereal, beautiful music that tore at her heart while visions of wild Scottish moors flashed across her mind. A mortal could never withstand the music of the fae without being lost to its spell forever; it was hard enough for a witch to resist the pull.

Before they reached the entrance to the hall, the page stopped and turned, gesturing to a small alcove tucked in the wall. They passed through to a broad oak door at the other side, and he bowed as he waved her into a small, comfortable room.

"You may go now, Dain. We will summon you when we have finished here," the voice was as musical as if the same instruments in the reception hall were contained in the speaker's throat, and Jessie met the Duchess' gaze, a smile spreading across her lips.

Duchess Mara Mac Gabhann of the Tuatha de Danann, possessed the beautiful, almost alien, sharply planed face characteristic of most fae with hair the color of ripe plums that fell in ripples past her slender waist, ivory skin, and emerald green eyes.

Mara was graced with an almost earthy character and a wicked sense of humor and deep appreciation for Jessie's knowledge and skills. She had brought her court into the peace talks with aplomb, offering insight and aid when Mikael needed to navigate the intricacies of Fae politics and diplomacy.

She came forward, hands outstretched and pulled Jessie into a warm hug.

"My dear, it has been too long! Of course we would love to assist you with this puzzling issue of yours. LaSalle is waiting for you with Annie. But how is dear Nicodemus?" she asked, her voice lilting with a centuries old Gaelic brogue.

"He's hanging in there. I brought the camera footage from the last two nights," Jessie replied, pulling her phone out of her bag. "My two big questions are these: is this the real Puck, and, if it is, could he be under a spell."

The Duchess frowned.

"Either are possibilities. That's actually in part why LaSalle is here. He came to warn that an attempt might be made to corrupt Robin and use him to sabotage the talks. But to bespell one of the oldest and most powerful Fae– particularly one under Oberon's direct protection– would take a tremendous amount of power from someone very unscrupulous."

Jessie frowned, choosing not to point out that sharing the knowledge of an impending attack might be nice.

"Like my level of power or stronger?"

"To place one of the Fae as old and powerful as the Puck under a spell of this nature would be very painful and would strip him of all free will. In short, you would make him a prisoner in his own mind. I believe you are strong enough, although I also believe you are too honorable for such an undertaking."

"What do you know of necromancers?" Jessie asked carefully. The Matagot were not the only ones to suffer at the hands of witches wielding death tools. The Duchess's lips thinned in rage, and her eyes flashed like green lightning.

"Why?" It came out as almost a snarl.

Jessie involuntarily stepped back from Mara's rage. The Duchess made a conscious effort to get herself under control.

"I am sorry, my honored guest. My anger is not directed toward you. Come, sit. Have some tea with no fear of trickery or deceit. Let me tell you about the ones you call necromancers and what has been done to our kind in that name."

She led Jessie to a small table which was carved from a single tree and topped with a beautiful silver and crystal tea service. When Jessie sat down in one of the richly upholstered purple chairs, she had a moment of panic that maybe she wouldn't stop sinking into the overstuffed cushion and be lost forever. Despite her pique, Mara laughed at the look on Jessie's face.

"These chairs are ridiculous, but I can't for the life of me convince my vassals to consider practicality over finery."

"Whatever makes them happy, I guess," Jessie remarked sourly, struggling to reach both her tea cup and her dignity.

"I assume that since a necromancer is made from a death omen or harbinger, there are a number of fae who have been involved in the process over the years."

"More than you know, and rarely of their own free will," Mara scowled, sipping a goblet of something Jessie suspected was much stronger than tea. Jessie was startled by the comment.

"Really! I thought that a necromancer could only be made of their own free will though."

"Yes and no. The one to be turned must come to the ritual willing to become a necromancer, but the witch performing the ritual does not have to tell them everything– like how painful the experience will be, that they too must suffer a karmic rebalance, or that after they're turned they can be killed as easily as a human can."

Jessie stared at her friend stunned.

"Greta is as close to an expert on this as we have, and I'm pretty sure she would have told me that if she had found out that they could be killed that easily. Or that it is painful."

"It is not common knowledge," Mara replied. "Those who are dark enough to practice these arts with such disregard for the beings they turn hid their secrets well. Can you imagine the Witch Council allowing such a thing to happen?"

"Not now maybe, but we definitely had members of the

council in the past who would rather sweep such knowledge under the rug," Jessie's voice carried a note of sorrow. "Especially if they benefited from the results."

Mara watched Jessie with sympathy.

"I imagine this is a painful memory to relive, my dear. After all, you and Greta had to spend decades cleaning up the corruption within the Witch Council and watch the imprisonment and death of hundreds upon thousands of witches."

"Oh, it gets worse," Jessie said, staring morosely into her teacup. "One of the darkest points was when we learned that council members had convinced impressionable, young witches, so young that their hair hadn't even turned silver, barely older than we were when we first began our training, to perform dark magic on the council members' behalf– a convenient way to gain all the benefit with considerably less karmic repercussions."

They sat in silence for a moment, neither sure what to say to make the other feel better.

"Well," Mara finally continued, taking another sip from her goblet, which conveniently refilled itself, "you are correct in that the Fae have their share of harbingers of death and death dealers who can all be used for necromancy. It's not hard to convince a banshee, for instance, to become a witch for a few weeks. Just point out that she gets a respite from screaming a call of impending death to those who despise her for what she is and has to do."

She took another sip before continuing, "All you have to do is leave out the little parts like if she is, in fact, allowed to live after the ritual is over, she will have to repay the karmic balance for the same amount of time as the witch by whatever means necessary. And definitely don't mention that chances are, you're just going to kill her before her time is up so that you don't leave a messy little trail. Because once a creature of fae is turned into a necromancer, they become as easy to kill as a mortal or a witch."

Jessie felt sick.

"I didn't know that."

Mara smiled sadly.

"Why would you?" she asked, putting the goblet on the table and rising to help pull Jessie out of her cushiony prison.

"But, come. Let us meet with LaSalle. And I will arrange for you to meet Brigitte at another time. She is a banshee who survived the massacre during the Witch Council rebellion. I believe Greta was the one who saved her life when those who used her for necromancy tried to inflict her untimely death. Not that Greta did her any favors. When the witch who turned her was killed and therefore unable to repay her end of the karmic balance, the whole lot fell to Brigitte. The universe will have its due whether the person responsible for payment was guilty or not."

Jessie followed Mara across the hallway to another small room just before the main hall.

"We weren't sure what would happen to the karmic repercussions if the witch died before the balance was repaid. Who pays the balance if both die?"

"Kindred, from what we've seen," Mara replied with a shrug of her slender shoulders. "The balance seems to be equally bestowed across all of the kindred though, so it probably seems more like a run of bad luck than real karmic blow back."

"'So you finally showed up. What do I look like, made out

of time? I have better things to do than sit around waiting for some witch, you know," a rough voice tinged with a flat Michigan accent greeted them as Mara pushed the door open.

Jessie came face to face with the Nain Rouge on the other side. Whatever she expected, this was not quite it. LaSalle looked for all the world like a disgruntled garden gnome in stature and appearance until she got closer and saw the surly expression, red eyes, and matted beard.

"What are you looking at, shorty?" he demanded.

"You," Jessie snapped back. "Funny, I thought you'd be taller."

He folded his arms across his chest and scowled as Mara choked on her laughter.

"Yeah, well someone has to make you feel big. Now what do you want? I haven't got all day."

"I don't think the Puck is who he says he is. I think either someone put him under a spell or the creature there is a shapeshifter. Someone brought up the Nain Rouge. I think that's a red herring. Am I right?"

He looked at her, nonplussed. He wasn't prepared for the blunt approach, and Jessie was secretly pleased that she threw him off balance.

"Aye, you're right. Might as well sit down while you're here. No point making yourself feel taller than you are by standing all day."

Jessie passed up on the purple chair for the wooden bench. She didn't feel like trying to have this conversation with her feet sticking up in the air. LaSalle chuckled, a cawing sound that was surprisingly pleasant.

"I hate those chairs. Hey, Duchess, tell your people to make something useful for a change!"

"I'll get right on that," Mara replied in a slightly strangled voice as she tried to control an indecorous fit of giggles. Jessie began to suspect that LaSalle's continued presence at court was more for entertainment value than anything else.

"Alright lass, tell me everything. And Duchess, get some beer in here! This wine wouldn't get a fly drunk," he demanded. To Jessie he added, "About the only useful thing they have in this place are goblets that never go empty. Now go on, tell me."

As Jessie talked through the events of the previous two nights, part of her wondered why she instinctively trusted this cantankerous little creature who she had never met. The Nain Rouge were known to be tricksters and malevolent, but as she warmed up to her subject and gauged his reactions, she began to wonder if maybe there was another side to them, much like the Matagot.

The Duchess listened in silence, and only her eyebrows, raised so high that they threatened to disappear into her hairline, gave away her surprise.

When Jessie was done, LaSalle took a long draught from his mug and sighed.

"I think you have the right of it, lass. Aye, we can be a mean bunch of pricks, but no Nain Rouge would stoop to being so underhanded. We take pride in putting our name on what we do, if you take my meaning."

"I do," Jessie nodded.

"This Madame Blanche. How well do you know her?" He looked at Jessie shrewdly.

"I don't," she answered. "I had never met her before. But Greta's experience with her was very different from mine. With Greta she was reserved and closed-mouthed, but admittedly that was only once and at an Alliance function."

"Seems to me you want to look the closest at those who point the furthest away," he emphasized his statement with a belch.

"Obviously, but that doesn't answer the question about the Puck," Jessie pointed out.

"True. Well, I can tell you it's not one of us. Besides, we can't shapeshift. That's not to say someone can't change one of us, but I don't know how it could be done without our permission. But you should know that I came here to warn the Duchess that someone was going to fiddle with these talks and tried to convince us to help. I never saw her face, but she met with our elders and wanted them to let her bespell one of us to look like the Puck and take his place."

"And you're positive one of your kind would never go behind the elders' backs and do it? Even if he thought it was for a prank?"

LaSalle stared at his beer.

"We know better than to let anyone take control of our bodies. Your Matagot isn't the only one who suffered from hunters. Back when this country was first getting settled, the cabal brought us from France to what's now Detroit so that we would wipe out the Sioux, and they wouldn't get their hands dirty. They wanted the land for themselves. We fought back though and wound up merging with spirits from this land to become who we are now. Still, you never forget something like that."

Jessie's lips compressed. She and Greta had both been born in Europe in the late tenth century and had their hands full dealing with the uprising and its aftermath at the same time the corruption spread to North America with the explorers and settlers. Although she had helped to bring the war to the cabalists who fled to the New World, it was too late for groups like the Nain Rouge who had been decimated by the fighting. LaSalle saw her expression and chuckled again, sounding much warmer this time.

"Don't get your knickers in a twist. I know it wasn't your fault. You did what you could, and you'll always be a friend to the Nain Rouge. Don't look so surprised. There are precious few of us who don't know who you are. I wouldn't have agreed to meet you otherwise."

"Jessie, show him the camera footage," the Duchess leaned forward. Jessie forgot that Mara hadn't had a chance to watch it either. She fished her phone out of her purse and pulled up the footage that Cassie had the foresight to download since the faery mounds didn't exactly get great cellular signals. LaSalle was fascinated.

"Hey, you think I could get one of these things?" he pointed at the phone, which Cassie modified for Jessie's use.

"I bet my girl could set one up for you," Jessie grinned, wondering what Cassie would say when she found out that she was expected to peddle electronic wares to the Fae community. Mara rolled her eyes and sighed.

"I suppose it was only a matter of time," she said, a hint of amusement mixed with resignation creeping into her voice.

They watched the security footage from the bar. Mara finally broke the silence when they were done.

"By the Goddess, I swear on my life that it is not the Puck, no matter how much that creature may look like Robin."

"Aye, even when I take him for all he's worth at dice he never has an ill word," LaSalle agreed.

"Can we rule out a shapeshifter or spell though?" Jessie asked.

Mara and LaSalle looked at each other.

"I don't know. I would have to be in front of him to better try to determine this," the Duchess said.

"The Ride is tonight," Jessie pointed out. "You usually wind up at my bar anyway."

LaSalle perked up.

"A bar, you say? Well then, this changes everything! Why didn't we just meet you there instead of this... fluffy place?" he demanded, unwilling to openly show his disdain for the overstuffed furniture and risk insulting the Duchess.

Jessie grinned.

"Because I don't have enough beer for that," she replied. "When can you get there? I can try to get Robin to the bar."

The Duchess shrugged.

"I would guess after midnight. The moon enters her zenith then," she said.

"Well, we'll try for a quarter after midnight and see what happens. Hopefully the vampire drama will be over by then. If not, this could be a very entertaining night," Jessie sighed.

"Vampire drama?" Mara lifted a perfectly sculpted eyebrow in a gesture that would make Charlie jealous.

"Ah, yes. You see, we're also trying to set a trap for Warsaw's killer, and we're luring him there by bringing in a vampire named Hathus."

"Why do I know that name?" asked LaSalle.

"You probably know the one he chooses now to use instead. Renard. The Fox," Mara said flatly.

LaSalle roared, spilling beer across the floor.

"The Fox! That old rascal is still around? You can count on me to be there tonight! I'll never forget when he came to Detroit! The drinking! The women! No one can party like he can!"

Jessie stared at LaSalle, sighed, and shrugged, turning back to the Duchess.

"I don't like it any more than you do, but it's only for a few hours, and we have to catch this kid. Nicky's too close to the situation and needs to stay away after almost losing control, and Mikael can't get involved because of his connection to ficwah."

"Ficwah?" LaSalle was confused.

"Yes dear, you see, Jessica and Nicodemus think they're cute when they make up little names out of acronyms," Mara primly smoothed her skirt. "She means the Fae, Cryptid, Witch, and Human Alliance.

LaSalle snickered. Mara sighed.

"Great. There goes another one," she threw her hands up. "Regardless, you are right. As long as he stays away from my nymphs, I'll tolerate his presence. I don't need a bunch of lovesick fae on my hands again."

Jessie hid her smile.

"I promise I'll do what I can," she agreed.

"What about this Madame Blanche," LaSalle asked with a sharp glance. "What are you going to do about her?"

"Keep watching. There's something off I can't put my

finger on, something nagging at the back of my mind, but I'll get there," Jessie said standing up. She still had a lot to do before everything was set in motion, and she could see dusk falling through the skylight.

To everyone's surprise, LaSalle reached out and shook her hand. It was like being engulfed by a rock. She resisted the urge to see if her fingers still worked when she got her hand back.

"The Duchess here can get hold of me if you have any trouble," he said, pushing his red hat back on his head and letting more unruly wisps of hair escape in all directions.

"Your help is definitely welcome," she said. Allies were hard to find and a welcome commodity. He puffed out his chest and turned red.

"Yes, well, gotta clear my name and all."

Mara tucked Jessie's arm in the crook of her elbow and started back down the hall, Dain the page anxiously running behind them trying to do his job.

"We will see you after midnight. Your ogre can reach me if you need us sooner," she bent to kiss Jessie on the cheek.

"Tug? Seriously?" Jessie was so surprised she almost fell off the front steps of the cathedral.

"Of course. Magic calls to magic after all," Mara replied in that gratingly annoying offhanded manner she used when she dropped little bombs like that. Jessie sighed in irritation.

"Fine. Don't tell me. Let me know when you can set up a meeting with Brigitte, and I'll see you tonight," she waved as she headed toward her car at the far end of the parking lot. Mara watched her go before turning toward the door.

"Come, Dain. I shall set the wards. I need you to send a missive to the High Court. Oberon has much to learn."

"Yes, milady," he replied with a deep bow. She smiled fondly at him as the door shut behind them both, cloaking the cathedral once more in an illusive veil of disrepair.

12

"We're all set?" Jessie asked for the umpteenth time while she paced back and forth behind the bar. It was eleven-thirty, and she had been on edge since she came back from visiting the Faeries four hours earlier. Her eavesdropping spell had picked up Belladonna making phone call after phone call to her fellow vampies. Her calls to Morticent, however, seemed to go unanswered.

Caroline and Jared did an admirable job of spinning out of her way since she, of course, decided to take up their main work space.

Caroline brushed a blonde curl out of her eyes and snapped in annoyance, "Yes, Jessie, everything is set, Jessie, we are ready, Jessie, can you *please* stop pacing and get out from behind the bar now?"

"Fine! I'll go somewhere else!" Jessie moved from behind the bar to the doorway of the storage room where she picked up her pacing again.

"Great! Now she's in my way!" Jared snapped in exasperation as he tried to get around her with cases of beer for the bar.

"You know, I'm your teacher and boss. You're supposed to show respect," Jessie protested.

"Then move!" they yelled in unison. Jessie stomped away, sulking.

LaSalle had taken it upon himself to bypass the Ride and show up at the front door. Tug looked him up and down, grunted, and moved over, giving LaSalle a front row seat to the festivities on the bench by the entrance.

"Hope you don't mind, but I took the liberty of bringing a little something from the Faerie Hall," he winked, holding up the endless goblet as Jessie approached. She laughed despite herself.

"Of course you did," she said, amused and secretly relieved that her beer supply was safe for the night.

"Hey, Boss. Time." Tug rumbled, jerking his massive greenish-gray chin toward the door.

She followed his gaze to the stream of cars cresting the hill toward her parking lot. The kids were early– and there were a lot of them. She spun on her heel and strode back to the bar, adrenaline coursing through her like fire.

"Caroline, you're up," she said as her apprentice nodded curtly and pulled out the vial of truth serum. She primed a glass with the serum as the first wave of vampies came through the door.

Jared gave a low whistle.

"Holy hell. You weren't kidding about what this Fox guy would bring in. Are we going to be able to control all of them?"

"Between you, Caroline, Tug, and me, we should be fine. This part is easy. These kids aren't aggressive, and they won't be focused on us, which makes it easier to manipulate them. We just need to get the information and get them back out the door. Get ready to cast the spell I taught you earlier."

They had decided the best way to handle the crowd was for Jessie and Jared to cast a glamour spell of complacency over the kids at the bar while Caroline kept them distracted with drinks. Jessie had spread the word for locals to stay away for the first part of the evening so they didn't have to worry about casting on any cryptids or regulars.

"Ready, with me," Jessie commanded as they ducked out of sight behind the door to storage and grabbed hands. Together they pulled from the leyline beneath the bar as they chanted the words of the spell in unison. Jessie felt the air in the bar subtly change as the vampies' voices became more subdued. They stepped back onto the floor and looked around.

"Jared, go help Caroline with the drinks. I'm going to see where the vampires and emissaries are," Jessie instructed her apprentice.

"Heard," he said, moving to the bar and using his considerable charm to pull some of the crowd out of Caroline's corner.

Jessie pulled out her phone and called Madame Blanche. She answered on the first ring.

"Jessica! How delightful to hear from you. Rupert was just insisting that we come by."

"Yes, that's actually why I called. I know things have been a bit hectic and strained for you. I thought maybe you could use a night off and come by for a drink. I understand that Robin hasn't had a chance to visit the local Fairy court, and they would be delighted to see him."

There was silence on the other end.

"What do you mean he did not visit them?" Madame Blanche finally asked in a guarded tone.

"I mean he didn't visit them. They'll be here tonight after the Ride. I thought you could bring him to get it out of the way."

"Jessica, he swore that he did make an appearance, and they were uncultured swine. He even said he refused to join them on their Ride because it would be below his station."

"Yeah, no. The Duchess is actually from Oberon's lineage, and they swear that he was never there during this visit." The gut feeling that something was off stopped Jessie from adding that he had visited the Duchess' Court many times in the past.

"I'm sorry to ask this, but can you bring him with you?"

Madame Blanche's voice took on a dark tone

"*Absolutement.* You can count on me, *mon amie.* We will be there in about forty-five minutes."

"Thank you! I knew you would understand," Jessie said as Madame Blanche hung up on her.

"One down, two to go," she muttered under her breath.

"You know, talking to yourself could be considered a sign of senility and old age," John murmured from right behind her. She yelped and jumped. He doubled over laughing as she punched him on the arm.

"Don't *do* that!" she yelled, punching him again when he laughed harder.

"What are we laughing at?" LaSalle sauntered over to them, sloshing beer across the floor as he went.

"*We* are not laughing," Jessie glared at the two of them.

"Have you noticed short people don't have a sense of humor?" LaSalle remarked to John who started laughing again, wiping tears from his eyes.

"Says the dwarf who wouldn't qualify for most rides at a carnival," Jessie retorted as she dialed Mikael's number.

"Jessica, do you wish for me to talk or fly? Because I cannot do both," Mikael sounded irritated. She heard whooping in the background.

"Just checking in. I can hear that Renard is with you. What's your ETA?"

"Sooner if I did not have to stop to answer phone calls. We will be there in fifteen minutes."

"Great! Shouldn't you be flying or something?" she hung up before he could start yelling.

"This is going to be a tight timeline," she said as she walked back to John and LaSalle, both of whom still snickered like little kids. She chose to ignore them.

"Madame Blanche is on the way with the Puck. She said he told her that he presented himself at Court, but it was full of bumbling hillbillies, so he left."

LaSalle whistled.

"Better not let the Duchess hear that," he said with another slurp of beer.

"I have to get one of those," John said, eyeing the goblet. LaSalle clapped John on the shoulder, making the werewolf stagger.

"I like you. I'll take care of that," he said before sauntering back to the door.

John rubbed his shoulder and winced.

"We need to meet weaker people. So what were you saying about the timeline?"

"You know, a simple pat on the shoulder shouldn't make you stagger around like that. It's probably a sign of old age," Jessie smirked.

He glared at her. She smiled beatifically back.

"Madame Blanche said to expect them in forty-five minutes, which should be about the time the Ride shows up. Mikael and the Fox will be here soon."

"How much do you trust Madame Blanche?" He could tell something was bothering her.

Jessie sighed, "I don't know. I want to trust her. I like Rupert. Something's just off about her and Robin. She seemed genuinely freaked out when I said Robin never visited the Court though."

"Interesting. I wonder if she meant for him to," John mused.

"But why? If she's the one behind this then his behavior would be a giveaway."

"Unless he's supposed to be the scapegoat," John pointed out.

"True, anyway–" Jessie was interrupted when the door swung open an a bellow filled the room.

"Ladies and gentlemen, brace yourselves, for the Fox has arrived!"

"Oh for fuck's sake," John groaned.

Jessie grinned from ear to ear. Yes, Renard could be an asshole, but he was one of her assholes, as he was fond of saying.

The Fox was rugged with wild, strawberry blonde hair that he wore long, a neatly trimmed beard, golden eyes, a crooked nose that had obviously been broken many times and added to his rakish air, and a stocky, muscular build. What he lacked in handsome features, he made up for with sheer animal magnetism; contrary to Hollywood's beliefs, not all vampires were model gorgeous. He drifted in and out of their lives on one escapade or another, always looking for adventure, and never settling down.

Renard crossed the room in long strides to sweep her up in a rib cracking bear hug, spinning her around in the process.

"Put me down, you heathen!" she yelled through her laughter. Renard grinned, kissed her noisily on both cheeks, and made a grandiose bow to the rapt vampies all waiting for his attention.

Caroline caught Jessie's eye and gave a curt nod. Morticent was suspiciously absent, but Belladonna was ready for them.

"Come, let me show you around," Jessie hooked her arm through Renard's and started to walk him back to the bar.

"Is he here?" Renard hissed without breaking his smile or moving his lips.

"No, but the girl is. She's the one at your eleven o'clock with the candy apple red hair and septum piercing. She already has a truth serum in her," Jessie's lips didn't move either.

"Understood. Love you, girl! Now let me save my brothers!"

"Love you too, you crazy beast. Go get 'em. Not literally though!" Jessie called after him as he moved like a beast on the prowl toward Belladonna, locking her in his golden gaze.

"I really hope he heard that last part," John said.

"As do I," Mikael agreed, joining them and downing a glass of whiskey. Jessie felt that it would not be prudent to mention that his hair was windblown for once in his life.

"Same here. Morticent is a no show. Madame Blanche is on the way with the Puck, and the Ride will be here shortly after midnight," she said and quickly filled them in on her visit with the Duchess and LaSalle.

"Does Madame Blanche know a Nain Rouge will be here?" Mikael asked.

"Nope. I left that part out. In fact, I think it would be best if he stayed out of sight just in case whoever tried to talk his clan into participating in all of this shows up." Jessie replied.

He nodded approvingly.

"Smart. There are a lot of those kids here. What if things go badly?"

Jessie frowned.

"I admit, I didn't think this many would show up. We will need to encourage them to leave. There's a complacency spell on the bar, so that shouldn't be too hard once we get what we need out of Belladonna," she said, just as Renard made eye contact with them and gave a nod.

"I believe your goal has been achieved," Mikael murmured in satisfaction.

"I believe you're right," she said with a smirk, heading toward the crowd and trailing her fingers along the bar. She began to move among the vampies while commenting that it would be nice to maybe go somewhere else. As one, the crowd began to move toward the door with only a few stronger willed stragglers remaining. Belladonna hung on Renard's arm, a rapt and adoring look on her face. He flashed his fangs at her.

"We can continue this later, my precious. Go. Now the big girls and boys play."

She sighed and reluctantly headed for the door as, on cue, the Suttons, members of the local wolf pack, and the matriarch of the Naga nest and her consort started to trickle in. Cassie ducked past and went straight to the office where she could keep an eye on the cameras unseen.

Renard wrote something on a piece of receipt paper, handing the pen back to Caroline with a wink. He joined the others and handed Jessie the paper.

"Your address. Do we go hunt down this bastard now?"

"Ah, you see, we like to save the hunting until after guilt has been determined," John hastily interjected.

"I like you, wolf! You are a good man. True, we should ascertain this fiend's guilt. To his abode!" And Renard began to run out the door as John ran after him, yelling for him to wait.

"Renard was your idea, you know," Mikael remarked to Jessie.

"Actually he was Greta's. I didn't hear you come up with anything better," she pointed out.

"Just making sure you remember whose idea this was," he said.

"Are you going to help me or keep making snide comments about whose idea was what?" she demanded with a modicum of irritation.

"Oh, did you have more ideas? By all means, I would love to help. Are we going after them?" he nodded toward the door where John tried to talk Renard out of flying off to Morticent's house.

"Do you even know where you're going?" he demanded as Jessie and Mikael approached.

"I would like to accompany the wolf and fox to track the circumspect young man," a deep purr rumbled behind them.

"A Matagot! By the gods! This night gets better at every turn! And here I thought it would be boring," Renard bellowed in delight, staring at Rupert, who groomed his front paws in equal parts delight at the recognition and disdain because he was a cat.

"Where are Madame Blanche and Robin?" Jessie asked anxiously.

"Close. They drove. I used my extreme dislike of cars as an excuse to come ahead. May I suggest that we leave now so you can deal with the Fae with no distractions?"

Jessie blew out a sigh of relief.

"Yes! That is an excellent idea! Rupert and Renard can ride with the sheriff since he knows where he's going, unlike the two of you, who are not actually from here. Mikael, you're with me. John, keep your phone close and come straight back here."

"Understood. Gentlemen, let's do this," John began walking toward the Jeep. Renard stopped.

"This is your chariot? By the gods, man! Haven't you heard of car wax and dent removal? I hear there's these things that will just pop dents right out for you!"

Jessie started laughing.

"I heard that," John yelled after her.

"I know," she called back.

"When are you going to let him court you?" Mikael asked as they stepped back in the bar.

"Is that really a priority right now?" she asked, irritated.

He shrugged.

"Just curious. So what exactly is the plan?"

"The plan is that we give Madame Blanche and Robin drinks and when the Fairies come in, the Duchess will approach Robin. Then we'll see what happens."

"Jessica, that is not a very good plan," Mikael said, doubt in his voice as they reached the corner of the bar.

"Again, didn't hear anyone else come up with something," she pointed out, pouring a glass of scotch for him and grabbing sweet tea for herself.

He sighed.

"Look, something is wrong here," she told him in her best please-be-reasonable voice. "It's either with Madame Blanche, Robin, or both. The one thing we know for certain is that Robin said he presented himself at court when he actually did not."

"Wait, but I took him to the Hill myself," Mikael objected.

"Did you go with him inside?" she asked.

He paused.

"No, I did not. Oh, I am an idiot."

"Don't beat yourself up. Whatever is going on involves very old and very powerful magic. Greta and I haven't come up against anything like this since the cabal's uprising.

"I wish she were here. There is strength in numbers, especially with power like yours."

"Agreed. We're meeting her later tonight though. Honestly, I hope nothing happens. I'm not really up for more surprises."

"Then now is probably a bad time to tell you we snuck Nicodemus into your office," he casually sipped his scotch.

"You did *what?*" Jessie stared at him in outrage. "The

whole point was to keep him away from all of this! Or do you not remember that he started to turn on that Morticent dumbass?"

"He is safer here than he would be alone with his thoughts. Now we can keep an eye on him," Mikael pointed out.

Jessie scowled but before she could say anything else, Tug called out from across the bar.

"Boss," he jutted his massive chin at the parking lot once more, this time as a stretch limo pulled in and triple parked.

LaSalle, who had moved to the bar where he could make raunchy jokes to the delight of the local wolf pack, craned his neck to get a better look before catching Jessie's eye. She jerked her head toward the back of the bar, and he grabbed his goblet and scurried across the floor to disappear in the storage room.

Tonight Madame Blanche wore a pale pink tea length silk dress with tulip sleeves. A thick, gold locket hung on a chain between her breasts, and she had pearl earrings and a delicate gold bracelet that matched her gold trimmed heeled sandals. Her long hair hung in a single braid over one shoulder. The Puck might have changed suits at some point. Jessie couldn't tell through the wrinkles and stains.

"No opal," she murmured to Mikael through a welcoming smile without moving her lips as the pair drew closer.

"Not that we can see," he replied, his smile equally immobile.

Talking without moving lips was an art mastered by witches and vampires alike through the ages.

Jessie took Madame Blanche's outstretched hands as she approached.

"How lovely to see you again. Please enjoy the hospitality of my establishment," she said. Madame Blanche kissed Jessie on the cheek and returned the smile. Robin scowled.

"It's always a pleasure, *ma cherie*," she said, gracefully sliding onto a stool. "I believe I would like a gin gimlet this evening, *mademoiselle*."

"Coming up," Caroline replied with a cheerful grin as she grabbed some limes and the muddler. "And for you? Don't worry, we have plenty of wine. Do you even want a glass this time? Or are you just going to chug straight from the bottle again?"

"Just gimme the wine, wench," Robin snarled.

"Oh, no. We don't do that here. You say yes ma'am, no ma'am, and please, or you can just leave," Caroline snapped.

Jessie inwardly cringed. This was, of course, the one time she needed the troublemaker to actually stick around. Luckily for their plan, the glow outside the door signified the Ride's approach.

"Fine! I'll find my own wine," Robin yelled, spinning around on the stool and coming up short when he realized he was face to face with Mara, the Duchess of Green Orchards, also known as Oberon's great niece, and her entire court.

"My, my. Imagine my surprise when we thought to enjoy the company of our dear friends after another lovely Ride only to see what appears to be none other than Robin the Puck, my uncle Oberon's own emissary, behaving like a common, ill-bred lout," Mara's eyebrow went up as the Puck squirmed under her sharp gaze. Jessie could almost feel Charlie taking notes.

"One would wonder why the Puck failed to present

himself at my Court," she continued, "although his obvious and sudden lack of manners and breeding answers that burning question."

"I don't have to take this! I'm Oberon's emissary," Robin fumed as he tried to push his way past the Duchess' line of courtiers.

He would have had more luck pushing through stone. Jessie could feel the hair on the back of her neck stand up in response to wild fae magic as Mara successfully blocked the Puck's escape at every turn.

"Let me go," he shouted, the words laced with panic. Madame Blanche watched in silence, tightly gripping her locket as though it were a lifeline.

"No, I don't believe I will. You see, this conclave is very important to my uncle. You, however, are proving yourself to be quite unworthy of his trust. I believe you shall come with me until we get to the bottom of this." Mara snapped her fingers, and he froze, falling to the ground like he had suddenly been encased in cement. His eyes darted around the room in a panic, meeting Jessie's with silent pleading. She stared back, refusing to give ground.

"Jessica, please accept my apologies for this sudden disruption of what surely was to be an enjoyable evening. I pray to the Goddess that you find it in your heart to forgive me."

"Please, Your Grace, do not trouble yourself," Jessica said, giving the Duchess an embrace. "I would love to share a drink with you, but obviously there are other matters to which you must attend in light of these events. Naturally the members of your court are welcome to stay and take advantage of my hospitality."

"You are too kind. Do come by for tea tomorrow. Dain would love to see you again, that dear boy."

"Of course! I would be delighted," Jessie said as they reached the door, the Puck floating a few feet off the ground in front of them with a terrified look on his face. She hugged Mara again.

"Did you get a good look at Madame Blanche?" she whispered.

"You're right, something's wrong there. It's right on the edge of my mind like a moth trying to reach a light. Come to me tomorrow at dusk. We will talk more after I reach my uncle," Mara whispered back.

Jessie walked back to Mikael and Madame Blanche, glad that the adrenaline was wearing off so she could look as shaken as she felt.

"Well. That was unexpected," she said as she looked for her tea.

"Robin knocked it over, along with half the drinks on the bar," Jared complained as he walked up with the mop.

"Yeah. I hope you weren't counting on a stellar liquor cost this week, Jess," Caroline said as she put fresh drinks down in front of Madame Blanche and Mikael.

"My, this has been a busy night, has it not? Where is Rupert?" Madame Blanche asked, reaching for her drink and looking around.

"He's checking something out with John. They should be back soon," Jessie replied. "Why would Robin be in such a panic over facing the Duchess?"

"I do not know, unless that is not really the Puck. Oberon will be able to see through such a disguise if that is the case."

"Who else would it be? The Nain Rouge?" Madame Blanche delicately lifted one pale shoulder in a little shrug.

"I do not know that either. Perhaps whoever is behind this has something to gain by sabotaging all of our efforts or perhaps they are simply working for someone else. It could be anyone for any reason. But we shall see. Ah, me," she sighed. "First my dear Warsaw and now my companion. Maybe we should reconsider these talks."

"No," Mikael said sharply. "If we back down now, then we show them that they can bully us into giving up. I will not let that happen, and nor should you. You are too strong and have fought too hard for these rights."

"You are right. Thank you. I must remember this is bigger than me. Than all of us," she waved her arm to encompass the room. "We have a fight, and we must win. We must!"

"Hear, hear!" Jessie raised her glass. As Madame Blanche raised her glass in return, she met Jessie's gaze with a tremulous smile.

"Your hospitality is, as always, perfect, my friend. I regret the actions of my companion. Please accept my apology on his behalf."

"Nonsense, it wasn't your fault," Jessie waved away the other's protests. "I'm just glad you're okay and ready to move forward. Would you like another drink?"

"No, I should get back to the hotel. I have much to share with the rest of the organization, and we need a new representative for the Fae if we are to move forward."

"Of course, and please let me know if I can help," Jessie

replied, giving Madame Blanche a quick hug as they walked to the door. Mikael followed behind.

"Would you like an escort?" he asked with a shallow bow.

"*Non, merci.* I will be fine. *Bonne nuit.*" she waved as she walked toward the limousine, her back straight, and her hair falling behind her like a silver cord.

"Do we trust her?" Mikael asked as they watched the limo pull out of the parking lot.

"I don't know. I just wish I could figure out what it is that's off. It's like Mara said, it's a moth trying to get to the light. Jared, Caroline, and the brownies are already looking for bugs though."

"The brownies?" he asked, startled.

"Of course," she said smugly. "You didn't think the Duchess and I would set this up without the world's best back up, did you?"

He glared at her.

"You can be very annoying, you know."

"I know," she smirked. "Shall we?"

As they turned toward the door, they heard the sound of an engine roaring into the parking lot and looked back to see John's Jeep come to a screeching halt in front of them.

"What on earth is going on?" Jessie demanded as John, Rupert, and Renard jumped from the Jeep and strode toward them.

"We found Morticent's house, or what's left of it," John announced grimly. Jessie stared at him in dread.

"What happened?" she demanded.

"Someone beat us there. The place was trashed. I mean, it looked like it had been taken apart by a wild animal."

"And Morticent?" Mikael asked.

"Gone. But there was blood everywhere, and by my guess, it's been there since at least late last night. I got a sample to test for DNA. Mikael, I'm sorry, man. But I gotta ask. Do you know where Nicky was last night?"

Mikael's eyes flashed quicksilver in anger. Jessie took his hand.

"No one thinks that he did it. John's the sheriff, so he has to ask. You know this."

He sighed. "I know. It's just… fine. As you say. He left here after the unfortunate incident and flew home. It takes half an hour to make the flight. Jessica informed me when he left. He was home when I arrived, perhaps five minutes later. He went straight to his studio and worked through the night. I checked on him myself frequently."

John gave a sigh of relief.

"Good. That gets him off the hook."

"Did any of you pick up a scent or see anything?" Jessie asked, considering that a Matagot, werewolf, and vampire probably made up the best CSI team imaginable.

"Yes, many scents," Rupert stretched. Jessie had been around him enough by now to know that the acts of nonchalance masked those moments when his brain was working furiously.

"The sheriff and I are fairly certain that the blood, among other things, belonged to Morticent. By the by, I thought we all agreed to stop calling him by that ridiculous name."

"What is his birth name?" Renard asked out of curiosity.

"Marshall," Jessie grinned.

"So much better," Renard muttered, shaking his head.

"Anyway," Rupert continued with a hint of irritation, "the blood was accompanied by something new. Or rather a new scent of something old. I mean an ancient creature– something that smelled of dust and decay and the moors and marshes."

"But you don't know what it is?" Jessie asked.

"There are many classes of Fae and cryptids alike who share such characteristics," he shook his head. "Jessica, I believe it would be a good time to summon your friend and compare notes," he said before sauntering inside.

"I agree," Mikael said.

"Ah! We call for Greta!" Renard beamed, clapping Mikael on the shoulder. Mikael scowled in annoyance. He had never been one for boisterous behavior, and Renard was another untidy package that irked him to no end. He could tolerate Renard in small doses, but he had the feeling this visit would last long enough to test his patience. Unfortunately, it didn't look like they had much of a choice.

Charlie had been joined by Nicky and LaSalle, who continued to show off the never ending goblet but without seeming to get any drunker. Jessie couldn't decide if the Duchess had watered down the beer, if he had that high of a tolerance, or if he had just been drunk from the beginning.

"Could it be? LaSalle! You old bastard!" Renard bellowed again, running to the Nain Rouge and swinging him in the air.

"Renard the Fox!' LaSalle yelled, the goblet's contents spraying across the floor. Jessie could hear Jared yelling all the way down the hall as he went back for the mop.

"I couldn't believe it when I heard you would be here!

When are you coming back to Detroit? That was legendary!" LaSalle grinned after he was finally back on his feet.

Caroline held up two more stickers like the ones Jessie had found in the bathroom.

"Bugs. Annie found 'em," she told Jessie who took them and looked more closely. She could feel the remnants of the listening spells fade away.

"You should have waited for me. The one in the bathroom was nasty," she said.

"Pshaw," Annie snorted, popping up over the bar like a very tidy jack in the box. "As if there was ever swamp magic that any brownie worth their salt couldn't dismantle in their sleep."

"What kind of magic?" Jessie stared.

"Swamp. It's what we call the old magic that the bogeys and banshees and swamp creatures who kept to themselves used to make. Nasty pieces of work if you don't know what you're doing, but easy enough to handle if you've a knack for it."

"Annie, you're an absolute treasure," Jessie exclaimed. "And you're sure you got all of the bugs?"

"Pretty sure. We didn't look in your office though," Caroline answered.

"I'll take care of that. Annie, tell the Duchess what you just told me about the magic!"

"Of course, and if you want help in your office..."

Jessie laughed, "Absolutely not. But believe me, you're getting a bonus for all of this." Annie sighed.

"Can't say I didn't try. I'll be back tomorrow, Jessie. Take care, and call on us if you have need," she said, giving Jessie a quick hug before popping out of sight.

Jessie looked around the bar, which had settled into its comfortable routine now that the drama was over.

"Caroline, you got this? I want to try to compare notes with Greta and see if she learned anything new."

"Yep, we're good. Go do your thing," Caroline said with a dismissive wave.

"You make me feel so useful. Okay, everyone who's coming along, come. Not you, Jared. You still have to work. And put the mop away. But probably somewhere close by at the rate the night's going."

Jared sulked all the way back to the mop sink as the rest of them started down the hall to the office where Cassie waited expectantly. Jessie walked to the desk and then turned to face her friends.

"I'm taking you to the Library, and you should know something first. I trust all of you to some degree or another. But if you have any ill will toward Greta or me, if you are behind what's going on, or if you have any desire to hurt us or our efforts to bring peace, you will be destroyed as soon as you cross the threshold."

"That seems a little dramatic, girl," LaSalle belched.

"Oh, she is quite serious," Nicky shuddered. "Literally destroyed. We will scoop what's left in a very tiny bag and send it back to your kin. And by 'we' I mean someone else because I am not doing that again!"

Mikael stared first at Nicky and then at Jessie.

"One day you have to tell me what the two of you get up to when I'm not around," he said.

"I don't think you want to know," Jessie grinned as she pressed the knot in the wall.

Considering that everyone made it through, she decided that her new found trust was justified. LaSalle blew out a breath as he crossed the threshold.

"You have a hell of a way of guaranteeing your allies' loyalty, witch," he said. John nodded in agreement but didn't say anything.

Everyone except the vampires and Rupert looked around in awe and fascination. Lucy tried to get in a standoff with Rupert and failed to impress him. He flopped down in front of the fireplace and began to purr. Aleister and Spot ignored him while Sunny and Lemur scattered.

"Jeez, Jess. You had this in the bar the whole time and never told us?" Charlie asked, floating up to the shelves and staring at the books hungrily. A panel on the other side of the room opened, and Greta stepped through, coming to a complete halt as she stared nonplussed at the group who stared back.

"Well! This is not what I expected," she started to say before Renard interrupted, charging at her full tilt.

"Greta!" he bellowed, which seemed to be his go to volume when he was excited. He grabbed her around the waist and swung her in the air. She laughed in delight as she hugged him back.

"Renard! I can't believe you made it! You were my idea, you know," she boasted as he put her down. Greta had always had a soft spot for him.

"And what a grand idea it was," he beamed. "They could never pull this off without the Fox!"

Mikael glared at Jessie who sweetly smiled back.

John sat down on the sofa, where, to everyone's surprise, Aleister immediately jumped in his lap and went to sleep.

Renard lounged in one of the armchairs, long legs stretched out and crossed at the ankle while LaSalle, ever present goblet in hand, stood nearby examining the contents of the shelves. Cassie nervously perched on the edge of the other chair, and Nicky and Mikael leaned against a wall.

"Okay, let's get started. We have a lot to go over," Jessie said, striding to the front of the room.

"I love it when she gets all instructor-y," Greta murmured to Nicky, scooting in between the brothers and hooking her arms through theirs while perching on top of a cabinet. Lucy, in an attempt to reclaim some of her dignity, jumped in her lap while pointedly ignoring Rupert. Jessie shot them a glare of annoyance.

"I like Greta," John grinned.

"Shut up. This is serious, and we're running out of time."

"How do you know?" Charlie asked.

"Because I think that we're dealing with a necromancer who might be a banshee, I think she has something very nasty planned, and she's running on borrowed magic."

"We already knew she had something nasty planned," Rupert pointed out.

"If I'm right, then her name is Brigitte. She arrived at Mara's court after an unfortunate incident we won't get into right now. She's under the burden of karmic debt and may be for the rest of her life." She glanced quickly at Greta, who looked sadly at the floor.

"Karmic debt?" Charlie looked lost. Jessie and Greta exchanged glances.

"Remember when you felt the wind when Morticent approached Nicky? That can only be caused by a necromancer.

A necromancer is made when a witch binds a death omen or harbinger, but in order to do it, the witch has to give up her power to the necromancer. She can put it all into a talisman or artifacts, and she gets back whatever the necromancer doesn't use. But once the necromancy spell ends, the witch and the being she used have to pay the price of karmic debt to restore the balance of the universe."

"I wasn't sure if the creature had to pay as well. That makes sense," Greta said.

"Yeah, Mara filled me in on a couple of things. For instance, you were right– if the witch dies then the creature bears the full karmic burden. Also the creature can be killed while they're turned. It makes them mortal– and vulnerable."

"I didn't know that part either. Unfortunately most creatures don't read the fine print," Greta winced before taking up the thread.

"We already know that Charlie felt the power of a necromancer," she jumped off the cabinet, much to Lucy's annoyance. "But to your point about a banshee, I finally found the site where the ritual was done in Ireland. It borders a marsh and a banshee's hut, which has been abandoned. The ritual was done by a *völva* who was left for dead."

"I take it she's no longer left for dead?" Jessie asked.

Greta shook her head.

"Nope. She is now in custody of the Council and in a death trance. I don't know if we'll get anything out of her. And for those of you who don't know, a *völva* is a Norse witch and a member of one of the oldest branches of witchcraft. She practices Seidr, which literally means to bind, and she can cast runes, see visions, and travel across dimensions and planes. She falls in the same class as shamans."

"How do you know she's the one who performed the ritual?" LaSalle asked curiously.

"I practice earth magic, and the Earth was repulsed by the act. She was more than willing to give up her secrets and show me what had taken place in hopes that I could repair the damage."

"Did you?" Rupert spoke up.

"Yes. Always," she answered with a note of finality. "But you're right, Jessie. It was Brigitte. There were two others there too, wearing deeply hooded cowled robes. I never saw their faces. One of them promised Brigitte that the karmic debt would be lifted if she kept her end of the bargain and then attacked the *völva*."

"Poor Brigitte," Jessie sighed. "I probably would have done it too if I didn't know better."

"Stupid banshee," Renard scoffed. "Did she not learn the first time?"

"Imagine doing something so repulsive to the natural order that you have no good, happiness, or peace for possibly centuries when you're already something that everyone hates. It's unbearable. I did her no favors when I saved her life, and if I had known the witch who bound her the first time was going to die, then I wouldn't have done it," Greta said, ignoring the shocked faces at her admission. "And now imagine someone says they can make it all better. She probably didn't even care. Maybe she was hoping that they would kill her when it was over."

"Then why doesn't she just kill herself?" Charlie asked.

"First of all, a creature of death can't just die unless they're turned into a necromancer. That makes them as vulnerable as the witch who performs the ceremony. I mean, to our knowledge, there's only one way to kill a banshee, and she probably wouldn't be able to do it to herself," Jessie explained. "Second of all, the universe won't let her get off that easily. Every attempt will be thwarted. It must come at someone else's hand or not at all."

"The woman who tried to convince our elders to let us impersonate the Puck wore one of those robes too. So what now?" LaSalle asked with a belch, passing the goblet to Renard.

"Now we compare notes," Jessie told him. "Charlie and I were able to recreate what happened when Warsaw was… well… we saw what happened. It was a very clever set up, but I don't think Brigitte is smart enough to pull it off."

"Jess, the runes on the syringe that was used on Warsaw were part of a binding to keep the needle from breaking and to ensure that he went down and stayed down." Greta said, hugging Nicky as she spoke. He looked at the floor, turning in on himself again. Jessie moved to his other side and wiggled under his arm until he was in the middle of a witchy hug sandwich.

"There is definitely someone else behind the scenes pulling the strings here," Jessie continued. "Someone who used her and the *völva* to try to stop the talks while implicating all of us in the process without getting their hands dirty. LaSalle, what are the chances the Nain Rouge would help us?"

"I hate to say it girl, but don't count on it. We'll fight when the fight is brought to us, but we don't stick our necks out for anyone."

"Fair. I'm meeting Mara at dusk to see the Puck. Supposedly Brigitte has been staying at the Hill too. I want to look into that, especially now that we know she was in Ireland being turned into a necromancer at the same time. John, we need to find Morticent's body. I think at this point we can't count on him being alive."

"No. He was a loose end, and that amount of blood was clearly staged to look like Nicky did it. Sorry, buddy."

Nicky shrugged. "It's a sound ploy in theory. But obviously whoever set this up doesn't know how strong willed a vampire as old as we are can really be. That could be to our advantage"

Greta started pacing around the room, much to Rupert's annoyance. After the third time she almost stepped on his tail, he hissed and jumped on the sofa next to John. Aleister couldn't be bothered to concern himself with Rupert's obvious distress.

"He's right," she said. "The key points seemed to be framing Nicky and making it look like a Puck was out of control, a vampire went on a rampage, and a witch was at the center of it all. But the Fae always look out for their own, and the age of a being dictates its ability to control emotions and reactions. A vampire as old as Nicky might turn to incite fear, yes. Lose control and go on a rampage against a kid, never. Maybe we can play on our stereotypes somehow to get an advantage. Okay, action list!"

"I love it when she starts making lists," Jessie murmured to Nicky who smiled. Greta shot her a side eyed glare.

"Charlie, see what else you can do and pick up on. By now they probably know that you have some abilities thanks to the bugs you found at the bar, so you need to be extra careful."

"We should talk to other witches we know like Isabel," Jessie added. "She probably has some ideas on ways to help him hone his abilities and experiments he can run."

"Good idea," Greta nodded.

"Rupert, watch Madame Blanche," she continued. "If someone messed with the Puck then we can't rule out interference with her too. If something is off with her, then my guess is that you were already in the States. I don't know that whoever is behind this could have sustained a spell on a White Lady during the time it takes to fly from France to here. Bespelling a living being is one thing, but the dead are a completely different matter. Does she know all of the ways you can shapeshift?"

"No," Rupert replied. "I never share that information with anyone."

"Good. Use that to spy on her and, more importantly, to escape if you find yourself in danger. LaSalle, I know it's a lot to ask, but just see if any other Nain Rouge would help us. And be careful! If you're recognized, you could be in serious danger. You and Annie will also be our go betweens for the Fae. See if you can verify whether or not Brigitte is definitely at the Hill, and see if you can find out what's going on with the Puck. I know Jessie is meeting Mara, but I want a first hand account sooner than that."

"Consider it done," he said with a bow.

"Renard, how long are you sticking around?" Greta asked.

"Until my brothers are safe," he said emphatically, jumping up and pumping his fist in the air while sloshing beer on the rug. Mikael gave a sigh of resignation.

"That's my Fox," she said fondly. "Keep working on getting information out of the groupies, especially Belladonna. She seemed to be the closest to Morticent. I want to know everyone they talked to in the last few weeks, where they met outside of the bar, everything. Make it look good, like she's your fresh blood for the night."

He licked his fangs suggestively. She wrinkled her nose in disgust.

"Nicky, you stay at the bar and at home," she fixed Nicky with a serious gaze. "Do not go anywhere else. Make sure you have an alibi at all times. We will come to you with everything we find, and you'll be our center of operations. Mikael, reach out to the Alliance and express concern over the Puck. See if you can get the talks postponed."

"Tell them he has food poisoning," Nicky suggested, ignoring his brother's glare.

"John, keep investigating of course," Greta continued. "Look into all of the vampies– love that, by the way, Jess– and see if anyone else has shown up out of nowhere. Like Jessie said, try to find Morticent's body, and for the love of the Goddess, can we please call him Marshall?"

"I don't know, the ridiculousness of Morticent is starting to grow on me," Renard grinned.

"It would. Cassie, can you adapt phones for all of us including the Fae?"

"Of course!" Cassie scoffed as if it was the easiest thing in the world. "I'll need a way to test one at the Fairy mound, but if I can figure out the electromagnetic fields then it should be easy enough."

"Yeah, I want one of those!" LaSalle toasted Cassie, sloshing more beer on Jessie's rug. Jessie glared at him to no avail.

"Good," Greta said. "Does anyone have anything else?"

"You didn't give me a job," Jessie said in her best little girl voice. Greta laughed.

"Just keep holding all of us together. I wish we had kept one of the bugs active so you could feed misinformation to whoever's listening though."

"Yeah. Maybe we'll get lucky and find more. I still haven't looked in the office"

"If you do, keep your apprentices in the dark. They're more believable that way. Jared couldn't act if his life depended on it."

"No. No, he could not," Jessie emphatically agreed.

"Okay, and…. Break!" Greta said before hugging everyone in turn and disappearing back through her portal. The rainy streets of London appeared briefly before the wall joined seamlessly together.

"Wait, if you have to use your office to get in here, then what does she use?" LaSalle asked in confusion.

"We both have a stationary and portable point of entry. Greta can't stay still for five minutes to save her life, so she always has her portal key with her. It can only be used so many times before it has to be charged though, which is why I don't use mine as much and we still do things like drive cars," Jessie explained.

"Hope she doesn't lose it," he burped, drinking more beer and passing the goblet to Renard as they followed the rest of the group through the portal and back into the bar. Jessie watched in fascinated revulsion.

"Are you two just going to do that all night?" she asked.

"What?" they said in unison, staring at her with identical looks of puzzlement on their faces. She started to laugh despite herself as the portal closed behind them.

13

Jessie woke up in the early afternoon after a fitful sleep with sandy eyes, a throbbing headache from sleep deprivation and nerves, a sense of impending doom, and the realization that she was not alone. Greta sat cross legged at the foot of the bed holding two mugs of coffee.

"Morning, sunshine!" Greta grinned as she held out a mug.

"I love you dearly, but what the hell are you doing here? I thought you were in London. And why are you so perky?" Jessie grumbled, taking the coffee and sipping it gratefully. "Mmm. This is good."

"I'm perky from sleep deprivation, jet lag, and too much caffeine, so I stopped off at that cafe in Paris we like for even more caffeine because why not? Don't worry, I'm charging my portal key. I decided that I want to see the Puck for myself. I think I know what was used to bind him. I found a spell to break it, but it's going to take all four of us and Mara to make it work."

"Four?" Jessie squinted at her friend in confusion, still trying to clear the cobwebs from her mind.

"I brought Isabel. She's chatting with Charlie at the bar

now. She may never leave. She's never gotten to really talk to a ghost who embraced his ghostdom."

"Ghostdom?"

"Okay, you need more coffee. And probably a shower. Go get ready. We need to see who we know that's a water witch who can come with us."

"Water witch?" At this point Jessie was just being annoying. It worked.

"Yes! Fire, earth, air, water. You fire, me earth, Isabel air. Need water. Go get ready! Stop repeating everything I say with a question!"

"Question?"

"Jessie!"

Jessie shrieked and scurried out of bed, miraculously saving the coffee, as a pillow flew past her ear.

"What about your friend, what's-his-face? The witch who moved to Puerto Rico to teach surfing," she called from the bathroom.

"Ivan? I can probably get him to come. I'll see what he's up to. Now get ready!" Greta yelled back. Patience was never her strong suit.

Jessie grinned as she started the shower, drowning out Greta's call to her witch buddy. Ivan and Greta had been friends for centuries. Originally from Scandinavia, Ivan had moved to the Americas early on at a time when men with the gift of Seidr were considered unmasculine and often put to death.

Twenty minutes later, Jessie was dressed, unceremoniously shoved into Greta's ancient Volvo that was usually kept in a garage behind Jessie's house, and on the way to the bar. When they walked in, Isabel and Ivan were engaged in a rapt conversation with Charlie. He looked up and beamed at Jessie.

"Hey, Jess! They want me to help with research into ghost and spectral abilities!" he said, glowing a faint rosy hue.

"Why is it when I bring up research you start talking about spirit abuse and being turned into a lab rat but when Isabel asks it's all something to be proud of?" Jessie protested.

"Because I'm nicer," Isabel replied, smoothing out the front of her slacks as she stood up and came to Jessie for a hug. A witch whose element was air, Isabel's tiny frame, ash-gray curly hair, huge brown eyes, and sharp features made her seem so birdlike that Jessie sometimes thought she could take flight at any moment.

"Hello, Jennet."

"Hello, Ysabell," Jessie grinned.

"Jennet?" Charlie asked in confusion. Jessie sighed.

"That's the name I was given at birth. Isabel and I were born at the same time in a tiny Scottish village that's been gone so long that I can hardly remember it," she explained. "You have to remember witches were persecuted, so when we didn't die, we usually moved to another region and changed our identities. Eventually I landed on Jessica, and it was common enough that I just stuck with it."

"People used to think we were sisters," Isabel chimed in. "But I'm nicer."

"Whatever. You're just so cute that no one can ever say no to you," Jessie grumbled. "Where's the spell?"

Greta pulled a polished quartz scroll case out of her bag and gently removed a yellowed scroll, unrolling it on the table. They bent over it.

"It's actually pretty straightforward," Greta said. "It just relies on intent, so we don't have to worry about memorization. All five elements must be present, and we need to each bring a sacrifice. It can be symbolic. We'll use our elements to create a binding that purges the spell from him from the inside out. It will be very uncomfortable for him, but that can't be helped."

"Five elements?" Charlie asked curiously.

"Yeah, we have earth, air, fire, and water," Greta explained pointing to each in turn, "and the ether makes five. Also known as the energy of the cosmos. That's what's used by the fae, which is why we need Mara."

"Have you reached out to her yet?" Jessie asked.

"No, I figured you could do it. I mean, I did find the scroll and all," Greta said and ducked as Jessie threw a coaster at her.

"So violent," Ivan grinned, shaking his shaggy gray hair out of eyes that were as blue and stormy as the ocean. He was tall and perpetually tan, and his beach bum mien hid a brilliant mind and talent for witchcraft. His love for water was almost legendary, and he had never lived farther than a mile from the ocean.

"You're next, surfer boy," Jessie warned with a mock scowl. "Can we just use whatever's lying around the bar for the sacrifices?"

"That would be best since this place seems to be a hub for everything going on," Greta agreed.

"Okay, everyone look around and see what you can use. Mara asked me to come at dusk, so we have a little time to make sure everything is in place. I need to call Cassie first and double check something on the camera. Has anyone heard from LaSalle or Annie?"

"They both came by earlier," Charlie informed them. "LaSalle said that he talked to his clan leader. The official stance is that they will not get involved. Unofficially though, if he happened to stick around and help us, no one would mind."

"That's good at least. I'm not really surprised that the rest of the clan is 'officially' staying out of it," Greta said with air quotes.

"Annie wanted to let you know that Brigitte is staying in a cell– she said it's like a monastic cell, not a prison– and pretty much keeps to herself, but she is definitely there," Charlie continued. "They have the Puck in a cell– like a prison, not a monastery– and bound with ash and holly."

Jessie winced.

"That sounds painful. Oh, Charlie, I have another test to do on you," she said.

"See, it sounds so much better when you do it," he complained to Isabel.

"Not listening," Jessie called as she headed down the hall toward the office.

"What are you looking for now?" he asked, curiosity getting the better of him, as he drifted in behind her.

"Well, I want to ask Cassie about the cameras around us and check something here, but remember when you picked up the emotions from the bathroom when we recreated that scene?"

Neither one of them wanted to put a name to it, but he knew what she meant.

"Yes," he nodded.

"Do you think you could do that in any other situation? I mean if it's not as concentrated? Or doesn't involve death"

He shrugged, "I can try. What are you looking for?"

"I want to see if we can find out what Madame Blanche and Robin felt last night when everything went down."

Charlie grimaced.

"I'll give it a shot, but I don't know if I can tell their emotions from everyone else's."

"See if Isabel has any ideas. She's been working on the art of isolating layers in time," Jessie told him as she pulled up the camera from the hallway on the monitor and started to dial Cassie's number.

"I also want to see if Morticent was here before the attack."

"Marshall," he corrected.

"Whatever. We never actually looked into that. Maybe I can get him on the infrared cameras coming into the building while invisible or maybe we can get footage of someone giving him the bracelet or instructions or anything."

Charlie sort of rested his translucent hand on her shoulder.

"Gotta stay busy, huh?" he asked. "I know the feeling. You'll get it, Jess. Don't worry. Holler if you need us."

"Thanks, Charlie. I will," she smiled as Cassie started yelling impatiently through the phone.

"Sorry, Cass. Hey, I have a question for you."

"I figured that was probably why you were calling me in the middle of the day and then having a complete conversation with someone else instead," Cassie snapped in exasperation.

"Be nice. Did you ever get any other camera footage of Marshall or Morticent or whatever we're calling him?"

Cassie giggled, "Marticent. No, Morshall!"

"What's so funny?" Greta poked her head in the door with a worried look on her face, clearly concerned that maybe her best friend had finally cracked from all the pressure.

"I'll tell you later," Jessie said, wiping the tears of laughter from her eyes.

"Anyway, Cassie, can you go back to George and anyone else you can think of and look for footage from earlier in the night? I want to see if we can get him arriving and see if he talked to anyone."

"I already did. He must have put on the bracelet before he reached the property, because I came up empty. He doesn't do anything at your place either after he slips past Tug except lurk in a corner until Warsaw heads for the bathroom. Oh, when are you going to the Hill?"

"Dusk. Why?"

"I think I got a phone working for LaSalle, but I need to test a few things first."

"No, you can't go," Jessie said, ignoring the indignant huff on the other end. Cassie's insane curiosity was going to get her in a lot of trouble one day, and Jessie was determined that it wouldn't happen on her watch.

"I can take it for you or you can give it to him here though."

"You'll have to take it. I need you to see if it works with the magnetic fields the Hill produces."

"Okay, meet us for lunch in about half an hour at the cafe and give it to me there," Jessie said, hanging up.

"Trying to get a better timeline?" Greta asked, perching on the desk cross legged. For as long as Jessie had known her, she had always eschewed chairs for a desk or table or cabinet or anything that was not considered a normal place to sit.

"Yeah. We were so hung up on Warsaw and what happened afterward that we never looked earlier, but Cassie said she didn't see anything on my cameras or anyone else's that showed where he got the bracelet or if he talked to anyone. She said he slipped past Tug to get inside and then just lurked."

Greta nodded. "Isabel's doing something involving dividing timeline dimensions that I don't really understand for Charlie. Do we have a spectral bloodhound now? Because that would be cool!"

"Yes, but we need a better name for it. Like Ghost Detective."

Greta raised her eyebrows.

"That's better?"

"You come up with something then! You're the writer," Jessie retorted. "Did Ivan find a sacrifice?"

"Yeah, he consecrated water in the herb garden out back and added some sea salt he carries with him. I have a pot of earth from our garden, and Isabel has incense she found behind the bar."

"Cool. I can grab a candle."

"Sounds good," Greta agreed before falling silent and watching the cameras with Jessie.

It wasn't hard to find. There was a brief moment when Tug's back was turned and the door opened just enough for someone with a slender build to slip through. Jessie switched on the infrared sensor, and sure enough, it was the same build as the figure she and Cassie had seen enter the bathroom. The timestamp was half an hour before the attack. They watched as Morticent settled into an out of the way spot close to the hall to wait for Warsaw.

"Okay, a few things," Greta frowned. "You were definitely right that he had to use a talisman. You would have felt a witch using that much power for that long. But how could he be sure that Nicky wouldn't show up and ruin his plan?"

"I don't think it would have mattered," Jessie replied. "The whole attack took less than two minutes. Nicky being here wouldn't have stopped Warsaw from going to the bathroom, and clearly Marshall used something that cloaked his scent too."

"Why would he have to?"

"My normal clientele is mostly made up of creatures that have heightened senses. Plus, I know he did it because an ogre's sense of smell is almost as strong as a wolf's, and a vampire's is right below that. We weren't super busy that night, so Marshall knew he could lurk without anyone bumping into him, but Tug– and Nicky, if he had been there– should have smelled him as soon as he came through the door."

"Since you have the only known ogre in existence living here, how common is the knowledge about his sense of smell though?" Greta was skeptical.

"Irrelevant, when you think about it. I have vampires, werewolves, werepanthers, naga, succubi, a ghost, and a kitsune here on a regular basis. It would be stupid not to mask his scent."

"True," Greta conceded.

"Well, so much for that," Jessie sounded dejected. "Cassie

has a cell phone for LaSalle to try. Do we need anything else for the spell?"

"No, just us. Goddess, I thought we were done with all of this intrigue and bullshit," Greta sighed, leaning back on her hands.

"Yeah, me too. I mean, I knew we were always going to be stuck with politics, but this is something else. Poor Warsaw and Nicky."

"Yeah. Whoever decided to make them pawns is going to pay big time," Greta said grimly, blackness starting to bleed into her eyes.

"Let's compare revenge fantasies over lunch. I'm starving."

Greta brightened at the thought of food, eyes shading back to normal.

"Does that really sweet Naga family still have the cafe? They have the best hand pies in the world!"

Jessie laughed fondly at her friend.

"You are so easy to please. Yes, and they make cappuccinos the right way," she said.

"You mean not a frothy latte? Be still my heart!" Greta said with a mock swoon as they walked down the hall and rejoined the group.

Isabel performed intricate gestures that looked like a cross between separating sheets of paper and tatting lace while Ivan studied the scroll. Charlie was a deep shade of indigo which Jessie was beginning to associate with concentration.

"How's it going?" Jessie asked.

Isabel smiled, pleased. "I think it's good! We're seeing how far back he can go."

"Great, what about last night?" Jessie asked, trying not to

let her exasperation show. She could be as giddy about learning and experimentation as the next witch, but they were on a deadline.

Isabel looked a little guilty.

"Sorry! Hang on, let me go back," she said, making flip book motions with her delicate hands.

"And you're going to teach us how to do that, right?" Greta asked eagerly.

"Oh, yeah! It's easy, see–"

"A-hem!" Jessie said loudly.

"Sorry!" Greta said, giving her friend her best side eyed puppy dog look. It failed to impress.

"Okay, here we are. Charlie? Wanna tell her what you found?"

Charlie turned indigo again.

"Definitely fear from the Puck. There's something else too, but I can't figure out what. Hatred or panic maybe? Madame Blanche was scared too. Scared and I think mad. I need to work on this a little more, but I think I can get it."

"If Madame Blanche was really behind this, then I don't think she would have felt a heightened negative emotion," Jessie was disappointed. "She made sure to stress to me that she thought the Puck visited the Hill, and, logically speaking, it was inevitable that he would get caught by the Ride. If I made a plot to frame Robin, then I would be pleased at this outcome."

"Although if she was behind this then the fear could be at getting caught," Ivan pointed out.

"True," Jessie nodded. "We can come back to it later tonight, see if we can hone the emotions a little better. Thank you, Charlie. That was great," she smiled at the ghost who blushed rose.

"Seriously, you never noticed he could do that before?" Greta was incredulous.

"Well, it's not like it ever came up," Jessie replied as she texted Cassie to let her know that they were on the way. She grabbed her keys and a candle from the bar top and turned on one of the bar TVs for Charlie.

"Everyone have everything they need?" she asked.

"Yes, and now onward to food!" Ivan cheered, Isabel right behind him giggling like a young girl and not one of the most politically and magically powerful witches in existence.

"What's she like when she heads up the Witch Council?" Charlie asked Jessie, nodding toward Isabel.

"Terrifying," Jessie grinned. "We'll be back later. If Annie or LaSalle stop by with more news, tell them we'll be at the cafe and then the Hill at dusk."

"Sounds good. Have fun storming the castle!"

"It'll take a miracle," she called back as they climbed in the car.

After more coffee and lunch and an hour long lecture from Cassie on how to tell if the phone was going to work or not and what diagnostic information she needed if it didn't work, at which point Jessie almost decided to say screw it and bring her along, they were on their way to the Court as the last rays of the autumn sun gilded the trees with golden-red light.

"I love this time of year," Greta sighed in contentment as she climbed out of the car. Dain was at his post, standing rigidly at attention. Jessie gave him a solemn half-bow.

"Greetings, good sir," she said. "Your Lady has requested

our presence. I bring those with me who only seek to help and never harm one of the Folk. I stand for them in all matters on this visit."

"Nice," Greta murmured.

"I know," Jessie murmured back.

"This way, milady," Dain bowed, leading them into the foyer.

Instead of the lush carpet and frescoes, Jessie had walked the day before, they padded along a gravel pathway lined with roses and asters. The Duchess waited for them at the end, dressed in a simple dark green velvet gown, her hair braided away from her face.

"It is a pleasure to see you as always," she said, kissing Jessie and Greta on the cheek.

"And for us," Jessie replied, gesturing Isabel and Ivan forward. "Your Grace, please allow me to present Ivan Erikson, a witch of our acquaintance who specializes in water. I believe you know Isabel."

"Of course," Mara smiled, greeting Isabel with a warm embrace. "Ivan, you are welcome as well. Please enjoy our hospitality."

Ivan gave a low bow and kissed her knuckles.

"My pleasure, my lady. I must say, I never dreamed that I would be honored to meet one as beautiful as yourself," he straightened with a little wink.

"Oh, I *like* him!" Mara said to Jessie with a laugh.

"Of course you do," Jessie shook her head in amusement.

"What do you want us to do first?" she asked, trying to get their visit back on track. Sometimes it seemed that she spent more time herding witches, fae, and cryptids than she did anything else.

"Let's start with Brigitte," Mara replied, sobering. "The Puck is likely to take all of our effort, and the moon needs to rise a little more before we begin the spell."

They followed the Duchess further into the gardens to a neat row of white stone huts. Ivan had to duck to go through the door when Mara gestured to the last one. Jessie followed, not sure what to expect.

The hut was larger on the inside and simply appointed. A cot was pushed against the far wall, and a desk with a lantern stood against the adjacent wall. A table and chair on a white, woolen rug in the middle of the room were the only other furniture. There were no decorations, and the only window looked out over the herb gardens that made up the back of the lot.

A banshee sat on the bed, staring unseeing into space. She acknowledged them with a glance when they came into the room. She was small with wild, dark curls, the golden cat eyes and sharp cheekbones that pegged her as one of the Fae, and an upturned nose covered with a smattering of freckles, and Jessie knew the minute she laid eyes on Brigitte that the real banshee was long gone.

"Well," she said, crossing her arms.

"Yeah," Greta replied, hands on her hips.

"I'm sorry?" Mara asked, looking between the two of them in confusion.

"That's a golem," Ivan explained.

Mara looked blankly at the creature on the bed and then

back at the witches, confusion warring with disbelief across her face.

"That's impossible," she said.

"No," Isabel said, "It's a very good golem. No one except a witch could tell the difference, so don't feel bad. But it's definitely a golem."

"How could you possibly tell? And how did this happen? Brigitte has been under our care since her unfortunate... incident," Mara said delicately, unwilling to bring up Greta's part in Brigitte's fate.

"All living beings have an essence that witches can sense," Jessie explained. "It's part of our tie to nature. We can tell immediately when something is alive or not. Golems are not living creatures, but a good one like this," she gestured at the creature, who had slowly moved its head to regard her with an eerily calm, unblinking gaze that gave her the creeps, "can be enchanted to act, look, and feel like a living creature."

"Are you positive Brigitte never left?" Greta asked.

"All of the Fae can come and go as they choose when they are our guests," Mara's voice held a defensive note. Jessie didn't blame her. It must be hard to realize that your impenetrable domain was actually full of ways to penetrate it.

"That's probably how it happened then," Ivan gently pointed out.

"But Brigitte never left of her own free will. Of that I know. She was too concerned for her fate to risk the outside world. She came here to try to do good for us and escape her home until the burden of the debt was lifted."

"Did she have visitors?" Jessie asked.

"None who sought her out," the Duchess replied.

"What about those who didn't seek her out," Greta asked, sensing that the Duchess held something back. Mara's sigh and the slump in her shoulders told them that Greta's hunch was right.

"There was one, a hobgoblin who studied herbology, or so he said. He spent much time in this garden and eventually began to strike up conversations with Brigitte when she would take her daily walks. But I never imagined that he did so with ill intent."

"We don't know for sure. Hobgoblins love mischief, ill intent or no. It probably wasn't hard for someone to convince him to befriend Brigitte as part of a prank and use him to convince her to leave the Hill. Then all it would take is some fast talking, smuggle the golem inside, and she's on the loose with a member of some shadow organization intent on destroying the world," Isabel said.

"Well, when you put it that way, how could I ever have doubted you?" Mara sighed, throwing up her hands. "What do we do with this creature?"

The golem continued studying each in turn with that unnerving gaze. Jessie backed toward the door, and the others followed.

"Well, chances are everything we said has been heard by the creator," Jessie said. "Not that it matters since anyone who can make a golem this good already knows we would have spotted it right away. But I definitely think that this is the point where it doesn't have to listen anymore."

"Agreed," nodded Ivan.

"What do we do with it? Should it be destroyed" asked Mara.

"Well–" Jessie began before an earth shaking bang interrupted them. She flung open the door to the hut, but it was too late. Fragments of clay were scattered across the overturned furniture from the golem's self-destruction.

"I guess that answers that question," she said, staring at the mess. "Lucky we weren't in there," Ivan said with a low whistle.

"Definitely," Isabel agreed. "Probably decided there wasn't any point wasting power on it anymore."

"Yeah," Greta said. "Still, it would have been nice to know how long the real Brigitte has been missing. I can see if the clay can tell me anything, but it may be contaminated."

"I can do better than that," Mara said smugly. "Our alchemist can tell you exactly when the clay was changed from earth to that creature."

"You have an alchemist?" Greta exclaimed, her eyes already glazing over with the thought of all of the possibilities of study.

"Focus!" yelled Jessie.

"Sorry! It's just... a real alchemist!"

"I know. Solve the mystery now. Play with magical science later."

"Right! Okay. I'm focused," Greta said brightly. Jessie sighed and turned back to Mara.

"We'd better get to Robin now. If the bad guys know that we know about the golem and they possibly infiltrated the Court, he could be in more danger."

"Right. Come with me," Mara spun around, moving across the garden in long strides matched by Greta and Ivan. Jessie and Isabel, on the other hand, had to scamper to keep up.

Jessie was glad Charlie and LaSalle weren't there to make short jokes.

Before they reached the main hall, however, they were met by Annie, looking frantic and disheveled.

"Your Grace! The Puck! He's been poisoned! You must come quickly!"

"No!" Mara gasped, breaking into a run, Greta and Ivan close behind. Isabel made a complicated scooping gesture, and Jessie felt pressure under her feet as a puff of air picked the two of them up, lifting them toward the window Annie pointed at on the second floor.

"Easier than trying to keep up with the tall people," Isabel commented.

"I'm not complaining," Jessie agreed as the little air puff deposited them in the room.

"Wait, how did you–" Ivan gaped as he burst through the door with Mara and Greta in tow.

"Worry about that later," Jessie said, running to the bed where Robin tossed, sweating and shivering in turn. His face was gray and his limbs contorted as he howled in pain, veins bulging and black.

"Iron," Mara snapped furiously. "We have to work quickly. Jessica, I need you."

"Tell me what to do," Jessie said, putting herself in Mara's hands. The Duchess shot her a grateful look.

"We have to stop it from solidifying," she said.

Ivan blanched.

"It will do that?" he asked in horror.

"In one of the fae, yes. Isabel, do whatever your little air trick is and take Greta to the garden. Greta, I need henbane, ligularia, and jewelweed, and I need you to purify the earth and bring that too. Here, take this," she said, thrusting a round, earthenware pot at Greta. Isabel grabbed Greta by the arm and dragged her out the window.

"Jessie, start raising his temperature. We need to keep the iron molten so we can get it out of him. Annie, bring a pot of water. Ivan, get it as cold as you can. We won't have a lot of time to get his temperature back down," she added as Annie ran out the door, another pot in her grasp.

Jessie set her candle by the bed and lit it with a thought. She could worry about a sacrifice for the spell later; right now she needed the focus it would give her. She stretched her hands over the Puck's writhing body and concentrated. She could feel the ugliness of the iron coursing through him like venom. Whoever had done this had meant for him to suffer. Her anger and frustration fueled her magic, causing her hands to glow with incandescent heat. Robin howled.

"Got it," Greta yelled as she and Isabel tumbled ungracefully through the window and onto the floor. She scrambled to her feet and ran to the bed.

"Good! Start packing the earth around him," Mara ordered. "Give me the herbs. Jessie, how are we doing?"

"Ready," Jessie gasped as Annie ran back in the room spilling water across the floor in the process. With a quick snap, Ivan pulled it back into the pot, poured in his flask of water he had consecrated in Jessie's herb garden, and began concentrating. Out of the corner of her eye Jessie could see ice crystals begin to form on the surface before Mara pulled her attention back to the Puck.

Greta overturned the pot of earth onto the bed, adding

her own pot from the garden behind the bar, and packed it around Robin while Isabel joined Jessie to begin the dangerous process of working the iron into his bloodstream from the surrounding tissue, using her incense to help guide it into the veins closer to the surface of his skin. Mara made incisions across both of his wrists with a silver dagger and combined her ethereal magic to that of the witches to use his blood to force the iron out of his body where Greta trapped it in the earth.

As soon as Jessie sensed the last of the molten iron leaving his blood, she yelled to Ivan, who cast the ice cold water across the Puck and joined his magic to theirs to draw the heat out of Robin's body. Mara quickly made a poultice out of the plants and packed them across the wounds on his wrists.

"There," she said, sitting down heavily on the floor. "He'll be weak, but we can get him back to my uncle's court where he can recuperate. You saved his life, you know."

"I think we broke the spell too," Jessie realized, trying to catch her breath. Witches didn't come with an inexhaustible reservoir of magic, and the spell had taken a lot out of her.

"Huh," Isabel grunted. "You know, I think you're right."

"Let's not use iron poisoning as a means of breaking enchantments on the fae though please," Mara winced, brushing her hair back from her face where it had escaped her braid.

"Agreed. I definitely do not want to do that again. We can get him back to Oberon through our Library portals," Greta said, gesturing to Jessie.

"We have our own portals," Mara told her. "He needs to rest. I will bring him to you when he awakens. You should be able to get answers before we take him home, if he has any to give."

"We need to figure out how he was poisoned," Jessie said, magic induced exhaustion seeping into her bones.

"Yes, who had access?" Ivan asked.

"The only one here today was Brigitte," said a little piping voice from the doorway. Mara turned toward the pixie hovering off the ground behind Annie.

"Brigitte was here?" Mara asked incredulously.

"Aye, she said she just came from the garden and wanted to give Robin something to make him feel better," the pixie replied.

"How long ago was that?" Jessie asked the pixie who cocked its head to the side and considered.

"After you went to the garden but before you came here," it told her.

"How much do you want to bet the explosion was a distraction so the real Brigitte could sneak into the tower and poison Robin?" Greta asked grimly.

"Not taking that bet," Jessie replied right before she felt a blinding white, ripping pain tear through her to her core, driving her to her knees.

"Jessie!" Greta yelled as Jessie screamed in pain before vomiting blood on the floor.

"Sorry, Annie," Jessie gasped, wiping her mouth. "The wards... the bar... we have to go..." Greta struggled to help Jessie to her feet as Isabel and Ivan moved to join them.

"No, you two get out of here. Isabel, call a council security meeting. Tell them about the necromancer and that the talks are in danger. Ivan, get to safety," Greta ordered, forgetting that Isabel currently outranked her.

"Right. Ivan, want a ride?" Isabel asked as she climbed onto her air puff. He shrugged.

"Why not? Might as well save the charge on my Library's portal key. Be careful and call me if you need help. That's an order," he waved as the cloud lifted them through the window and out of sight.

"Can I leave my car here? It's going to be faster if I can get us back through the Library portal," Greta asked Mara, struggling under Jessie's weight while Jessie tried to find her footing on a world that wouldn't stop tilting. Whoever had come through her wards hadn't just broken into the bar. They had set out to destroy her magic that was interwoven into the wards in such a way that the backlash would be guaranteed to render her useless.

"Of course! What can I do?" Mara asked anxiously.

"Hold her up for a second. For someone who's so tiny she can weigh a lot when she goes deadweight," Greta gasped trying to reach the bracelet she used as her key to the portal.

"Work out more," Jessie slurred, falling into a heap in Mara's arms, almost sending them both crashing to the floor.

"Well, she can still make smartass comments. I guess that's something. Mara, you and Annie don't come until I get word to you that it's safe. Keep a guard on Robin at all times. I only trust the two of you and LaSalle at this point. You hear that, Annie?" Greta looked around the Duchess to fix Annie with a stern gaze, forgetting that maybe she shouldn't bark orders at the local Fae nobility. Greta tended to forget things like that a lot.

Annie held up her hands. "You don't have to worry about me, milady. I know better than to go around jumping into danger, but I will guard the Puck with my life."

"At least one of us has common sense. Okay, Jess. Here we go. Please don't throw up on my shoes," Greta begged as she got the portal open and stooped to haul Jessie to her feet.

"No promises," Jessie muttered, trying to get her feet under her as Greta half lifted and half pulled her across the threshold.

14

Jessie did, in fact, throw up on Greta's shoes. And the rug, and the Library floor once Greta, in an act of desperation, finished dragging her best friend by one leg through the portal. She deposited Jessie on the sofa and kicked off her ruined shoes. She preferred being barefoot anyway.

She put both hands on Jessie's temples and whispered a command of sleep while using her earth magic to begin healing the bleeding lesions inside Jessie's body caused when the wards tore apart. Then Greta edged toward the portal to the bar, silently thanking her mother for pushing her to take dance lessons in the eighteenth century in an attempt to make her ungainly daughter more graceful. Dancing may not have much of a practical application, but it helped her move like a cat when she needed to, and right now she definitely needed to.

Her eyes adjusted quickly to the darkness as she eased the door open and slipped into the office. Grateful that the bar was closed and Jessie's apprentices and clientele weren't in danger, she began to make her way down the hall and toward the front of the building. Although, she reminded herself, having the bar closed had made it easier to attack the wards—and Jessie. She trailed her fingers along the wall as she went, drawing on the leyline to build a shield between herself and whatever waited for her.

As she drew closer to the bar itself, she reached out guarded tendrils of thought to the plants growing in the windows. Jessie's affinity for fire made it possible for her to be in tune with the fire-cured wood of the building, but Greta had to rely on the window beds she had planted years ago to give her the power of the earth she needed. All she could hear was the sound of dripping water and creaking wood.

"Not safe!" the ivy screamed in her head.

"Shit, shit, shit, shit, crap!" she hissed under her breath. Earth magic was great for healing and defense, but it was nothing compared with what Jessie could do with fire attacks. Her mind raced.

"I know you're there," a woman's voice came out of the darkness ahead. "You can't fool me, earth witch. We're sisters, after all."

"Sorry, I already did the dysfunctional family thing," Greta called back, the anger curling in her gut giving her the strength to keep her tone light.

"How's your little friend? I hope I didn't hurt her too badly. I couldn't leave those pesky wards up though," the voice sounded so pleased with itself. Greta funneled the anger into her core of earth magic. Losing her cool wouldn't help anyone now, but she could use the heat from her rage to temper her shield and build a slightly unorthodox attack strategy.

"Oh, you should come see! She would love to chat. Did you check out the office yet? There's all kinds of fun stuff to play with," Greta pushed off from the wall and began strolling back to the office in plain sight, a crazy idea forming in her mind.

"I don't recommend turning your back on me," the woman's voice turned cold as it drew closer. Greta ignored it as she continued to saunter away without looking back or hesitating.

"I said, don't ignore me!" the voice cracked.

"Danger!" the ivy screamed, and Greta, without slowing down, caught the attack aimed at the spot between her shoulder blades in her shield and bounced it back to where it came from like an arrow. The woman shrieked in pain.

"Bitch! You'll pay for that!" she screamed. But Greta had already reached the office when she heard the woman start to run down the hall. Launching herself over the desk, Greta pushed the knot in the panel and opened the portal just as the witch burst through the door. Greta had enough time to glimpse a pale face hidden in the depths of a cowled hood before the witch lunged, mouth widening and hands morphing into talons. Greta spun out of the way at the last second as the witch realized her mistake too late, her screams of rage turning into a squeal of terror.

"No!" she cried right before she ran into the barrier to the Library and exploded into a fine, pink mist of gore.

"Jessie! Where are you?" Greta heard Nicky's terrified voice and the sound of running feet– a welcome sound this time.

"She's in here. Watch your step," Greta called back as the vampires, LaSalle, and Rupert came through the door and skidded to a halt. Nicky barely kept his balance when his feet hit the gory slime.

They stared at her. She stared calmly back– not because she actually felt calm, but because she was covered in dead witch and really wanted to scream, vomit, and scour herself until her skin came off, not necessarily in that order. Mikael cleared his throat.

"Um…" he trailed off at a loss for words.

"Yes?" she asked, still as calmly as if they had all met for tea and she wasn't dripping with aerosolized witch.

"The Duchess sent me to get these guys," LaSalle jerked a stumpy thumb at the vampires and Rupert, "and told me to get you to safety or she would make me wish my ancestors never left France."

He shuddered at a memory. Mara could be terrifying when the occasion called for it.

"What in the seven hells happened here?" Renard demanded.

"Well, the bar was attacked, someone ripped through the wards and made Jessie so sick with the backlash that she started throwing up blood, she's in there passed out," Greta gestured toward the Library, "and I don't know where Charlie is. Now this is what we're going to do. I am going home where I will take a very thorough shower and put on new clothes. Nicky, you are going to clean this part up."

"Not again," Nicky moaned.

"It's this or where Jessie threw up all over the rug and floor. Your choice."

"I'll take the witch," Nicky said hastily.

"Good. LaSalle–"

"Oh, no. I am not a cleaning service," the little dwarf swore, beginning to back out of the doorway.

Greta felt what was left of her patience start to slip away, which must have shown in her face because he stopped very quickly.

"LaSalle," she continued as if he had not interrupted,"you get the vomit. Renard, you help him, and make sure you two get all of the beer you spilled on her rug."

"Rupert, we just saved Robin from a very serious case of iron poisoning, one of the worst any of us has ever seen, including the Duchess. Brigitte did it after her golem blew up and tried to kill us. When's the last time you saw Madame Blanche?"

"At dinner. She said she was going to go over notes for her speech tomorrow night and that she wanted to be alone."

"Does she eat?" LaSalle asked curiously.

"Of course not. I, however, am quite fond of the steak tartare at the Waldorf," Rupert sniffed.

"Great. Wonderful. So glad to hear it," Greta said evenly. "Go back and see if she's there. Try to figure out if she left at any point or if she seems to be in danger. Mikael, you have to go *now*. See if you can delay the talks by another day. Tell them Robin was attacked and we need time to get him on his feet. I'll hold the portal open for you."

Mikael blinked at her.

"Did you say her golem tried to kill you?"

Greta closed her eyes, counted to ten slowly, and tried to get the urge to scream under control.

"Yes. Yes, I did. Now, I am going to wash the dead witch off of me. When I get back in half an hour, I will tell you everything. Oh, and see if you can figure out how bad the damage is to the bar and look for Charlie."

She turned on her heel and crossed the Library, carefully stepping around the mess on the floor and pausing only long enough to make sure Jessie was still asleep and the lesions were healing. She could hear arguing behind her.

"Why do I have to help clean up?" Renard complained. "I fought Romans and led armies of Gauls!"

"Well, you can fight Greta too, but I think I'll take my chances with the rug instead of a pissed off earth witch who's covered in a disintegrated person and could probably bury me alive," LaSalle replied.

There was a pause.

"Where is the mop?"

Half an hour later, Greta came back through the portal to find Mikael waiting for her. Jessie was still asleep. The lesions had healed, leaving only faint scars behind.

"The talks will take place in three nights' time," he said without preamble. "Oberon had already arrived, outraged that his emissary had been tampered with in an attempt to sabotage peace. He spoke with me afterwards to ascertain that Jessica is safe and to express gratitude for your part in saving Robin's life. Was it really that bad?"

Greta sank down on the floor in front of Jessie and sighed.

"It's like Brigitte just pumped iron into him. Jessie had to heat it up until it was almost molten and then keep it that way so we could get it out. Mara said it was the worst case of iron poisoning she had ever seen. The only good thing is we broke the original binding spell in the process, but Jessie had to do so much magic so quickly that it made it easy for whoever this was to attack the wards and completely take her out. In fact, I'm pretty positive that was the plan because the wards could never have been breached if she had been at full or even half strength."

"That seems an unnecessarily cruel thing to do to the Puck," Mikael looked down at his clasped hands.

"So was what happened to Warsaw," she pointed out. "But Robin was not very kind to those who allowed themselves to be made necromancers. He felt that they should have known better, even though realistically they had no way of knowing. It's not like they had access to libraries and information like the witches or high fae did. Regardless, I don't know if this was revenge or Brigitte's karmic curse coming into play, but it was nasty."

Mikael nodded.

"And you? How are you holding up?" he asked gently.

"I'm okay. Come on. Let's let her sleep. I want to see what other kinds of damage that bitch of a witch did."

"We still can't find Charlie," he told her as he followed her back through the barrier and into Jessie's office.

"If she did anything to him, I will resurrect her and force her through the barrier over and over and over again," Greta snarled.

They joined the others in the front room. The bar was untouched– there was so much magic poured into it that a hundred witches couldn't destroy it– but the rest of the room was in shambles. Chairs and tables were overturned, glasses smashed, and scorch marks covered the walls. Greta went to the ivy on the window and stroked the leaves.

"Shh, there, there. It's safe now. You did so well!"

She turned back to the group, who stared at her un-certainly.

"Oh, the ivy warned me that I was in danger," she explained.

"She talks to plants?" LaSalle asked Renard.

"Earth witch," Renard shrugged.

Greta stopped listening. Something about the scorch marks on the wall across from the bar was wrong. She stared, head cocked and eyes narrowed, trying to put her finger on what exactly bothered her while chewing on her thumbnail. The others watched her expectantly, seeing the wheels turn in her head.

Without speaking, she slowly walked away from the bar and turned to look in the huge antique mirror hanging on the wall behind it.

"It's a miracle that wasn't broken," said LaSalle.

"No," Greta replied. "It was intentional. Look. See the scorch marks? They're runes, and they're backwards. We need the mirror to read them."

"That seems overly complicated," Nicky said doubtfully.

"All of this is overly complicated, Nicodemus," Greta snapped as her temper frayed.

"I'm sorry," she said, trying to get herself under control. "I think it's meant to be a message just for Jessie and me. No one else would think to look in a mirror to read burn marks on a wall."

"This is true," he conceded. "I certainly would not. What do they say?"

"Oh, no. This is bad. This is so bad."

"Greta, what *is it?*" Mikael demanded.

She turned to him with tears in her eyes.

"They took Charlie. It's a ransom demand. If we don't back off, they'll destroy him."

"How did they get him out of the bar?" Nicky demanded. "I thought ghosts couldn't leave the site of their death."

"They would have had to use a spirit trap. It's the only way. It's so cruel. He'll be trapped until either we get him back or he is destroyed. The trap is devouring his soul piece by piece as we speak."

LaSalle and Renard started to swear in unison. Mikael ran a hand over his face.

"How long until we can get Jessica back on her feet?" he asked.

"Now," said a voice from the hallway. They turned to see Jessie, pale and shaken, slowly make her way into the room. She took in the damage and went to Greta, tears streaming down her face. Greta folded her into a hug, and they held each other in silence while the others stood awkwardly, unsure of what to do. Finally Jessie pulled away.

"John called and woke me up," she told them. "They found Marshall's body in the woods off of 75. It was mauled pretty badly. He said it looks like a stereotypical vampire attack but feels like a rage killing. He picked up the same scent from Marshall's house, the old, musty swamp smell."

"He was a loose end," Mikael shrugged. "Who better to use as a target for rage while trying to frame us?"

"Yeah. Still, no one deserved to die like that," she said sadly. The vampires were silent. Being warriors in a past life made them consider how people deserved to die a little differently than the witches did.

"Has anyone heard from Cassie?" Jessie asked, looking

around. "LaSalle, she gave us a phone for you, but I don't know where it is."

"It's still in my car at the Hill," Greta told her. "I need to go back and get it anyway. We can check in with the Duchess too, see how Robin is doing."

"Yeah," Jessie looked around, lost as her phone started to ring. She fumbled to try to answer it before just giving it to Greta.

"Caroline, hey. It's Greta. No, she's right here. It's just… it's been a hell of a night. Hang on, I'm going to put you on speaker," Greta said, hitting the button.

"Hey, I'm with Jared and Cassie. We're safe. She saw everything on the cameras before the attacker took them out. They missed two though, the one over the storage room that points at the front door and the one in the office. Maybe you can get something out of them. She saw them take Charlie, Jessie! She showed us! It was horrible! The way he screamed!" Caroline broke down sobbing as Jessie stared numbly at the wall. They heard a low murmur of voices and shuffling sounds before Jared's voice came through the line.

"Hey, Jess. It's Jared. Look, don't worry about us. We're safe. We're going to lay low for a while. These guys are no joke. If you need us though, whatever you need, we got your back."

"No, you stay wherever you are. Don't tell any of us where it is. Is Tug with you? I don't see any sign of him, but I don't know if they tried to get into his apartment over the bar," Jessie finally spoke.

"He spends the days we're closed doing his own thing. He won't be back until dawn," Jared replied.

"See if you can get in touch with him and have him come stay with you," she ordered.

"Yes, ma'am," Jared didn't even try to argue, which was a testament to the severity of the situation.

"Where's Rupert?" Jessie looked around, a slightly dazed look on her face.

"I sent him to check on Madame Blanche. How are you feeling?" Greta asked carefully.

"I think I was hit by a truck. They took Charlie?" Jessie asked in a tiny voice, her bottom lip trembling.

"We'll get him back. You know we will. Come on. We need to figure out a game plan," Greta said, hugging Jessie to her again.

"I made this for you," Nicky came up behind them with a cup of hibiscus and rosehip tea. If there was anything he had learned about the witches over the centuries it was that tea solved pretty much everything.

Jessie sniffled and gave him a tiny smile and hug. "Thank you," she said, taking the cup and sipping it gratefully.

"So what now?" LaSalle asked in a subdued voice.

"I need you to go back to the Court and fill Mara in on what happened here. Tell her we'll be in touch and we may need help," Jessie told him, feeling better as she wrapped her hands around the mug to soak in the warmth and comfort of the tea.

"You got it, boss," he popped out of sight. Jessie looked around.

"I don't even know where to start," she said. "We need to get this place cleaned up and see if there's anything we missed."

"Be careful though," Greta warned. "We don't know what they left behind."

"Did you get a look at her?" Jessie asked.

"Just a glimpse of her face, but I didn't recognize her. She started to shapeshift before she hit the barrier though. I wish I had gotten more information. Like how did she know exactly when you were weak enough to take out the wards," Greta's voice was bleak.

"You got her to try to go through the barrier? I bet that was epic," Jessie's smile was cold and bitter.

"Yeah. It's probably on camera in your office somewhere. You'll love it. Especially the part where I wound up wearing her."

"She made me clean it up," Nicky complained.

Renard snorted. Greta shot him a warning look, and he suddenly found the runes very fascinating.

"Did you finish translating these?" he asked. "They say that there is a deadline. They'll give Charlie back if we stay out of the peace talks. That's three days' time, yes?"

"Well, Mikael got it extended to three days. This was written when they were supposed to take place two nights from now. We have to assume he won't last much longer past that," Greta pointed out.

Renard grunted. "I see," he said, crossing his arms across his barrel of a chest. "Well, my friends, this has been fun. I think it's time for me to move along now. Greta, I need your assistance if you would be so kind as to let me leave through the portals."

Greta and Jessie stared at him shocked. He stared blandly back. Mikael and Nicky did not react at all.

"Fine," Greta snapped, her voice shaking in anger as she stalked past him and down the hall. She slammed her palm against the knothole, and the Library opened up. After they stepped through, he grabbed her arm and spun her around.

"Don't be mad, I have a plan," he said hastily.

"Oh, I know," she said. "I wanted to make it look good. There's no telling what that witch left behind."

He roared with laughter and gave her another rib cracking hug. "Greta, girl, you are a gem! I take it you already figured this part out, but you need to look for more of those listening spells. Get the brownie to help you. But leave them be. Use them to send worthless information back to these assholes."

"It would be nice to have the upper hand for a change," Greta agreed.

"I am really leaving, but I'll be back," he told her. "I know someone who may be able to help free Charlie. A shaman. Get the Fae to lend you some doppelgängers too, and bring the ogre back to help. You need to open the bar like it's business as usual but keep your little apprentices out of sight. They're smarter than rabbits. Jessica taught them well."

"Oh, I know," she said wryly.

"One more thing," he continued. "Belladonna told me that she saw Marshall meet a woman who wore a hood and never showed her face but who gave him a small gift. She said the bracelet appeared on his wrist after that and he never took it off. However, the longer he wore it, the more obsessed he became with Nicky and the more he raved that he was better than Warsaw and someone needed to show Nicky even if he had to do it himself."

"How long ago?" Greta asked.

"A little longer than a week. This plan went into action very quickly, but I am certain the bracelet was not only the source of his invisibility but also his obsession. To her knowledge though, he was the only one of her acquaintances who had this encounter. It seems he was brought here for that purpose."

"I don't doubt it. Renard, thank you. I don't know what to say. You did so much more than we dreamed of asking, and we are in your debt," Greta threw her arms around his neck.

"Nonsense, girl. You're my family, and I have great love for you. Now I must go! My brothers still need to be saved, and so do you," he hugged her back.

"We love you too," she said, leading him to the opposite wall.

He stepped through the door that opened up into a swank hotel room in Manhattan. "I will send a message when I have found the one I seek if there is time. For now the Library seems the safest place to meet. Don't forget what I said," he warned, kissing her on the cheek as the portal closed behind him.

"I won't," she said to an empty room.

15

Jessie was losing her mind. That was the only way she could describe it. Her brain wouldn't turn off, and all she could think about was how to get Charlie home, what was she going to tell Mary Jo, she never should have taken on apprentices, this was exactly what she was afraid of, what if something happened, she would never forgive herself, that's it, when all of this was over she was going to reassign their apprenticeships, it was for their own good.

"Jessie!"

She snapped out of her reverie. Greta stood in front of her looking exasperated.

"Come on. We have to get everything cleaned up."

"We're cleaning up?" Jessie asked blankly.

Greta sighed and pinched the bridge of her nose.

"Not this again. Yes. It's late. The boys have to leave soon. If we're going to get this mess cleaned up with their help, we have to do it now. Come on. Help me pick some sage," she commanded, taking Jessie by the hand and leading her out into the garden.

"Since when do you need help picking sage?" Jessie asked, exhaustion and grief creeping into her voice.

"Since I need to fill you in on Renard's plan without tipping off any new listening devices that might be in the bar," Greta smirked.

"Ha! I *knew* he wouldn't bail on us!" Jessie crowed triumphantly, a sliver of hope starting to creep back into her heart.

"No, he didn't," Greta confirmed. "He needed to get me somewhere safe so he could tell me his plan and then go for back up."

"Well. Now I feel bad for having any doubts," Jessie winced.

"It's okay, You had a pretty rough night. You would have realized what he was up to if you hadn't still been dealing with the repercussions of what that bitch of a witch did to you."

"What's his plan?" Jessie asked as she bent down to pluck a branch of sage. The harvest moon was on the waning side of full, her banishment powers at their peak.

"He's getting a shaman he knows to help us get Charlie back. He also said to get Annie to help us look for any new listening spells the witch might have stuck around the bar before I got there and leave them be."

"Feed them misinformation. It would be nice to have an advantage for a change," Jessie sniffed.

"Agreed. He also suggested that we open as if nothing happened."

"I will *not* put Caroline and Jared in danger!" Jessie spun around, tiny hands clenched in fists and in full mama bear mode.

"No, we're not! But the fae can help. Like it or not, they

owe us one. Big time. If they can send us some doppelgängers, we can make them look like Caroline and Jared. We are going to want Tug back though."

"I agree with everything except Tug. I don't want to leave them undefended," Jessie objected.

"We can hide them in the Library," Greta pointed out.

"Yeah. I guess that's our only choice," Jessie sighed.

"I need to recharge my portal key. It got a work out tonight," Greta continued. "I'll do that, and you grab them at some point this afternoon. You still have your key?"

"Of course," Jessie said. "Besides, I just realized that we'll have to have Tug. We don't know enough about his strengths and weaknesses to replicate him with a doppelgänger, and it would look too suspicious if he wasn't here."

"Also true. Okay, I think we have enough sage. Let's get the bar put back together as much as we can before Mikael and Nicky have to leave," Greta said, leading the way back to the shattered back door.

Jessie grimaced as they passed through, the residual traces of the shattered wards bringing with them a fresh wave of nausea.

"I hope Rupert's okay," she said, worried about the big cat.

"Me too," Greta agreed, dropping the armful of sage onto the polished bar top. "Here, light these and start smudging."

"Yes ma'am," Jessie said with a straight face. Greta gave her a mock glare that hid her secret relief. If Jessie could make jokes then she was already feeling better.

Nicky had rolled up his sleeves and dug out a bucket from somewhere. He had filled it with soapy water and industriously scrubbed the scorched runes off of the wall. Mikael had found the broom and swept up broken glass. The furniture had been pushed off to the side.

"Can either of you repair those?" Mikael asked, nodding toward the pile of broken tables and chairs.

"I can if they're made of wood," Greta said, walking over to inspect the damage.

"Of course they are," Jessie replied. "I had to make sure I could get the furniture fixed whenever there was a bar fight."

"Of course," Greta said wryly, giving her friend a sideways glance. She sighed as she got to work.

Repairing broken wood was a lot like trying to build a 3-D puzzle when half of the pieces were missing. It was amazing how much one splinter was integral for the whole piece, especially if the piece in question was weight bearing. Like a chair.

Luckily the mystery witch had, for all intents and purposes, just thrown it around rather than blasting the furniture to smithereens. Most of it was still intact, and Greta was able to convince the wood to repair itself around the splinters and jagged edges so that the end result was as good as new.

"That's a handy skill," Nicky remarked, eying her progress.

"No kidding," she agreed.

"Is that why the furniture in the library looks like it's ready to fall apart in a good wind? You just keep patching it back together with spells?" Mikael asked innocently.

"Pretty much," she replied with equanimity, refusing to take the bait. If he couldn't see the value in restoring something that was perfectly comfortable, that wasn't her problem.

"The back door is going to be harder," Jessie said. "It's shattered."

"Yeah. We're going to have to improvise something," Greta agreed. In the end they took the door off of the storage room, and Greta performed some neat little spell work to convince the wood that it was really supposed to fit the door frame. Jessie reforged the hinges and lock, and together they set new wards and reinforced the remaining old ones.

"There. Those assholes are in for a nasty surprise if they try to take those down," Greta smirked as they stood in the garden and inspected their work.

The new wards gleamed like platinum as the first rays of the morning sun touched the building. Jessie had intertwined strands of fire throughout an earth defense system Greta created. Combining the effort meant that if someone tried to tear through these wards, the backlash wouldn't be as concentrated. Plus they threw in an added bonus spell that guaranteed that the intruder would get a healthy dose of the backlash too.

"Well, I think this is about as good as we're going to get until the brownies come this afternoon," Jessie said as they went back inside. She glanced at the brothers.

"The sun's coming up. Are you going to be able to get home okay?"

Vampires could function during daylight, but their powers were greatly diminished. They wouldn't be able to shapeshift and fly.

"Yeah, I figured Greta could, you know..." Nicky trailed off with a vague wave of his hand. Greta sighed.

"I should start charging for fares," she complained. "Fine, I'll port you back. Jessie, will you be okay for a minute?"

"Actually, I want to go home too. I want a shower and a good cry and my bed."

"Understood. I'm going to pick up my car and then do the same. You and I used a lot of magic tonight, and we need rest– you more so than me. I'll tell the page at the Hill to let us know when the brownies are on their way, but in the meantime, try to get as much sleep as you can. Come on, boys," Greta commanded, pointing down the hall.

"Boys?" Nicky protested. "You know we're older than you, right?"

Jessie listened to them bicker as their voices faded before being cut off by the Library portal. She looked around, tears filling her eyes before digging her keys out of her pocket and locking the front door behind her.

Her Prelude sat forlorn and alone in the parking lot. She checked it over thoroughly. Satisfied that it had not been tampered with and nothing was lurking in the back seat, she drove to her little stone cottage, blasting Toadies and singing at the top of her lungs.

Her house hadn't been messed with either, reinforcing her belief that the attacks were aimed at the group as a whole and not her specifically. She stood under the hottest water she could stand before falling into bed and passing out in a deep, mercifully dreamless sleep.

Not nearly long enough later, she woke up for the second day in a row with the sense that she wasn't alone. Rupert was next to her pillow, every hair on his body standing on end, prodding her with one huge paw.

"You have to get up now," he said as soon as she opened her eyes.

"What's going on?" she asked, struggling to sit up. Somehow she had managed to completely wrap the blankets around her legs, and that, combined with a giant cat taking up half the bed, made it a little hard to maneuver.

"You are in danger. *We* are in danger. You must get up now. We must get the others to the Library as soon as possible."

"Okay, just... can you please move? I can't do anything as long as you have me trapped in the bed like this!"

He snarled in frustration and jumped off the bed, pacing up and down the bedroom floor. She rolled out of bed, narrowly missing the end table, and pulled on her jeans and a t-shirt while tripping over his tail as she tried to move past him and out the door.

"If you don't get out from under my feet, I will make you wait outside," she finally snapped in irritation.

"Fine, please hurry!" he begged as he ran out the door.

She grabbed her phone and keys and struggled to lock the door and call Greta at the same time. Greta answered the third time Jessie called while she pulled into the empty parking lot of the bar after driving one handed and yelling at Rupert to stop blocking her mirrors.

The bar was closed two days a week so the staff could have a few days off and Jessie could train her apprentices. She had planned to finish restoring the bar and fleshing out the doppelgängers this evening. She suspected that was going to have to wait.

"Jessie? What's going on?" Greta's voice finally came through the other end, sounding as groggy as Jessie felt.

"Rupert woke me up. He's panicked. He said we all need to get to the Library right now, that we're in danger. I'm going to call the boys. Do we have a way to get in touch with LaSalle?"

"Yeah, I gave him his phone when I picked up my car. What time is it?"

"Goddess-forsaken-o'clock. Oh, and bring coffee," Jessie added before hanging up and calling Mikael while dropping the wards so she and Rupert could get in. It was pointless to try Nicky at this time of day. He could sleep through a war.

"Jessica, I swear by everything holy and otherwise, if this is not a matter of life or death, then I will not talk to you for a year after all this is over," Mikael snarled into the phone as she opened the entrance to the Library, almost getting knocked over by Rupert who ran past her, tail still double its size, and his ears flat against his head.

"It's a matter of life or death. Get Nicky up. I'm sending Greta to come get you. She's bringing coffee. Do you drink coffee? If not, then I'll drink your coffee."

"Touch my coffee and die, witch," Mikael growled before hanging up on her.

She called Greta again.

"I'm up!" Greta yelled.

"Bring the boys coffee. They're very grumpy."

"I can't imagine why. If it were anyone other than Rupert, I would have said to fuck off."

"Does anyone actually have LaSalle's number?" Jessie asked, watching Rupert pace in front of the fireplace. The rest of the cats had scattered except for Sunny and Spot who came running as soon as she opened the cat food and dug out their bowls.

Silence.

"Crap. I did not think about that," Greta finally groaned.

"Yeah, let me try Cassie and see if she remembers what it was. See you soon. Do not forget the coffee."

"I'm getting the coffee!" Greta snapped before hanging up.

Jessie dumped food in the bowls as all five cats came out of hiding and tried to trip her by running underfoot and screaming.

She dialed Cassie's number and frowned as it went straight to voicemail.

"That's weird," she said as she tried again. Same thing. "What is it?" Rupert asked.

"Cassie's phone. It's going to voicemail. She never turns it off," Jessie told him, fighting down the wave of trepidation that crept up from the pit of her stomach.

She pulled up Caroline's number and called. Caroline finally groggily answered.

"Jessie? What's going on? Why are you calling so early? Is everything okay?"

"I don't know. Did you say Cassie was with you yesterday?"

"Yeah, we grabbed her when she called me in a panic because she couldn't reach you. You really should start checking your messages, by the way."

Jessie chose to ignore that.

"Her phone is going straight to voicemail. Are you sure she's still there?"

"No, you just woke me up. Hang on..."

Jessie heard the clunk of the phone being put down and voices in the background, then running footsteps before Caroline grabbed the phone again.

"She's gone! I don't know when she left, but her shoes, keys, and bag are all gone! I don't see her car either!"

"Damnit" Jessie yelled. "I bet you anything she figured that no one would be up and that it would be safe to leave. Why the *fuck* couldn't she stay put for just one day?"

"I'm so sorry Jessie. I should have known. I should have watched her!" Caroline wailed.

"Stop blaming yourself; that's not going to help anyone," Jessie snapped. "Get Jared up. Where are you? I'm coming to get you right now."

"Jared's apartment."

"I'll be there in exactly thirty seconds," Jessie hung up the phone as she crossed the room to a battered desk in the corner and rummaged through the drawers before pulling out a decrepit, extremely gaudy ring that looked like it came out of a bubble gum machine (because it did) and slipping it on her finger.

"I have to go get the kids. Cassie's gone. I don't know where she is, but if she's not answering her phone, then it can't be good. If Greta and the boys get here before I get back, tell them to stay put."

She didn't wait for a response before twisting the ring three times, picturing Jared's living room, and stepping through the portal that opened up in his apartment.

Half an hour later, they were all in the Library with a large amount of caffeine and joined by John and LaSalle. Jessie couldn't stop pacing, wracked with worry. Caroline was a miserable huddled ball on the sofa, face splotchy with tears. It had taken all of Jessie's considerable powers of persuasion to get her apprentice to abandon her plan to run out the door and start a world wide manhunt for Cassie.

"I need everyone's attention, for we do not have much time," Rupert said, watching Jessie's pacing with his emerald gaze. "I am now certain my companion is not the true Madame Blanche."

"I could have told you that," LaSalle shrugged.

Everyone stared at him.

"Would you care to elaborate?" Jessie asked incredulously.

"She drinks," LaSalle said and then stopped, as shocked by his words as the rest of them.

Jessie and John stared at each other.

"That's it!" she yelled. "That's what I couldn't put my finger on! She can drink a drink, and when I took her to the morgue, she fainted!"

"She hit the ground like a ton of bricks! I am so stupid!" John started pacing too, almost walking into Jessie.

"Do not blame yourself, Sheriff," Rupert said. "I have traveled with the real Madame Blanche for centuries, and I knew something was wrong, but every time I tried to think about it, the thought slipped away like trying to look at something in the dark."

"Exactly, I always knew something was wrong, but I couldn't figure it out until you said she wasn't the real deal. Then it was crystal clear," LaSalle added.

"How *did* you figure it out?" Greta asked Rupert.

"I had flown back to the hotel and had just landed outside her window. She took off her opal, and when she did so, her real face was revealed. She does not know about my crow form."

"Then where is the real Madame Blanche?" Nicky asked.

"The *völva* who turned Brigitte into the necromancer was extremely old and very powerful. With that kind of power at her fingertips, Brigitte could have helped the cabal imprison Madame Blanche anywhere," Greta said. "We should ask Mara if she has any ideas. It might be a place that's only accessible to the Fae."

"You're right. Where's the paper?" Jessie asked, rummaging in the desk drawer.

"I don't know. I thought you had it last," Greta said, bending down to look in a drawer under her feet. She looked up to see everyone staring at her in disbelief.

"We have two of the most powerful witches in the world at our disposal, and they can't find a piece of paper. This is great," LaSalle muttered to Rupert.

"Found it!" Jessie exclaimed triumphantly. "Where's the pen?"

"Oh for fuck's sake! We'll be here all night," John complained to Mikael who sighed and rubbed his temples.

"Found it!" Greta held up an ancient quill. Jessie scratched out a message, folded the paper into an airplane, and threw it out a little window that appeared next to the fireplace and opened into blackness.

"Centuries of technological advancement, and we're talking to fairies with paper airplanes," Jared shook his head.

"Technology doesn't always work between this plane and the faery mounds unless it's one of Cassie's phones. Paper airplanes do. Moving on," Greta said, pointedly ignoring the skeptical looks. "We're obviously dealing with a very complicated cloaking spell."

"Can she do it to us again?" John asked.

"No," Jessie replied. "Cloaking spells only work on a person once. Now that we know the truth, the spell can't deceive us again. But we need protections in place, and I kind of want to know why she chose to kill Morticent."

"I don't think Madame Blanche could have produced the amount of blood we found or did the damage that was done to his body," John said doubtfully.

"Madame Blanche couldn't do that kind of damage. But assuming that Brigitte is the one masquerading as Madame Blanche and we don't have more than one necromancer out there, a banshee can shred a person in seconds," Greta pointed out. "He probably came really close to blowing it for her the night he made Nicky start to turn and had to go. My guess is she lost control of the obsession 'love' spell she placed him under."

"Because she has an immense amount of power and no idea how to control it," Jessie added.

"What do we do now?" Rupert asked, settling into a loaf position in front of the fire. "We can't let her know that we're on to her."

"I need to let the Witch Council know as soon as possible," Greta said, jumping off of the cabinet and starting to pace around the room too. "And we need to see if we can bring the *völva* back. She's the only one who can tell us exactly how much power Brigitte has at her disposal and what she can do. Rupert, what does she travel with? We already know about the opal– that's probably one of the primary talismans. Is there anything else?"

Rupert considered.

"Her jewelry case. It stays with her always."

Greta nodded, "Makes sense. It would be a logical thing for a woman in her position to have at all times, and they could have channeled power into each piece. I wish we knew more, like how much she's already used and what she has left."

"How much power does it take to do her cloaking trick and keep herself changed like that?" Nicky asked.

"The initial spell would have been hefty, but it doesn't take much to maintain in short bursts," Jessie said. "The power source for the spell is probably tied to the opal, which is why she always wears it. I'll bet you anything it was inside the locket she had on last night."

Rupert stood up and stretched, unfurling his giant pink tongue.

"I will go back to the imposter and play the role of the comforter as I have done before. But I must ask. What do you think she did with the real Madame Blanche? I do have a fondness for my companion, and I would like to know her whereabouts."

"I don't know," Jessie said, exchanging glances with Greta. "She can't be killed since she's already dead, and White Ladies can't be caught in spirit traps like regular ghosts," her voice faltered before she continued.

"Try to think back to the last time you remember her acting, well, normal. We can start from there. Like Greta said before, it was probably after she reached the States. Maintaining that kind of spell in plain sight of everyone for an international flight would be risky and a drain on her magical resources.

"I will ponder on it," he replied. " But for now, I must go back lest she become suspicious."

"Yes, you do. I'll find a way to reach you if we learn anything new. But be safe! Do not stay there if you're in danger."

"You are an exceptional being, Jessica. I am grateful to know you," he said solemnly.

"Same goes for you," she smiled. "No matter what happens, you always have a place here."

Greta opened a portal onto Peachtree Road a block from the Waldorf, and he stepped through, tail high, without looking back. They watched him go in somber silence.

"Now what?" John asked.

"LaSalle, I need you to go back to the Duchess and find out when the doppelgängers will be ready," Jessie said. "Greta–"

"I'm taking your apprentices to Isabel," Greta told her in a tone that brooked no argument.

"Which is exactly what I was going to ask."

"I know," Greta said flippantly.

"Why do we have to leave?" Jared demanded.

"Because you're not trained enough to go up against a cabal of witches with Goddess only knows what kind of power and talismans at their disposal, and while the Library is probably the safest place for you to be, eventually you're going to want things like food and bathrooms," Jessie told him.

"Isabel sounds nice."

"I thought you might feel that way. Also you can help her find Cassie," Jessie pointed out.

Caroline looked up hopefully.

"Do you think so?" she asked.

"Yes, but you need to go now while you can still get

Cassie's trail," Jessie said as Greta began to push the pair through another portal. This one opened up on a beautiful, airy room lit by skylights and with a barn owl on a perch by Isabel's desk. Isabel looked up without surprise.

"Took you long enough," she said. "Do you need my help there?"

"No," Greta shook her head. "But you need to let the council know that the cabal is back– or at least a new one is– and Madame Blanche is missing. A necromancer has been masquerading as her for a while under a very slick cloaking spell."

Isabel sat back in her chair and looked at them.

"Ah," she said finally. "I'll handle it. What else?"

"Find our friends," Jessie growled. "My apprentices can give you more information, and Renard is coming back with a shaman he thinks can help rescue Charlie."

"Charlie is gone," Isabel said flatly. "I see. This is very bad. Go take care of it. I'll protect the young ones."

"Thank you," Jessie said as the portal closed behind Caroline and Jared. She turned back to the remaining members of the group.

"You got one of those portals for me? I can't seem to be able to reach the Hill from here," LaSalle said, red faced from the effort. Greta opened a third panel that looked out on the parking lot of the cathedral.

"I'll be back as soon as I can with the doppelgängers," he promised as he stepped through. "And then there were five," Nicky said ominously.

"Yeah. Let's hope it's enough," Jessie said. "Wait– did anyone remember to get LaSalle's phone number this time?"

"Aw, crap," John groaned.

16

Jessie knew something was wrong the minute she passed back through the portal into her office. She froze, causing John to run into her.

"What is it?" he whispered.

"I don't know. Please tell me we reset the wards when we came in," she whispered back.

"Um, I don't think we did," Nicky hissed.

"Fuckity fuck fuck, everyone go back!" she started to turn when the spell hit her, freezing her where she stood while blackness descended on them.

"Leaving so soon?" Madame Blanche's voice came out of the darkness.

"I left the stove on," Jessie retorted, her mind racing.

The effort to freeze two powerful witches, two ancient vampires, and a werewolf had to be huge. Either the necromancer had access to more magic than they thought or she was close to the end and just didn't care anymore. She decided to take a gamble.

"Brigitte, we know it's you. Why don't we sit down and talk face to face?"

"Face to face... Interesting idea," the voice changed from Madame Blanche's urbane Parisian accent to a wild, soft Irish brogue.

"The last time I was face to face with your ilk was when your noble Greta tried to save me. I'm not even mad anymore. She tried to do what she thought was right. But now I'm doomed for all eternity. Do you even know what it's like? Everything you touch crumbles. Everything you care for is destroyed in front of your eyes over and over. You're afraid to leave your cell because you might care about something that is taken away, so you pass every day in hiding."

"We can find a way to help you. This wasn't your fault. You were tricked. There has to be a loophole for that somewhere," Jessie said, her heart twisting as she listened to the unspeakable loneliness, bitterness, and pain in the banshee's voice. The darkness lifted, leaving them all blinking in the sudden light.

Out of her peripheral vision, Jessie could see John, Greta, and Nicky right behind her— but Mikael hadn't made it through when the spell hit. She wondered if Brigitte realized that he wasn't there.

She could feel the bar's protection magic begin to worm its way through the forcefield that held her captive. If she could just get one finger free and get Mikael out of the library, maybe they would stand a chance.

The banshee walked into her line of vision, her diminutive form in Madame Blanche's clothes giving the impression of a child playing dress up. Jessie had to remind herself that this was actually a creature who wielded a tremendous amount of power and not a vulnerable caricature.

"Oh, lass. If I hadn't made the devil's bargain the second time, then I might believe you. But you know as well as I that there is no coming back for me now. I'm going to do what I was sent to do so that she'll kill me and end it all."

Out of the corner of her eye, Jessie saw a tiny hog-nosed bat start to make its way across the floor. She desperately thought of anything to keep Brigitte talking and distracted so she wouldn't notice Mikael creeping up behind her.

"Who's she and what is it that you are supposed to do?" Jessie asked, trying to keep Brigitte's eyes on her. She felt the binding around her left hand give way.

"Kill you and Greta and make it look like the wolf turned on you. I admit, I wasn't counting on the vampire being present. At least now I get to say how sorry I am to your face," she nodded to Nicky, who watched in silence, his face a mask of rage.

"Warsaw was a good person and kind to everyone. I swear on the Goddess and my home that I did not know that he was to be killed or hurt in any way. I didn't know anyone was supposed to be hurt in the beginning except for Robin," she said. "If I had known, I would have never agreed."

"Did you order it to be done?" Nicky asked softly.

"No. I did not. I was told to use the magic I was given to make a spell that would hide whatever happened in a room and to make a talisman for Marshall so that he would become obsessed with you. I didn't know until after he was gone that the gargoyle was meant to die. You were supposed to turn on the human and kill him here in the bar, proving that cryptids and witches and humans couldn't get along. Then the talks would have to stop. But you have to believe me, I never would have ordered the gargoyle to be killed. I would have found another way."

"I see. And did you kill Marshall?" Nicky asked.

"No. I did not know he was dead until you found him. I was not the only necromancer they made. The one who took down your wards and tried to attack you last night was one of my sisters, but she craved power and begged for them to turn her. 'Twas she who slaughtered the boy. Robin… well, he was no friend of mine. I admit I knew that it was iron in the syringe, but I didn't know he would get that sick. I swear I didn't want anyone to die. I have to live for death. I do not have any desire to bring it about myself."

"Well then," Nicky said sadly, "If you want to make it right, tell us who is behind this."

"And tell us where Madame Blanche and our friends are being held. We already know that the *völva* wasn't behind this or she wouldn't have been attacked and left for dead," Jessie chimed in. "She's not, by the way. That's not on you– yet."

Brigitte drew a sharp breath.

"She lives? But I saw the killing blow be struck!"

"Which is why you should never underestimate an ancient and powerful witch's will to live," came Mikael's voice, cold as winter, from behind the banshee as an iron blade appeared at her throat. She screamed as the iron burned her skin, and her scream was terrible, full of agony and pain. Jessie could see angry red welts bubble across her neck right before Brigitte's purloined magic exploded.

"Mikael, don't," Greta begged as the binding spell broke, ducking as a shaft of lightning barely missed her head and blasted the wall behind her. "She's already suffered more than any being deserves to."

John staggered into Jessie, almost knocking her over, and jerked her out of the way of another lightning bolt that threatened to fry them where they stood.

"What do you mean making it look like I turned on them?" he demanded angrily.

"When the first plan failed, I was told to create a distraction," Brigitte gasped, struggling in Mikael's grasp against the iron. She had wrapped her hands around his arms, fire flaring between her fingers as she tried to break his grasp. He didn't flinch.

"If it looks like you, a cryptid leader in the community, killed two ancient witches, then the talks will be stalled long enough for the ones behind this to take power. I do not know what they did with your friends or the White Lady. After what they did to the gargoyle, I didn't want to know anymore. I just did what I was told and hoped they would kill me too."

Mikael was losing his grip as Jessie fought to control Brigitte's fire. Brigitte may have the power of an older witch, but Jessie had centuries of training behind her. Springing forward, Jessie grabbed Brigitte by the wrists, forcing the fire back inside Brigitte's skin and causing the banshee to shriek in pain and fear.

A banshee may look small, but like gargoyles, they possessed a tremendous amount of strength that belied their size. Sensing how close she was to freedom from the iron blade, Brigitte redoubled her efforts and slammed her head back into Mikael's chin, sending him reeling while flinging Jessie across the office as if Jessie were a rag doll.

She whirled on John, the change into her true form beginning. Her mouth widened until it was impossibly big for her face, and her fingers elongated into talons. She lunged for his throat as she drew in a breath for the death wail– that never came.

Staggering back in disbelief, she looked down at the holly inlaid silver dagger protruding from her side and then up at Nicky who met her wondering gaze with quiet sadness, his hand still on the hilt.

"I forgive you," he said. Tears welled in her eyes as she reached out a trembling hand. He gently kissed it and clasped it to his heart. "Be at peace, Brigitte."

He gave the dagger one last twist, and she sank to the floor at his feet. The office was silent except for Greta's muffled sobs.

Jessie sat down heavily, oblivious to the tears streaming down her face. John dropped down next to her and pulled her to his chest. For once, she didn't pull away. Nicky sat down on the other side of her, and she wrapped an arm around his shoulders while Mikael held Greta. They were still like that when LaSalle and Annie burst through the office door and froze at the scene before them.

"Oh, Brigitte," Annie gasped, a tiny hand going to her mouth.

"It was merciful," Jessie said dully. "I mean, there was an iron knife being held at her throat because we had to, but her death was quick and merciful."

"I forgave her," Nicky said softly. Jessie stroked his curls. LaSalle roughly cleared his throat.

"Well. I suppose the Duchess needs to be told," he said.

"Yes. And we still don't know where Madame Blanche is, and we still don't know where they have Charlie and Cassie. We're running out of time," Greta said in a subdued voice.

"The doppelgängers are ready for you," LaSalle said. "We weren't sure if it was safe to bring them now or not, so they're still at the Hill."

"We need to let the Duchess know what happened here," Annie added. "We got the letter you sent, and Her Grace asked me to try to help. I'm sorry, but that needs to wait. We need to take Brigitte home.

"You should do that now," Jessie said, pushing off of John's shoulder to lift herself to her feet. LaSalle bent down and gently lifted Brigitte's body. She looked like she was simply asleep except for the dark green stain the color of marsh water at night that spread across her blouse.

"Wait," Greta pushed past Jessie. "We need the opal! If we're right, then it's one of the main sources of the *völva's* power. We can't let whoever's behind this get their hands on it."

"Goddess, I'm glad you remembered that!" Jessie exclaimed. "Is she wearing any other jewelry?"

"Here, take these," Annie said, gently removing a simple pair of emerald earrings and a delicate gold filigree bracelet.

Jessie took the jewelry from the brownie. She could feel the power in each piece. "Do you need one of us to go with you?"

"I think it's for the best if the Duchess hears what happened from you. Can you come?" she asked with pleading eyes.

"Of course," Jessie said, squaring her shoulders and lifting her chin. "Nicky and I will go."

"I'm going to find Rupert," Greta said.

"I'm going with you," Mikael informed her in a tone that had no room for argument, which was fine because she had no intention of arguing.

"Actually, none of us should probably move around alone right now. Take John too. And hide these in the Library vault," Jessie decided, handing the jewelry to Greta.

"Good call," the sheriff nodded. "Also, LaSalle, we all need your phone number. There's no point in you having a way to communicate if we can't actually reach you on it."

"Can it wait? My hands are a bit full at the moment," the Nain Rouge said, struggling awkwardly under the mound of Madame Blanche's clothes that shrouded Brigitte's body.

"I'll get it when we get to the Hill. Come on. We need to go," Jessie said, pulling Nicky toward the door, Annie close behind.

"Annie, can you get us there? Or do we have to drive?"

"No, I'll get you there. But you know how you are with vertigo, Jessie. Do not throw up on the Duchess' clean floors!"

"Why does everyone think I'm going to throw up all the time?" Jessie complained as she followed them through the portal to the cathedral on the other side.

17

Death was never an easy thing for a witch, especially when it involved a being who should have lived forever. Poor Brigitte had suffered for so long though, that it was almost a mercy at this point. Still, that didn't make facing Mara any easier.

Annie's portal let them out at the stairs to the cathedral where Dain waited, rigidly at attention. He was so pale that he looked almost translucent. Death hit the immortal Fae much harder than even the witches. Their little group paused at the base of the steps, Brigitte cradled in LaSalle's arms. Dain swallowed hard as he looked down at them.

"Milady Brownie, Milady Witch, Milord Vampire, and Milord Nain Rouge, I greet you on behalf of the Duchess of Green Orchards on this saddest of days. She bid me tell you that all but the witch and vampire are welcome in these halls," he announced, his voice cracking at the end.

"I understand," Jessie bowed her head. It wasn't that she was suddenly a pariah. The death rites were so sacred and private that not even a witch as old as her had ever witnessed them.

"I know this is a difficult time and I am asking a lot, but I need to speak with the Duchess. There is very important news I must share," she said, palms up in supplication.

Annie stepped forward.

"Aye, I'll vouch for that. Be a good lad and fetch Her Grace," she ordered.

Dain bowed and slipped inside the building. LaSalle followed without saying a word. He didn't have to.

Jessie wiped tears away again, trying to regain her composure in the face of everything they were up against and still yet to come. She could mourn the senseless death later. Right now she needed to rally their allies and brace for what looked like an upcoming war.

"Jessica, please come with me. Nicodemus, if you would be so good as to wait for us here," Mara's voice spoke from behind them. Jessie turned to see her friend dressed in a simple gown of green velvet that was so dark, it was almost black.

"Like Brigitte's blood," her mind whispered before she pushed the thought down and stepped forward to take Mara's outstretched hand. Mara tucked Jessie's hand into the crook of her elbow as she led the little witch along the path to a simple herb garden filled with plants Jessie hadn't seen in centuries.

"This was her favorite place. She was afraid to come here too often though. When you live in fear that you might destroy something because the universe must have its due, then are you really living?" The Duchess mused.

"She didn't know what they had planned when she agreed to be turned a second time," Jessie told her. "By the time she realized what they were doing, she was too far gone."

"If she wielded the power then did they control her though?" Mara asked.

"You can have all the power in the world, but if you don't know what you're doing, then you aren't really in control. If she had come to one of us once she was changed into a necromancer again, then we could have helped her and probably restored some of the balance in the process. But she let this group, whoever they are, make her believe that they had all of the power."

"And so they did," Mara said quietly.

They sat on a simple wooden bench under an old oak after Jessie finished telling her friend everything they learned from Brigitte about the cabal's plans and the second necromancer.

"She wanted to die," Jessie sighed. "She really believed there was no way out. She tried to attack us hoping we would kill her, and Nicky did it in the most merciful way possible in the end."

She paused, fighting back the tears that threatened to spill over before continuing, "I need to ask, do you have tabs on any other harbingers from Faery who might be used in the same way? Especially ones who were used in the past?"

"Not many survived that massacre," Mara shook her head. "The Witch Council probably knows better than we do. Brigitte came to me, but she was the only one. However, any harbinger can be used. We must speak to the High Court as soon as possible, especially if there are Fae like the one who attacked your wards begging to be turned."

"Yes. I have one other request. We're running out of time to find our friends. If we don't find Charlie by tomorrow night, he may never come back. And we don't know where they put Madame Blanche. Do you have any ideas? Anywhere that would be used in Faery?"

Mara stared thoughtfully into the distance. "I don't, no. How did you discover what happened to Brigitte?"

"Greta found out from the Earth at the site where the ritual took place. That's also where she found the *völva*."

"Then my advice is go there and see what can be discovered. Tell me where it took place, and I'll reach out to the Fae in that region for assistance. This concerns us all and should not be hidden."

"It was close to a marsh in Ireland, probably Brigitte's home. From a magic standpoint, that would have been the best place to turn her if they wanted her to be as strong as she possibly could," Jessie said. "How is Robin?"

"I'll make sure the Fae in that area are ready for you," Mara nodded. "Robin is better but still weak. He hopes to return within a fortnight to show his gratitude to you personally for your part in his salvation."

"That's not necessary," Jessie protested.

"Not to you maybe, but he quite holds himself in your debt for life, you know."

"Great. First a half-cocked Visigoth vampire and now a puck," Jessie's mouth quirked. Mara smiled and patted her hand.

"Do not discount your allies, my dear, nor those who owe allegiance to you. I fear that we are in for quite a long battle, and we will need all the help we can get."

"Truer words were never spoken. I've taken too much of

your time already," Jessie said, coming to her feet. Mara rose gracefully beside her.

"Of course, and you are always welcome here. Well, not at the moment, but you understand."

"I do. I'm sorry again that we couldn't save her."

"Try as you might, you can't save everyone, my little witch," Mara said, leaning forward and kissing Jessie on the forehead.

"Take these. They contain the living essence you need to create your doppelgängers," she handed Jessie two carved wooden puzzle boxes. "Now go save your friends. We will be in mourning for three nights' time, and then we shall come to your aid if you need us."

"Okay. Oh, and have LaSalle text me with his phone number so we have it," Jessie added, hugging her friend as the path dissolved, leaving her and Nicky in the parking lot. They looked at each other as she realized that neither of them drove, and her Library portal key was sitting on her desk.

"I really hate flying," she groaned as he gave a little chuckle, scooped her up, and let his large, bat-like wings that morphed from his shoulder blades carry them into the air.

18

Greta looked at John and Mikael after Jessie and Nicky left with the fae.

"We can go through the Library," she said. "Come on. We need to hurry. If Rupert's at the hotel when they figure out that Brigitte's dead, then he'll be in serious danger."

"Ready when you are," John said, and they turned as one back through the portal, leaving a pool of brackish, green blood behind as the only evidence of what had happened for anyone who came looking.

The portal let them out in Madame Blanche's suite at the Waldorf Hotel. The rooms looked like a tornado had touched down. Clothing and furniture were scattered everywhere.

"Someone was looking for something," John said grimly.

"Let's hope they didn't find it– or Rupert. Stay close and search everywhere," Greta ordered. Mikael looked at the sheriff.

"You know, it occurs to me that we have an excellent opportunity to take advantage of our supernatural senses," he remarked. John grunted.

"Yeah. I guess you're right," he said, shaking himself into a huge red wolf with golden eyes.

"Look– or smell, rather– for Rupert and Madame Blanche. Also catalog any scents you pick up so we can come back to that later," Greta said.

John gave her a look that clearly said, "stop telling me how to do my job" before lowering his nose to the ground. Mikael frowned.

"We do not know how many other necromancers or members of the cabal are here. We need a way to get that information."

"Yeah, and I bet they've all come through here at some point or another," Greta agreed thoughtfully. "Our good sheriff already has the scent of the one who killed Marshall. John, did you get Brigitte's scent when she attacked us earlier?"

The sheriff sat back on his haunches and regarded her with his golden gaze before yawning, scratching himself behind an ear, and putting his nose back to the ground. Greta and Mikael stared at each other baffled.

"Was that a yes?" Greta asked.

"Either that or he has spent too much time around Rupert. Or both," Mikael shook his head.

John's nose led him to the bedroom, its furniture hidden under the chaos of strewn clothes and upended bags. There were still no signs of Rupert or anything that even faintly resembled a jewelry case.

"Can you do anything... witchy to see if you can recreate whatever happened here?" Mikael asked with a vague waving motion of his hand.

"Witchy?" Greta asked, amused. "I haven't mastered

recreating events in time. That's Isabel's thing. I don't have the control to fine tune what I'm looking for, and frankly, I'm pretty sure there are probably things we don't want to see here."

"Can we ask her for help?" Mikael asked.

"Yeah, but I don't know when she can get here. We kind of dumped a couple of kids on her and then told her to call an emergency session of the Council. I think we need to get as far as we can on our own."

"We may not have to," John called from the bathroom, back in his human form and sounding insupportably smug. "I just picked up Rupert's scent, and I'm pretty sure I know where he went. That is one smart cat."

"Show us," Greta ordered, leading Mikael into the marble tiled room.

"Look," John said, pointing to a small vent close to the floor. "The screws are a tiny bit loose."

"Wait, so you're telling us that somehow he got through there?" Mikael asked, baffled. "How did he get it unscrewed?"

"Jessie told me that he can shift to human form very briefly," Greta told them. "I bet that he unscrewed it, became something smaller, and then just pulled it back into place."

"And if he was carrying the jewels when he shifted, they'll still be with him wherever our clothes and belongings go when we change into animal forms," John finished her thought, gesturing to include himself and Mikael.

"Oh, good cat," Greta breathed. "We have to figure out where this goes."

"Oh, if only one of us could become a small animal," John

deadpanned, glancing at Mikael out of the corner of his eye. Mikael sighed.

"Fine," he snapped before changing into a tiny white-winged vampire bat.

"Oh, you're so *adorable!*" Greta squealed. John started laughing as Mikael squeaked indignantly at them.

"Better go to it, buddy, before she cutes you to death," John said, pulling off the grate so Mikael could get into the duct.

"Wait, how are we going to know where to find him?" Greta asked.

"He'll come back," John reassured her. "Good call on the scents too. This place is full of them. Unfortunately it would take hours to try to narrow down what I'm smelling, and that's time we don't have. Brigitte and the other necromancer are only part of it."

"It was worth a shot," she sighed as he shifted back into a wolf and trotted toward the living room, nose on the ground again. She settled herself on the edge of the tub and waited.

About ten minutes later, although it felt like an hour, Mikael rolled out of the grate and popped back into his vampire form.

"That was surprisingly not as filthy as I thought it would be. Let us gather John and get out of here."

"Did you find him?" Greta asked.

He shrugged. "The trail went cold. I honestly have no idea where he is. We should leave now though."

Greta swallowed against the lump of disappointment in her throat.

"We really have to leave, *now*," he snapped, pulling her to her feet and half dragging her out the door.

"John! Come! It's dangerous to stay here, and we need to keep looking elsewhere," he called out as he strode to the front door, Greta in tow. John popped up from behind the upturned sofa, confusion written across his face.

"What's going on?"

"Just come!" Mikael snapped exasperated.

"Okay, okay! I'm coming," John hurried across the room.

It wasn't until they were out the service door behind the building and across the street that Mikael stopped, turning to them.

"He is on the roof, and there are cabal agents all over that hotel and listening spells planted all over the suite. Greta, we need a beacon and your portal" he ordered.

"What kind of beacon?"

"Anything to signal our location to the cat. Blow out the streetlight if you have to. Something that will let him know where we are."

"Okay, here goes," Greta put her hands on the pole of the streetlight over their heads, forcing her magic into the conduit beneath the metal. John swore and ducked as the light shattered, showering them with sparks. Greta nervously twisted her bracelet, ready to open the door.

"There!" Mikael called out, seconds later, pointing up toward the rising pale moon that still rode nearly full in the sky.

They could see the crow outlined against it, but right behind him was a spreading field of black that quickly eclipsed the moon's light. Greta's eyes widened in horror as she fumbled to get the portal open and pushed John and Mikael into the Library just as Rupert shot through like an arrow.

As she ran through and sharply cut the connection, she saw scores of blood red eyes and yellow, razor-like fangs accompanied by empty howls of madness and screams of rage and hunger.

She sank to the ground against the panel in the Library, shaking hard. Mikael sagged against the wall next to her. There weren't many things that could scare a three thousand year old vampire, but this was definitely one of them. They clung to each other as John began to furiously pace around the room.

"What the *fuck*?" John yelled. "They summoned *ghouls*! What the actual fuck is *wrong* with these people?"

"This is insane. This is so insane." Greta couldn't stop shaking. "Is everyone okay? Did they get any of you? I need to know right now so I can get the anti-venom if they did."

Rupert shifted back into a giant black cat, clutching a jewelry case barely the size of Greta's palm in his jaws. He shuddered, eyes wild, before dropping the case on the floor.

"I am unscathed. I have not seen a ghoul in centuries. Why would they summon a mindless battlefield carrion eater? Do they not know that if the ghouls cannot find a food source then they'll simply make one?"

"And now they're loose in downtown Atlanta," John added.

"I'm starting to feel like we're missing a piece to this puzzle," Greta shook her head. "But they're not all loose in Atlanta. I trapped most of them in this plane when we came through the portal. Eventually they'll be able to find their way back to a populated realm, but for now, we're safe."

"What about the ones you didn't trap?" John demanded.

"When they're denied their prize, they turn on the ones who summoned them. Let the cabal worry about those."

Mikael hadn't moved, and neither had Greta when Jessie and Nicky walked through the portal from the office. John still paced furiously around the room.

"Oh thank the Goddess, you're safe!" Jessie cried, running to Rupert.

"Yes. However, the three of them seem to be broken," he replied testily.

"What happened?" Nicky asked, perplexed, staring from one to another.

"Oh, nothing. Just your every day night trying to rescue a Matagot and a thrice cursed jewelry case while fleeing a squall of ghouls," John snapped.

"They summoned *ghouls*?" Jessie stared at them in horror.

"Yes, ghouls, now you can see why I'd like to get away from that damn case as soon as possible," he snarled, pointing.

They stared at the simple, innocuous case on the floor like it was full of venom.

"Rupert, tell us what happened," Jessie finally said.

"I barely beat the cabal agents to the hotel. One of the first things Madame Blanche– Brigitte I suppose– had done was hide this case in the bathroom. Now I see that it was very peculiar, but then I was under her glamor and thought nothing of it. I was able to remove the case, shift into a mouse, and get into the duct just as they came through the door. I didn't stay to see how many there were. I simply ran. Luckily Mikael found me on the roof right before the ghouls arrived. I thank you for your timely rescue, sir. It seems I owe you my life once again."

"Oh, I am certain that I will owe you mine before the night is out," Mikael inclined his head to the regal cat.

"Great, now that we know whose life is indebted to whom, what are we going to do about this? How safe is the Library against these things, especially if they're trapped on the same plane?" John demanded.

"Pretty safe, actually," Greta told him as she and Mikael finally released their death grips on each other and came to their feet. "The only way to get through is for both Jessie and me to be killed. The magic set in this defense system will hold up, even if our reserves are depleted. It's a lot more complex than the wards on the bar."

John looked skeptical. "Considering how easily they took out the wards on the bar, that's not exactly reassuring."

"It wasn't easy! They had to force me to do enough magic to drain my magical reserves until they were almost depleted, and besides those wards were fairly basic. They were more in place to deter wanna-be thieves, not a power hungry group of renegade witches," Jessie snapped back.

"As much as I too would love to know exactly what you've done differently here, may I suggest that we operate on a suspension of disbelief and come back to the matter at hand, which is that we were chased by a squall of ghouls and why is this case so damn important? Surely it can't be just because of a witch's power," Mikael interrupted their glaring match.

"He's right," Greta admitted. "A witch's power can only be used by that witch. The only exception is if she makes a necromancer. Why do they want it?"

"Didn't you say the *völva* is still alive?" John frowned.

"Yes. She's at the Council headquarters," Greta said. "But

they left her for dead. Until now, no one knew she had survived except us."

"Unless they have a spy in the Council," he pointed out. "Or maybe they found a way to harness that power for themselves. If they go around making witches create necromancers and then killing both, it seems a waste to let all of that power go back into the universe."

"That's a chilling thought. But spy or not, we have to assume they know by now she's still alive," Jessie added. "And if you agreed to undergo the karmic reckoning caused by creating a necromancer and then the people who recruited you tried to kill you and you had a chance to reclaim your powers, what would you do?"

"I would kick some serious ass," Greta said with a grim smile. "I think maybe we should pay a little visit to a certain unconscious witch."

"We don't have time for that tonight," Jessie shook her head. "I have the doppelgängers in my office. We only have until the end of tomorrow night to get Charlie back. We have to move now."

"You're right. I'm sorry. I got caught up in revenge fantasies," Greta said remorsefully, crossing the room to hug Jessie. "But I want to get the case and the rest of the jewelry to Isabel. It will be safer in her personal vaults than anywhere else in the world."

"Yes, and Isabel can decide if she wants to revive an ancient, powerful witch who practices Seidr and might like to help destroy a few shitty witches who tried to screw her over," Jessie agreed.

Rupert shook himself. "Come, let us meet the dopplegängers and, how do you say, get this party started?"

John snorted. "Leave the vernacular to the young kids," he told the big cat as they walked toward the opening to Jessie's office together.

"The dopplegängers are so realistic that it's extremely unnerving. I will never get used to it," Nicky said to his brother as they followed.

"You're probably going to need me if you want to get out that way," Jessie called after them. She stopped to hug her friend back.

"Tell Isabel to hurry," she said.

"I will. Be safe. I'll be back before you know it," Greta promised.

Jessie sighed as Greta's portal closed behind her before turning back to her own and her friends who waited impatiently for her to open it.

"Okay, let's do this," she said grimly.

"Agreed," Nicky said, baring his fangs in an ugly grin.

19

"Wow," John stared in disbelief.

"I know, right?" Nicky agreed.

Perfect replicas of Caroline and Jared stood behind the bar, looking and moving for all the world like the originals down to the little flair Caroline used when she picked up a glass and the wrinkle that formed between Jared's eyes when he concentrated on a task.

"It's so freaky," Jessie said as she joined them. "If I didn't know any better, I would swear they're the real thing."

"Did you find Tug?" Mikael asked, walking over to their little group.

"Jared did," Jessie replied. "He's on his way."

"Good," Rupert purred.

"I'm back," Greta said from behind them.

They turned to look at her.

"What did Isabel say?" Jessie asked.

"The *völva* is already awake. Isabel said she knows you. Her name is Gertrud. Does that ring a bell?"

Jessie's eyes widened.

"Oh you have *got* to be kidding me!" she exclaimed. John looked at her, puzzled.

"Who's Gertrud?" he asked

"Oh, just the witch who started to train me in the art of Seidr before she decided to join the original cabal. She's so old and powerful that she predates the Icelandic Saga period. She joined the cabal because she didn't believe that witches would ever be allowed to exist in peace and therefore they should claim the power of the world for themselves."

"I mean, I'm not saying that she's right, but out of all of the reasons why anyone joined that group, that's the only one that made any kind of sense. Greed and being power hungry were the dominant reasons from almost everyone else," Greta shrugged.

"What else did Isabel say?" Mikael leaned against a table.

"Nothing yet. She said she would give us more information as soon as she got it. I don't know if she's going to give the case back to Gertrud."

"Well, there's no telling how much of the power was even touched if she's that old," Jessie pointed out. "It's very possible that Brigitte didn't put a dent in it."

"Yes, and we still don't know if the old cabal is reforming, if it's a new group, who they are, why they tried to kill her, and if she's ever going to want to rejoin them," Nicky pointed out.

"Well, if it's questions you have, I would be happy to answer them for you," a Scandinavian accented voice spoke from behind them.

They turned and looked at the woman in the doorway of the bar. She was voluptuous with thick blonde hair that fell over her shoulders and high cheekbones. She regarded them with ice blue eyes.

"I take it you're the reason why we're all here," Jessie said, a dangerous edge underlying her pleasant tone.

"Indeed," the intruder said.

She strode into the room and settled herself at the bar, resting her gloved hands on the bartop. DoppelCaroline and DoppelJared looked at each other and then at Jessie for guidance. Jessie casually walked behind the bar as if the witch at the other end was just another customer.

"Tea?" she asked.

"You're too kind. I believe I'll pass though," the other was just as polite.

"And may we ask to whom we have the honor of speaking?" Mikael asked. The tension in the room was so thick that it could be cut with a knife.

"Where are my manners? Of course you want to know who has dogged your heels for the last week and will soon be responsible for righting the world order. I am Astrid," she inclined her head.

Jessie swallowed a sigh. Great. Another world domination plot.

"Our pleasure," Greta spoke up. "I don't suppose you'd be interested in telling us where our friends are. It's just that we really want them back and all. I'm sure you understand."

"Oh, Greta, always the impatient one," Astrid tsked disapprovingly. Considering that this woman was, by all appearances, a very young witch, her superior attitude was ridiculous, and Greta didn't try to hide her amusement at the other's hubris. Nicky openly grinned.

"Go ahead and laugh, vampire," Astrid hissed, her facade cracking. "I single handedly destroyed my mother, who was older and far more powerful than any of you could ever dream of becoming, and I will destroy you!"

"Your mother. That would be Gertrud I assume? Who's not very thrilled right now, from what I understand," Jessie leaned against the bar, cradling a cup of hot tea in her hands. Sometimes being a fire witch was very convenient.

Uncertainty and fear flashed across Astrid's eyes for a split second, but that was all Jessie needed to know that not only was she right, but Astrid did not, in fact, know that her mother was still alive.

"Tell me, when did you 'kill' your mother?" Greta asked, using air quotes. "Oh, right. After she made your necromancer. But wait. She was powerless then, wasn't she? How does that make you a badass? And while we're at it, how many members of your little group did you lose to the ghouls? Because after we eluded them, I imagine they decided to turn to other sources for food."

Astrid scowled.

"The ghouls were nothing," she sneered, attempting to regain the upper hand. "We easily put such creatures in their proper places, as we shall do to all who cross us."

"In other words, you ran away" Greta said, still leaning against the wall. Astrid looked from one of them to the other, growing more and more unsettled.

"You're not really behind this, are you?" Jessie cocked her head as she fixed Astrid with her piercing blue gaze. "Someone else convinced you to be the face of the new regime but neglected to mention little things like if a ghoul is summoned and denied their reward, they will hunt those who summoned them to the ends of the earth and beyond. Or that if you're going to try to distract a couple of really fucking old cryptids and witches then you should do your homework. Maybe get to know them a little better."

"No matter," Nicky said, moving toward Astrid like a cat stalking a mouse, the flighty, vain vampire persona replaced by an apex predator. "We'll just ask Gertrud after we finish taking care of you. Oh, did we forget to mention that whoever is pulling your strings knows that she's alive and at the Witch Council along with the banshee's talismans? You. *Failed.*"

He was on her at the last word and had her by the throat just as she let out a terrified squeal. And then all hell broke loose.

Witches in cowled hooded robes poured through the door in a mob. Greta and John launched themselves over the bar, and Greta pulled on the leyline beneath the bar to throw up a shield around them.

"Now would be a good time to go all wolf," she shouted at John.

"Where's Rupert?" he yelled back.

A roar that could only come from a lion broke out on the other side of the room.

"Found him," Jessie called out as a witch bounced off of Greta's shield and went flying into Mikael's waiting razor sharp talons and mouth full of fangs.

John shifted into his wolf form and caught the nearest cabalist by the throat, ripping it out and dowsing Jessie and Greta in arterial spray.

"Oh, nice!" Jessie groaned, shooting a wave of flame darts

into the crowd, catching the witches' robes on fire and piercing their bodies.

"Don't hit the boys!" Greta yelled, using her shield to deflect magical attacks back into the enemy while opening up the floor under a group of cabalists' feet and trapping about half of the mob in the stone beneath the bar.

"Greta!" Jessie protested in horror.

"What? They're not going to die! They're just trapped," Greta defended herself as she caught another magical attack and launched it back where it came from. The cabalist went down like a lead brick.

"Fine, but you had better let them all out when we're done," Jessie scolded, a wave of flames rippling from her fingers and setting fire to the row of cabalists pressing in on them.

"Wait, how come you can set them on fire but I can't bury them alive?" Greta objected as the burning cabalists ran screaming out the back door and toward the pond behind the building.

"Because I said so."

"That is so unfair," Greta sulked.

Mara had done a good job with the doppelgängers. They fought back just as hard, pulling from the ether to create missiles that they flung in the faces of the cabalists, causing them to stumble backwards disoriented. Some began fighting their compatriots, mistaking them for the enemy.

"Get the apprentices! Kill the witches!" Astrid shrieked hysterically. Somehow she had gotten out of Nicky's grasp. Her army, face to face with fully turned vampires for the first time, fell back from his fury as he stalked her, oblivious to the rest of the mob.

"Yes, get the apprentices!" her voice rang out next to Greta, who almost dropped the shield in surprise.

DoppelCaroline, now DoppelAstrid, grinned at her.

"No one said we had to be locked into one form, you know," it said as it jumped over the rail, followed by DoppelAstrid number two. Together they waded into the crowd, yelling out random commands and sowing chaos.

"Listen to me! I'm the real Astrid," she shrieked, red with fury.

"No, I am!"

"No, I am!"

"Oh, this is beautiful. It's too bad Charlie's not here to see it," Jessie marveled.

"Yeah, well, we may not be here either if this goes on too much longer. They're young and unorganized, but there's a lot of them, and we were already pushed pretty close to our limits," Greta said.

"Tug should be here any minute," Jessie gasped as a wave of magic burn and exhaustion swept over her. The constant attacks and distractions of the last week on top of the spell to purge Robin of the iron poisoning had done their job, keeping her and Greta's energy levels low enough that they wouldn't be able to keep this up much longer. She blasted another wave of fire darts at a row of cabalists trying to attack John from behind as he ripped through a witch's hamstrings before taking out her throat.

"I hope he gets here soon," Greta snapped.

"Wait, what was that?" Jessie asked as the room collectively froze in response to a massive bellow that shook the bar. "It's Tug! He's here!"

"Oh, thank the Goddess!" Greta almost sobbed in relief, her shield beginning to falter under the constant onslaught.

Tug burst through the door, ripping the frame out of the wall, and waded through the cabalists, dropping them with blows from his massive fists and bellowing all the while. Jessie had never seen an ogre rampage. "Epic" was the first word that came into her head. He had grown so big that his horns brushed the ceiling. The cabalists' attacks bounced off of him like his greenish-gray skin was as hard as diamond.

"Get the ogre! Kill it!" Astrid's voice screamed in panic from somewhere in the crowd.

"Okay, we really need to do something about her," Jessie snarled.

"I think we're good," Greta started laughing as Tug trampled the crowd to form a path to Astrid, who scrambled backward over her fallen comrades right before his giant fist popped her on top of the head, laying her out like a sack of potatoes.

Unfortunately, this just enraged the cabalists even more, who doubled their efforts. Even though Tug had put a sizable dent in the enemy's forces, Jessie, Greta, and their friends were still outnumbered.

Rupert and John fought back to back, the witches' attacks bouncing off of Rupert's coat. John was limping badly, and bloody froth dripped from his muzzle. Mikael and Nicky were still going strong, but daylight was less than an hour away, and they would lose more than half of their strength once the sun came up. All the cabalists had to do was stall for time, and the vampires would be finished. Jessie's leyline worked against her as a trio of cabalists used it to power a magic net designed to hold down the ogre, whose bellows grew louder as he struggled to free himself.

So when John suddenly raised his head and howled, Jessie was so surprised that she almost missed her target.

"Jessie, focus! Shielding both of us is hard enough," Greta snapped, fatigue coloring her words.

"No, listen!" Jessie yelled, her exhaustion forgotten in her excitement.

There, behind the screaming of the cabalists, Greta heard it too: the call of the pack.

"*Yippee ki-yay, motherfuckers!*" Cassie screamed as she burst through the door wielding a saber and on the back of a centaur who loosed arrows from his long-bow into the crowd so fast that his fingers were a blur. Greta and Jessie stared in shock as the werewolf pack, claw of werepanthers, the Suttons' clan, a Lamia, and two more centaurs entered the fray.

In seconds, the tide had turned with Cassie and the succubi leading the charge. Cassie screamed commands, looking for all the world like a tiny Mexican general, her long hair rippling behind her like a shining mane. If Caroline had been there to see her, she probably would have swooned.

The Suttons stunned their prey into submission while the werewolves and panthers ripped through the cabalists like a hot knife through butter. The doppelgängers constantly shifted, now an enemy, now a friend, creating chaos and confusion.

If Warsaw and, more importantly, Charlie had not been collateral damage, then the death toll might have been very different. As it was, there was no mercy, and the near decimation of the cabalists who tried to fight back was brutal.

Rupert and a gray wolf guided John to Greta's shield behind the bar.

"He's hurt," Rupert told them, worried. "I think he is wounded on the inside."

Jessie went white.

"Greta, please. You have to help him!" she begged.

"I know, I'm trying! John, hold still, I need to see how bad the damage is," Greta snapped in exasperation as the big, red wolf whined and twisted away from her grasp.

"I swear by the three rings, if you bite me, then I will muzzle you!"

He whined again.

"I don't care! Do you really want to bleed out on the floor of a bar?"

He stopped trying to escape her grasp and stood still, flinching as she slowly ran her hands over his sides, using her earth magic to sense the damage.

"You have two broken ribs, and one of them is very close to puncturing a lung, you have a bruised kidney, and I'm pretty sure you have a broken toe. You're definitely out of the rest of this fight. We need to get you to a hospital soon because you're not changing back on your own, and I can't heal the ribs without setting them first."

He whined and snarled.

"So help me, if you talk back to me one more time or even think about fighting again, I will make a crate and put you in it!"

The gray wolf sat on her haunches, tongue lolling out in silent laughter. John limped behind Jessie and sat down, sulking.

"Um, I think he's going to stay put," Jessie informed her friend, trying to control a fit of slightly hysterical giggles.

"Men!" Greta muttered, turning to see what was going on.

The fight was pretty much over. The remaining cabalists and an unconscious Astrid had been herded against the wall where they were held prisoner by a snarling ring of were-beasts. The Lamia watched hungrily.

"Surely no one will miss one or two," she hissed to Mikael.

"They did destroy the cameras when they tried to attack the bar the first time," he pointed out. "I will not say anything if a few of them go missing."

"We are *not* eating them," Jessie admonished the pair as she and Greta joined them. "Not yet, anyway. Hi, Despina. Thanks for helping out. I'm amazed that everyone rallied so fast."

"And turn down a free meal plus a chance to show these children what true power is? I wouldn't have missed it for the world!" The Lamia glided off to melt back into the shadows.

"That wasn't at all creepy. Where's Nicky? And Greta, you promised," Jessie reminded her friend, looking around.

"Fine," Greta huffed, snapping her fingers. The floor obligingly spit out the rest of the cabalists who lay stunned before being unceremoniously herded together with the rest of the survivors.

"Nicodemus is teaching some of the children, as Despina so aptly put it, a few things about manners, respecting their elders, and why killing his lover was a bad plan," Mikael replied.

"Slaughter. Got it. Did anyone other than Astrid seem to be in charge?" Jessie frowned.

"No, and that makes me uneasy. I suspect we were right

and that she's not the true power behind these attacks. She's too young and full of ego to mastermind everything for which this group is responsible. She is also much too careless. Furthermore, when I discovered Rupert on the roof of the Waldorf, he told me that he found listening devices in the hotel room, and we have to assume they were placed here as well after the wards were attacked. She lacked knowledge that she should have had."

"Plus this fight was too easy, even as exhausted as we were. We never would have made it as far as we did if a seasoned witch had been here. Granted, we wouldn't have made it at all without Cassie or Tug, but if we had been at full strength, we wouldn't have needed them," Greta added.

"I agree," Jessie nodded. "And she didn't know that her mother is still alive, and I'm pretty sure things would have been handled quite a bit differently if she had. Keep an eye on her. We need to make sure that we get her back to the Council and see if we can get some answers out of her."

"Yes, I am certain that her mother has a few choice words for her as well," Mikael bared his fangs.

"Oh, hi, Jess. Nice night, isn't it?" Cassie walked up to them, covered in blood and grinning from ear to ear.

"You do realize that I am going to kill you, right?" Jessie asked in a conversational tone. Calm even. Not at all like the near hysterics she and Caroline had felt hours earlier when they realized that Cassie was nowhere to be found.

"I'm sorry. I know you were probably worried sick, but I knew I could bring everyone together. I've been helping all of the packs and tribes with things like computers and phones so they can be more a part of this world, and, well, not to be insulting or anything, but you're not really one of them or part of their lives like I am, and you were so worried about everything going on and caught up in it, and you were already a target, and I just knew they would listen to me and help. I was afraid that if I told you or Jared or Caroline what I was going to do then either you would try to stop me or someone from the cabal would find out," Cassie said breathlessly, the words coming out in a rush.

Jessie sighed before grabbing Cassie in a hard hug.

"You're right, and if you *ever* pull a stunt like that again, I will definitely... I don't know. But I'll think of something. Nice entrance, by the way. I didn't know you even knew *Die Hard.*"

"I can't breathe," Cassie gasped.

"Shhh...." Jessie squeezed harder.

"Jessie! Let go of me! You psycho!" Cassie squirmed free and scowled at her friend.

"Oh, hey. What did we miss?" Isabel asked from the hallway. She looked around the room, wrinkling her nose at the gore that plastered the floor, walls, and ceiling. "It's going to suck cleaning this up, you know."

"I just fixed all the furniture too," Greta moaned.

"Yep. Well now you can do it again," Isabel patted Greta on the shoulder.

"Thanks," Greta said sourly.

"Jessie, I believe you two know each other," Isabel stepped aside. Behind her, surrounded by an armed guard, was a tall, statuesque woman with silver hair that hung to her knees. Runes were tattooed across her face, and her eyes were such a pale shade of gray that they were almost white.

"Hello, Gertrud. It's been a while," Jessie crossed her arms and gave the other woman a level gaze.

"Jessica," Gertrud acknowledged, inclining her head.

"I believe this one is yours," Jessie nudged Astrid with her toe. "Why did you let her talk you into doing this all over again? Did you learn nothing from the chaos and destruction before?"

"It is not what you think," Gertrud said softly, sorrow heavy in a voice accented from a language that had been extinct for many centuries.

"After we failed, I was content to live in solitude at the edge of the world, alone with my runestones and visions. I saw the error that lay in thinking that the solution to a life spent in hiding was a life spent trying to dominate and rule. I was happy to continue to learn the secrets of the universe and nature. When I decided to birth a child, I planned every step to have my perfect girl. Life was good for me after that, but as my daughter came of age, she became discontent with her lot and disappeared not too long ago. I was distraught. My spirits could reveal nothing.

"Then I received a message telling me that a new cabal had formed and that she was their prisoner. That I had to do what they said or she would die. They were very convincing. Apparently it was nothing for her to lose a finger here or there if it meant furthering her cause because when I started to receive packages of her body parts, I did not think twice before I agreed to do what they asked."

Cassie walked over to Astrid and pulled a glove off of her hand. Sure enough, all that was left of her pinky finger was a bandaged stump.

"For what it's worth, if that is the case then I'm sorry you were dragged back into this," Jessie said.

"Thank you. I am sorry you were as well. I have agreed to remain at the Witch Council until my powers return for my safety. In exchange for protection, I will provide every assistance and piece of knowledge I have to give," Gertrud said, refusing to look at her daughter.

"That will be very valuable. Thank you," Jessie inclined her head in a shallow bow. "Do you know where Charlie was taken?"

Gertrud shook her head, "I know not where they took anyone or where they are headquartered."

"If Astrid took him then do you think she might have put his trap at your home?" Greta asked.

"It is possible, but the only way for me to find and access my home is with the use of my magic, which, as you can see, is no longer mine to command," Gertrud replied with a sardonic twist of her lips.

"I am sorry that your magic is gone, and I hope that your assistance ends your debt to the universe that much sooner," Jessie inclined her head again, swallowing against the lump of disappointment in her throat.

"Come on, let's get these back to the Council. I can't wait to chat with them!" Isabel said, gesturing toward the huddled cabalists and gleefully rubbing her hands together.

"We'll never talk," a witch who bore the ghosts of acne scars across his face and who was young enough that his hair was still brown spoke up.

"We'll see," Isabel said as she waved the armed guard into place. One of them slung Astrid over his shoulder in a fireman's carry. They herded the group through a portal Isabel opened up to the Council Chambers where a room lined with stern-faced witches waited. Gertrud followed as the portal closed behind them.

"They recruited children again," Jessie said sadly.

"I know," Greta said, giving her friend a side hug.

"How can you tell how young they are?" asked Cassie.

"A witch's hair turns gray by the time she's thirty," Jessie explained.

"Oh. Wow. They're as young as Caroline and Jared," Cassie realized, wide-eyed as she took in the scene in a different light.

"I hate people sometimes," Jessie sighed.

"Same here," Greta agreed.

"And we're still no closer to finding Charlie," Nicky said as he joined them. He was covered from head to toe in blood and gore.

"I believe I can help with that," a voice soft with a Louisiana drawl and as rich as dark chocolate and as expressive as a night of jazz on the wind of the Mississippi said from behind them, followed by Renard's trademark bellow as he exclaimed, "Brothers and sisters! We have arrived!"

20

Renard bounded into the bar, stopping short to take in the carnage. For the first since Jessie had known him, he was speechless.

"What in the seven hells happened here?" He finally asked, looking at each of them in turn. Jessie could feel the blood start to dry on her skin. She was not a fan of the experience.

"Well, a bunch of cabalists showed up, then Tug showed up, then Cassie showed up with a bunch of cryptids and succubi, then we kicked a bunch of ass, and now it's over," she leaned against the bar. "How was your night?"

"I am truly sorry I missed it," he said with a slow whistle.

"As are we," Mikael admitted. Renard may get on Mikael's last nerve, but his prowess as a fighter was legendary.

"Why is the sheriff still a wolf?" Nicky regarded John with curiosity.

"Because he has two broken ribs, and he can't attempt the transformation until someone can set them and hold them in place. Otherwise he might puncture a lung, which, I would like to point out again, is an absolute miracle that he didn't do during the fight," Greta spoke up.

"Not for lack of trying," Jessie shot the giant red wolf a dirty look. He whined.

"Come on, let's get you to the hospital," the gray wolf, now a young woman with a long, dirty-blonde ponytail, and no-nonsense attitude, said with a grin. John whined again and limped out the door behind her, pausing long enough to glance back at Jessie who watched him go with a worried look in her eyes.

"Are you the shaman Renard told us about?," she turned back to Renard and the person behind him.

The shaman, a beautiful Black woman with a kind face, regarded them with light brown-green eyes that sparkled with a lively wit. Her hair was cropped close to her scalp, and a simple linen robe draped elegantly over her curves, cinched around her waist with a colorful belt that held a leather pouch on one side. She wore strings of wooden beads around her neck and both wrists.

"I am Caliste," she said, coming forward to clasp Jessie and Greta's hands together. "My dear Renard told me of your troubles. I am very sorry to see this darkness rise up again. I thought we had put it behind us."

"So did we," Jessie said bitterly.

"Don't waste your energy on dark emotions," Caliste fixed Jessie with a calm gaze. Under those eyes, Jessie felt the world of pain and exhaustion she had lived in for the past week slowly drift away.

"Excuse me for asking ma'am, but are you a witch too?" Ruth Ann sauntered toward them. Somehow she made even the obscene amounts of blood covering her look alluring, something Caliste obviously did not mind.

"I am a shaman," she said. "We fall within the realm of witchcraft, but our connection to nature allows us access to the spiritual plane. Some among the other communities of the world consider us to be mystics in that respect. We can heal the spirit and travel through the spiritual realm when needed."

"I see," Ruth Ann pursed her lips appreciatively.

"Excuse me, if I might cut in here," Jessie interrupted, "Ruth Ann, just give her your number or however you can be contacted like a normal... well... I don't know what's normal anymore."

"I'm sure I'll think of something," Ruth Ann said with a throaty laugh.

"I'm sure you will," Caliste smiled enigmatically as she turned her attention back to the two witches.

"I need space to concentrate, and I need a connection to Charlie," she told them.

"I might be able to help with that," Mary Jo said from behind her. Caliste turned, an eyebrow arched in surprise, the gesture filling Jessie with a pang. What if they were too late and Charlie was gone? As if hearing her thoughts, Caliste glanced back and gave Jessie's hand a squeeze.

"It is not too late, but finding him is going to take a little time. May I suggest that the two of you clean up? We will be traveling through the spirit world, and your current state could attract some undesirable attention," she gestured at their blood soaked clothes and matted hair.

"You know what? I think that's a wonderful idea," Greta wrinkled her nose in disgust as she looked down.

"I don't hate that idea," Jessie agreed.

"Wonderful. I will see the two of you back here in half an hour. Come, let's chat," she turned back to Mary Jo and gestured toward the door. "It's much more pleasant outside."

"I can't believe we did this much damage," Mary Jo remarked as they walked out together. She laughed, a sparkling sound. "I haven't fought in a battle like that in quite a while."

"You never really think of the succubi as warriors," Renard commented, watching Mary Jo walk away. Jessie rolled her eyes.

"We'll be back. I'm not saying you *have* to clean up, but if at least some of this was not as... gooey, that would be nice," she batted her eyelashes at the vampires.

"No," Mikael said flatly.

"Absolutely not. I had to clean a disintegrated witch the last time," Nicky scowled.

"I was stuck with your sick the last time we had to clean, and besides, I didn't even get to join in this battle," Renard objected.

"I didn't say you *had* to," Jessie pointed out. "I just mentioned that it might be nice."

"How *are* we going to clean that up?" Greta asked as they walked down the hall toward the library. "It's pretty bad, even for us."

"We're not that bad!" Jessie protested.

Greta snorted.

"Okay, I'll meet you back here in half an hour," she said, going to her panel on the other side of the Library. Jessie waved good-bye as she pulled on her ring and pictured her bedroom.

Half an hour and two glorious showers later, they walked

back down the hall to the bar. The vampires were nowhere to be seen, which was not surprising since the sun was already up.

"I guess your cuteness failed us for once," Greta sighed, looking at the mess which was still as gory. The smell wasn't pleasant either.

"It was a long shot," Jessie agreed. "Where's Caliste?"

"Right here," Caliste drawled from the doorway to the garden. "I believe I have what I need to begin. Are you ready?"

"Yes," Jessie said fervently.

"Good. Let's go outside. The circle is complete," Caliste led them out the back door.

"Aw, man! They shattered that too," Greta complained.

"Yeah, but I think our guys did it this time," Jessie pointed at the carnage in the yard where the cabalists had tried to escape Nicky's wrath.

Muttering under her breath about the lack of appreciation some vampires had for craftsmanship and hard work, Greta followed Jessie and Caliste to a circle of quartz and feathers sprinkled with sea salt and lake water that was set up in the middle of a tangle of herbs and roses. Caliste sank gracefully to the ground, and they followed suit.

"Now. The spirits have told me that Charlie is in a place far to the north, but I cannot see the clear path. So we must find it another way," she said, getting comfortable before pulling out a bottle of red wine, five black candles that she set at the four corners and center of the circle, and a dove from her pouch.

"Mary Poppins had it right," she added with a grin.

"The local fae Duchess told me to go back to the site where

Greta healed the Earth after the necromancers were made. She thought maybe the Earth would help us," Jessie said.

"That seems like a good place to start," Caliste agreed, pulling the cork out of the bottle. She poured it over each candle until the bottle was empty, the wax absorbing every drop, before lighting the candles on fire with a gesture.

"The spirits appreciate a little fine wine every now and then," she explained. "Makes them more inclined to help out."

"Makes sense," Jessie agreed, smiling as she thought about Charlie's portal mug.

"You know, I bet I could help them with that," she said, an idea dawning on her. "I made a mug for Charlie that exists in the spiritual plane so he gets to have his beer. Maybe we can use it to send the spirits in the garden some good beer or wine every so often."

"They would appreciate that," Caliste approved. "Spirits have feelings too. Just because they're not physically here doesn't mean that they don't miss the things they had in life. It can't hurt to get on their good sides either," she added with a little wink.

"This journey is a long one," she continued. "You will see and hear many things that are not meant for the eyes and ears of the living. Whatever you do, never leave the path, and never eat or drink anything that is offered to you. Keep your mind clear. The dove will help us find the way, and you can use your keys to your Library to return home. Do you understand?"

"Yes," they said in a chorus.

"Then let us begin."

She pulled a staff carved from a cypress tree from her

pouch and slammed the butt of it on the ground. The world fell away into velvet blackness studded with twinkling lights like stars. Jessie and Greta both had studied shamanism and mysticism as part of their studies in the many fields of witchcraft, but it had been many centuries since either had walked in the spirit world.

"The lights you see are entry points between the spirit world and the mortal plane," Caliste explained. "We are looking for the one where Greta healed the earth. There are a lot of them, I know, but the Earth in that place remembers you. Concentrate and let her call to you."

Greta cleared her mind and slowed her breathing, reaching deep into her core to the place where her magic rested beneath her breastbone. Jessie had once described her fire energy as an ever moving current, but earth energy was slow and still. She pulled a thread and cast it into the darkness, ignoring the voices whispering around them.

"Come play with us" and *"Just for a little while, the banquet awaits,"* they tried to entice the witches from the path to no avail. Maybe it would have worked if Jessie and Greta were a couple of centuries younger, but the urge to explore when someone tells you not to was gone a long time ago.

"There," Jessie called out as Greta's line of energy glowed bright green and strained toward a point of light.

"Hold on," Caliste warned, neglecting to tell them exactly what they were supposed to hold on to in that vast, empty darkness. She clapped her hands together and slammed the butt of her staff on the path beneath their feet again. The howls of the spirits grew louder as the wind picked up. Jessie's hair flew about her face, and Greta squinted against the gale. Caliste was unperturbed.

"They're going to take us there," she shouted over the literally howling wind. "Don't be afraid."

The witches slowed their breathing and stilled their minds as Jessie intertwined her fingers through Greta's. They felt the ground fall away from beneath their feet, a sensation that was both dizzying and exhilarating.

The point of light became brighter and larger as they shot through the void, opening in front of them until they fell through and tumbled to a halt on a cold, boggy marsh. Well, Jessie and Greta tumbled. Caliste stepped through the entrance of the world as casually and gracefully as if she were out for an afternoon stroll, which, Jessie reminded herself, was probably because the shaman did this sort of thing on a regular basis.

Greta rose to her feet and tried to brush the mud and bracken off of her sweater and jeans.

"So much for the shower," she sighed. "But this is the right place. They did the ritual there," she pointed at a scorched circle of earth. Jessie walked to the site and knelt down, reaching out to sense the ghost of the fire.

"Everything here screams out against the travesty that took place," she shook her head as she stood up.

"That ritual was a very bad mistake," Caliste agreed, looking around them. The marsh lay still under a heavy layer of gray clouds. Not far from the cursed circle was a shack that looked like it would blow over with a strong breeze.

"That must have been Brigitte's home before she went

to Mara's Court," Jessie pointed at the ramshackle building–although calling it a building was generous.

Greta bent down and scooped up a handful of earth. She raised it to her face, closing her eyes and concentrating. Jessie watched.

"The earth will have our answers, I hope," Caliste murmured.

"I hope so too," Jessie said. "Fire moves too quickly to remember. I can tell that the ghost of the fire that was here was in pain at what it was forced to do, but it doesn't know what happened after the ritual was over. Mara said she would ask the Fae in this region to help us."

"And so she did," a lilting Irish brogue spoke behind them. Jessie and Caliste turned to see a slender Fae standing there.

About Jessie's height, maybe a little shorter, he had the alien features and sharp facial bone structure that most Fae possessed along with copper curls that brushed his shoulders, a neatly trimmed beard, and a mischievous twinkle in his amber colored cat eyes. The set of tools in his belt underneath his red coat pegged him as a leprechaun. The discovery that leprechauns were not little men who gave away gold was one of many shocks when the Fae's existence had become known to mankind.

"Greetings," Jessie inclined her head. He returned the gesture with an elaborate bow and cheeky grin. She couldn't help but grin in return. Greta gently returned the handful of earth to the ground and came to join them.

"Did the Duchess tell you why we're here?" Greta asked, the corners of her lips twitching despite herself.

His grin faded. "Aye. I left my Court in mourning to offer you my aid."

Jessie bowed her head in acknowledgment of his sacrifice.

"Just so you know, before you agree to help us, one of our friends had to kill her. She attacked us because she believed there was no other way."

"We know. We do not bear you any ill will. She could have taken many paths, and you are not responsible for the one she chose," he shook his head. "Besides, we know you. You helped many of us when things were worse than they are now. You will always be a friend to the Fair Folk. You may call me Tam."

Caliste remained quiet, watching the exchange and leaning on her staff. Greta glanced at Jessie and then back at the leprechaun.

"We're trying to find our friend. He's a ghost, and he was trapped in a spirit ball. He's being kept somewhere in the far north, and we hoped that the earth could help us. Do you know anything about what happened here?" she gestured at the scorched earth behind them.

"Very little," he answered, scowling at his feet. "What do you know about the witch they used to turn Brigitte?"

"She is a *völva*, an ancient witch from Scandinavia," Greta said.

"Then I would go to that part of the world next," he shrugged as if it were obvious. Jessie bit back a sigh of exasperation.

"We don't know where though. It's a pretty big area. Is he trapped in Norway, Finland, Iceland, Greenland? We need to narrow it down."

"Ah. Aye, you do. Isn't Iceland the green one and Greenland the icy one?" he mused. Jessie fought back the urge to shake him.

"I think the witches are looking for more precise information. Did anyone observe the ritual? Anyone who might have heard something useful?" Caliste stepped in before Jessie or Greta lost their patience.

He sighed.

"Apologies. Sometimes all the entertainment we have is teasing witches and mortals. It's just second nature to me now. There is a Fae who lives close by in the swamp, a Fir Darrig. He is willing to speak with you if I deem you worthy of his time. But be warned, he easily takes offense, so watch what you say and the words you use," Tam advised them.

"Oh, don't worry. We will," Jessie said hastily. Caliste glanced at them, puzzled.

"The Fir Darrig are a wee bit sensitive," Tam told her with his dazzling grin. "And being part rat and all, they can be a bit nasty as well. So best watch yourself. Good luck," he bowed, turning back to Jessie and Greta.

"Return here once you speak with Matthias. His hut is in that direction," he pointed across the marshland where watery rays of sunlight tried to break through the gloom, "and we will help you on the next step of your journey."

"Your aid is invaluable," Greta said, a bit taken aback. It showed in her face; his smile dimmed.

"Brigitte was one of many who were duped time and again. If helping you helps our kind, then that is what we must do," he said.

"True. We shall return," Jessie said.

"We shall hope so," his cheer returned and he winked before blinking out of sight.

Jessie shaded her eyes as she turned and looked out across the marsh.

"I guess it's the little lump out there?" she asked.

Greta shrugged, "your guess is as good as mine."

Caliste settled on the ground and pulled a pipe out of her pouch.

"Watch your step," she said as she lit the pipe and drew a deep lungful of smoke. "I'll be here when you get back."

"You're not going with us?" Jessie asked in her best little girl voice to no avail. Caliste snorted.

"And get my feet cold and wet? I'll be right here waiting for you," she said, drawing on her pipe and leaning back against a rock.

"Well, let's get this over with," Greta sighed as together they started out against the chill wind coming off the marsh.

About a quarter of a mile later, complete with countless slips, two falls by Greta who was completely covered in mud at this point, some very cold and wet feet, and a lot of swearing, they reached a well built, low slung mud hut rising from the marsh grass.

"Do we knock?" Greta whispered, eying the wooden door.

"I guess," Jessie whispered back before steeling her nerve and walking up to the door.

It swung open as she raised her hand, and she barely avoided knocking the short, plump, rat faced, dark furred creature in the doorway on the nose. She stared at him nonplussed.

"Ah, you must be the great Matthias we heard about,"

Greta stepped in. He blinked at the two of them, long nose twitching.

"What of it? And who are you" He snapped in a thin, high voice.

"My apologies, please allow me to introduce us," Jessie bowed, regaining her composure. "I am Jessica, and this is Greta. We are on a quest to rid the world of the witches who seek to use the fae to their own ends, and we were told that your wisdom and insight could help us achieve our goal."

"*Nice! Very smooth,*" Greta's voice said in Jessie's head

"*Quiet, I'm trying to work here,*" Jessie replied.

"Hmph," Matthias snorted, seeming unimpressed although his tail arched over his head with a flourish.

"Please forgive us if this is too painful a topic, but we hoped we could speak with you about Brigitte," Greta joined in.

He became very still. For a moment, Jessie was afraid that he would slam the door in their faces. Then his face fell, and he stepped back, motioning them inside.

Despite the Fir Darrig's reputation for shabbiness, Matthias kept a very neat home. The floor was swept clean and covered with a reed mat, and a nest made of scraps of fabric, wool, and grass took up one corner. A questionably smelling stew bubbled over a fire pit in the middle of the room. Jessie remembered learning that the Fir Darrig were carrion eaters and fervently hoped they wouldn't be asked to dinner.

"Sit. You make me nervous with all that standing around," he gestured toward two sturdy chairs along one wall. They each took one. He drew up a third and positioned it so that he faced them.

"What about Brigitte?" He asked curtly, pulling a long

stemmed pipe from somewhere among his patched clothing and lighting it with a coal from the fire.

Jessie and Greta glanced at each other.

"We're not going to insult you by trying to beat around the bush," Greta spoke up, leaning forward in her chair. "The witches who turned her into a necromancer are back, and they're doing it with more fae harbingers. They prey on the fae who feel cursed or alone, and they target those who want a reprieve from their lot in life. We want it to stop. We want to protect the innocent or at the very least, make sure they know what they're signing up for. We also want our friends back. They were taken by this new cabal to try to force our surrender and submission."

Matthias hmphed at that but did not speak.

"What we need from you," she continued, "is to find out if Brigitte spoke to you about her plans to allow herself to be turned again or if you saw the ritual. Anything that could tell us where to go next would help."

He sat in silence puffing furiously on his pipe and staring into space.

"I know you," he said finally, looking up at Greta. "She told me all about you. You're the reason why her lot became so hard."

Greta paled but did not answer. He sighed.

"I see the guilt you feel in your eyes, girl. It's written all over your face. I know it wasn't your fault. She did too, but what's done is done. I'll help you. Not for you, but for her and for all like her. She was as close to a friend as I'll ever have. We're not the pretty ones. We're the ones that make everyone run screaming. So we have to stick together, her and me and everyone else who lets themselves get used because they don't want the world to be afraid of them or hate them anymore."

Jessie swallowed back a lump in her throat at the self-loathing and sadness in his voice, but when she spoke, it was with nothing but respect.

"Our goal is to make anyone who plans to exploit the misunderstood or feared Fae and cryptids think twice. In a perfect world, we could teach Fae like Brigitte to stand up for themselves, but for now we have to settle for protecting them as best as we can."

"And we hope to avoid the mistakes we made the last time," Greta added. "We had to learn too, and unfortunately fae like Brigitte often took the brunt of our lessons. But we're not here to beg for forgiveness or seek atonement. We need to know everything you can possibly tell us about the witch who performed the ritual and everything you witnessed or Brigitte told you."

"Did you know that you did save some of them?" he asked, nose twitching as his tail curled around his body. "Most in fact. You beat yourself up over condemning Brigitte to a lifetime of misery, but you seem to forget that she could have worked to reverse the curse. So maybe you should stop getting so hung up on atonement and forgiveness."

Greta stared at him, startled. He shrugged and took another pull on his pipe.

"We may have a reputation for living like rats and being nasty pranksters, but the thing is that rats are pragmatic, and we have no room for bullshit and dwelling on the past. My advice to you? Move on, get over it, learn from it, and focus on now because that's where the shite is really getting deep.

"Brigitte left to stay at a Court over the seas to try to find a way to get rid of the curse," he continued after a moment. "I heard she came home, and I went to see her. I was there when the ravens came to warn her that the witch was on her way. I watched the ritual. I hid in her hut, and I saw everything. They never even thought to look for trespassers," his lip curled in derision at the sloppy methods Astrid had employed. "I heard the marsh scream when it was done."

"Three of them came, two of them wearing these ridiculous robes with hoods so deep you couldn't see their faces. They stepped out of a rip in the air. They sweet talked her, promised her the moon and stars and absolution until she gave in, and then the oldest of them, the one with the runes on her face, did the ritual. Oh, how Brigitte screamed and wept. She screamed like she was on fire. I don't know what happened to make her change, but it was not a kindness. Have either of you seen or done this thing?"

The witches mutely shook their heads. He sighed and tamped more tobacco in his pipe. It smelled like earth and wet grass and was, on the whole, not unpleasant.

"When it was done, Brigitte was too weak to move, and she just laid there on the ground surrounded by jewelry I guess, although I can't for the life of me think why that mattered," he continued, lighting the tobacco with a fresh coal. "One of the witches snuck up behind the old one and hit her over the head with a stone. She took her hood off then. She wasn't a bad looking one, but her hair was too yellow to be older than thirty if she was a day. They have children running this thing, can you imagine?" he snorted and shook his head before going on.

"The yellow haired one said, 'Now I will have what's rightfully mine, my legacy, Mother. You thought you were so powerful, but look how easily I defeated you.'"

"Yeah, really easy to defeat a witch who just lost all of her powers and is now completely mortal and weakened to the point of near death," Jessie was scornful. Matthias looked at her in surprise.

"Is that what happens, now? Then why would anyone agree to that? You lose your power for a curse?"

"In this case she was tricked into thinking they had kidnapped her daughter and were holding her hostage. The girl even cut off her own fingers to send to her mother to sell the story," Greta told him.

"And when the first cabal rose up, the older witches tricked both death related Fae and cryptids and young, impressionable witches into performing these rites and then killing both once they had no use for them. That's what happened to Brigitte. Greta saved her from being killed by the cabal, but the cabal got the witch who turned her anyway, so Brigitte had to bear the karmic curse for both of them," Jessie added.

He gave a low whistle through his sharp front teeth.

"That's a nasty bit of business. Now I understand a little better why you did what you did and why she felt that there was no hope anymore," he said with a little nod to Greta. "I still think you need to stop beating yourself up, but that's neither here nor there."

"I'll take it under advisement," she said with a wry twist of her lips. "What happened next?"

"Well, Brigitte was unconscious by this point, so they gathered up all of that jewelry, slung Brigitte over the yellow haired girl's shoulder like a sack of potatoes and then they opened another rip in the air and left. The third witch never said a word."

"What did you see through the portals?" Jessie asked.

"The second one was just a dark room. I'm afraid I won't be much help there. But the first one was in the far North. I saw the dancing lights over the fields and mountains in the distance."

Jessie and Greta looked at each other. Matthias watched them anxiously, desperate to help and knowing that he was giving them little to go on.

"Would you recognize the scene if you saw it again?" Greta asked slowly. Jessie cocked her head and looked at her friend, puzzled.

"What are you thinking?" she asked.

"I'm thinking that we ask the Earth to lend us a hand. If Charlie is in the north, then maybe going through their portal is the next step," Greta replied with an ever-so-slightly smug smile.

"You want me to describe what I saw and have the Earth make it for me?" Matthias asked, a gleam in his clever black eyes as realization set in.

"Exactly," Greta said. "We need to go back to the spot where the ritual took place. It's where the Earth will remember the portal and where it is in the most pain and therefore is the most eager to help us. If that causes you discomfort or any anguish, then we can try it elsewhere."

"No, I will do this for Brigitte and for all of us who are feared and taken advantage of," his voice was defiant as he hopped to his feet and plucked a patchwork red overcoat and red cap from a hook by the door as protection from the late afternoon autumn wind.

They had a much easier time crossing the marsh; it turned out a guide who knew where to step was very convenient, and a few minutes later they stood in front of Brigitte's hut again, staring mutely at the scorched circle in the ground. Caliste joined them.

"So our plan is to use this fine personage's memory to recall the formation of the earth and thus our destination?" she asked, drawing on her pipe. Matthias' nose began to twitch almost violently.

"I don't believe we have met," he said with an extravagant bow that rivaled Tam's. He pulled his own pipe out of his coat pocket. "I see you are a connoisseur of tobaccos. Perhaps I could interest you in a trade?"

"Alright, I could get on board with that," Caliste said approvingly, taking his offered pipe and drawing from it before handing him her own. Jessie and Greta stared at them.

"Excuse me," Jessie said, not bothering to hide her annoyance. "While I would love to help create a tobacco trade route, I would also like to find my friend before his soul is ripped apart forever and stop the evil cabal bent on destroying harbingers around the world."

"Of course, of course. Where were we?" Matthias hurried back to the circle.

"What do we have here?" Tam's voice came from behind them.

"Goddess, please give me patience and strength," Jessie muttered before turning around again. Tam stood next to a familiar Puck, one who looked much more pleasant and clean than he had when Jessie had first met him in her bar.

"Robin!" Jessie cried with delight, her urgency forgotten for a moment.

"Jessica! When I heard that you were in need of assistance, I had to help. I owe you my life, my sanity, my reputation, and so much more," he exclaimed, coming forward, hands outstretched. Matthias watched, jaws agape.

"The Earth is ready for us if you are, Matthias," Greta helpfully nudged them back on track.

"Of course! My, the Puck here in my little swamp, what will the others think," he muttered as he scampered to Greta's side.

"What are you trying to do?" Robin asked.

"Matthias witnessed Brigitte getting turned and saw the portal they used to enter this site. He's going to help Greta recreate the landscape he saw so that we know where we need to go to look for Charlie," Jessie explained.

"Did you ask Gertrud if she knew?" he asked. "And, yes. I know she was involved. I was by Oberon's side when Isabel sent an emissary to let him know what happened at your bar."

"But I thought the courts are in mourning," Jessie said, fighting down her uneasiness. Was this another ruse?

"They are," he said sadly. "However, in times of war the mourning rites may be interrupted in the face of a threat so dire that our home and lives are in danger. And I think we all can agree that this counts as one such event. I also feel that I am to blame for I was... unkind before. I believed that the ones who were hurt should have known better than to agree to these rituals, but I never tried to teach them."

"It seems none of us did a good job defending those who could not defend themselves," Jessie conceded. "Gertrud doesn't know where Charlie is. But she also said the only way she can enter her home is through her magic. What if he's there and we can't get to him?"

"Let's find Charlie first and worry about where we can and can't go second if it becomes a problem," Caliste, the voice of reason, pointed out.

"Okay. Yes. That makes sense," Jessie calmed her breathing.

"No, make that one a little higher. No, this part is flatter and broader. No, the mountain is here, you dolt!" Matthias snapped at the Earth in frustration.

"Can we please not insult the element that provides us with shelter and protection and is the source of my magic?" Greta asked, sweating profusely and unable to keep the irritation out of her voice.

"Fine, have it your way. If you so please, your earthness, this mountain is higher than that one. There, is that better?"

"Oh, sure, the sarcasm helps a ton," Greta rolled her eyes. "Is this close to what you saw?"

"It's not quite right, but it's the closest we've gotten yet."

"Okay, stand back," she spread her hands over the tableau. Jessie felt a tremendous surge as Greta's magic pushed through the earth. Matthias swore and stumbled backward, tripping over his tail.

"What is she doing?" he demanded.

"My guess would be asking the Earth to search for the place that matches what you just created," Jessie said.

Matthias swore again and even Caliste stared in surprise.

"She can do that?" Tam asked in awe.

"Ancient earth witch," Jessie shrugged offhandedly and resumed watching in silence.

As Greta concentrated, the landscape under her hands began shifting, the mountain range snapping into clearer focus, the fields rippling with autumn flowers and grains and studded with herds of reindeer, the trees forming black against the sky.

"That's it! Stop!" Matthias yelled, his irritation forgotten in his excitement.

"Lapland," Greta said with a grunt of satisfaction, trying to hide her exhaustion. Neither she nor Jessie were even close to their full power after saving Robin and fighting the cabal. She was worried about what they would find in the far north and how much of her flagging power she had left. If they wound up in a fight, they weren't going to last long.

"The Earth can't open a portal for us, but she can guide us there. It's dangerous for us to use our own portals without knowing where we're going unless we want to wind up stuck in the middle of a tree or reindeer," she told them.

"Then let's go," Caliste said. "But first I want to do something."

The others watched in silence as she knelt down and scattered rose petals around the circle of scorched earth and sprinkled water over the top.

"There. That combined with your aid will help the earth heal more quickly," she stood up and brushed her palms off on her robe that somehow remained pristine. Jessie and Greta, still covered in mud from their trek through the swamp, felt a bit resentful. Caliste grinned.

"Now you see why I stayed behind," she said, reaching for

one of Jessie's hands as Greta took the other one. "Hold on tight. We're still in the protection of the circle at your bar, but the spirit world gets wilder the further north we go."

"I'll reach out to the Northern Fae to help you," Robin called.

"Glad you're feeling better and come visit me soon. Matthias and Tam, that goes for you too," Jessie called as the world dissolved into darkness. The last thing she saw was a pleased grin spread across Matthias' homely face.

2 I

They hurtled through the spirit world again, only this time the wind ripped at their hair and clothing with dagger-like fingers made of ice and screamed in their ears. Speech was impossible. Calista's grip tightened on Jessie's hand until Jessie thought her fingers would fall off.

"Don't let go," Calista's voice warned inside their heads. *"I can't promise that I could get you back this far to the North."*

"The North is the realm of Earth," Greta replied, exhilaration coloring her thoughts. *"I can get us home if we get separated. I know the way."*

"Or we could just not let go," Jessie interjected.

"Well, yeah. Obviously."

Wild music and tantalizing scents of roasted meat and sweet fruit wrapped around them as the spirits tried to entice them off the path.

"Caliste, I can't feel my fingers," Jessie objected.

"Oh, sorry." Caliste didn't sound sorry at all.

Greta's magical cord glowed a brilliant forest green that lit up the darkness like a beacon, drawing them to a rapidly approaching point of light. The spirits' efforts to distract them intensified, visions of dancing, feasting, naked men and women beckoning to them, even their library with the cheerful fire and cats draped across the sofa circling around them in a cacophony of light and noise.

They finally burst through the point of light and rolled to a stop at the base of a silver birch tree reaching up to a brilliant blue sky. Jessie blinked, trying to adjust to the mid afternoon sun. She sat up and shook the leaves out of her hair. Greta and Caliste were a few feet away, trying to get their bearings.

"Does anyone have any idea where we are?" Jessie climbed to her feet, brushed herself off, and turned to realize that they were in the middle of a stunned herd of reindeer.

"Huh. Well, that's something you don't get to experience every day," Greta remarked, eying the stag who couldn't decide whether to charge them or pretend that three complete strangers hadn't just fallen out of the sky.

"So, Miss The-North-is-the-realm-of-Earth, where do we go now?" Caliste asked, smirking as Greta flushed red.

"I got caught up in the journey!"

"We should have brought Matthias. Does anything look like his tableau?" Jessie asked, looking around.

"It's hard to tell through the trees," Greta admitted. "Maybe we should take a step back."

"Hello," said a tiny clear voice from behind them. Greta jumped, and Jessie shrieked. Caliste swore.

They turned to see a small gnome-like Fae staring at them out of one eye in the middle of his forehead.

"Um, hi," Jessie said, regaining her composure. This must

be the Fae Robin had enlisted to help them. The Nisse held out his hand.

"I am Olav. I believe you are expecting me. We are here to aid you in your journey. These are my companions Ingrid and Sharaya," he gestured to the Hulda whose cow tail twitched as she bobbed her head and the Keiju who tried to hide in Ingrid's hair.

"I'm Jessie, a fire witch, and these are my companions, Greta, an earth witch, and Caliste, a shaman. We seek the home of the *völva* Gertrud. We believe my friend is imprisoned in a spirit ball there. We have until the sun sets to find him before his soul is destroyed."

Despite her best efforts, Jessie couldn't control the tremor in her voice.

"We are familiar with Gertrud. We have been her companions for many years, assisting her in her home and with her magic, tending to her when she enters the death trance. And we are familiar with her spawn," Olav spat in the dirt. "Your friend is indeed here. We will guide you, but the way is treacherous. Only one with Gertrud's magic or the Fae that assist her can walk the path unhindered. Our magic lets us see the traps that block your way. We will do the best we can to show you how to avoid them. Come, we must not delay."

He turned on his heel and plunged into the undergrowth. Jessie hesitated, but Greta grabbed hers and Caliste's hands and dragged them forward.

"The path is hidden," she said over her shoulder. "The woods and earth are showing me the way, but they won't be able to show me the traps. By the way, do we have gifts for the Fae who are helping us? Because I'm pretty sure that's expected here."

"Your hair is a pretty gift," a musical voice like bells rang in Jessie's ear as the Keiju danced through the air by her head. "I am Sharaya. Can I have this lock of your hair? It would make the most beautiful silver dress."

"I think we can make that work," Jessie smiled.

"Oh, I can't wait! How I shall shine in the sun and moon!"

"Keiju. So easy to please and so easily distracted," Olav snorted, appearing next to them. "Sharaya, you're supposed to be helping them watch where they're going."

"The earth witch can see the path," Sharaya shrugged, her delicate wings casting a kaleidoscope of images through the air as she spun the pilfered lock of hair through her fingers.

"But not the traps, you empty headed dolt," Olav snapped, irritated.

"Oh, right. I'm sorry, Olav. But this one said I could have her hair as a gift! Isn't that lovely?"

He sighed and rubbed the bridge of his nose.

"Yes, that's just lovely. Please focus! The first trap is coming up."

"Oh, I know what it is! Let me tell them, please!" she begged, clasping her tiny hands.

"That's the point!" he yelled, his face turning red.

"The first trap is in the ground," Sharaya continued, oblivious to Olav's ire. "If you step in it, you will be dragged under the ground and buried alive!"

The witches froze.

"I don't suppose you know where this trap is located," Caliste asked.

"Here, there's a trick," Sharaya said. "Pick up that rock and throw it right there," she instructed, pointing to a spot about three feet ahead of them. Greta touched her palm to the earth and whispered a few words before tossing a rock at a spot in the path hidden under leaves and twigs and swore as it was immediately swallowed up by the ground.

"How many of these traps are there?" Caliste demanded.

"This many," Sharaya held up a four fingered hand, fingers outstretched.

"This one wasn't all that challenging," Greta's voice was colored in doubt. "The Earth told me she would release us at the base of the mountain if we fell."

"Gertrud was more concerned with keeping people out than harming them," Olav explained. "The first two traps are in place for that purpose, as you shall see when we reach the second one."

"What about the last two?" Jessie asked.

"The spawn is responsible for those," Olav's disgust was palpable. Astrid clearly was not a favorite.

"Well, one down and three to go," Jessie commented as they climbed up the steep embankment and edged around the trees to either side of the path, trying not to fall.

Greta sighed.

"You know what I miss?" she asked.

"No, what?" Jessie replied.

"Being able to just walk up to someone's house and say something like, 'Hi, we'd like our trapped friend back now please.'"

Jessie stopped and stared at her friend's back.

"When have we ever been able to just walk up to someone's

house without going through a labyrinth, alternate plane of existence, or trap filled path in the woods?" she demanded.

Greta considered.

"Surely it happened at least once," she objected.

"Not in this lifetime," Jessie shook her head as they resumed their trek up the hill.

The path opened up into a meadow dotted with more herds of reindeer and late fall blooming flowers. A dark forest waited for them at the far side, and about halfway up the side of the mountain, they could see a clearing with a neat, stone cottage nestled among the trees.

"That's Gertrud's home," Jessie said, feeling a pang as memories of studying in this place under the *völva* came flooding back to her. "I wasn't sure if she ever left or not."

"Where's the next trap?" Caliste asked, looking around warily.

"It is here," Ingrid called from the center of the meadow. "You must cross the meadow. That is the trap."

"I see. I don't suppose you have any words of wisdom?" Jessie asked hopefully.

"Yes. Watch where you step. The reindeer have no consideration for others," Ingrid wrinkled her dainty nose as she wiped a delicate hoof on the grass.

"Great. Well it seems simple, which means it's probably really hard," Greta sighed.

"Yep. How do you want to do this?" Jessie looked at the others. Caliste picked up another rock and tossed it into the meadow– where it rolled to a stop at her feet.

"Okay, so we're up against a dimensional rift," she said.

"Would the spirit world be able to help us?" Greta asked.

"Not likely. As you pointed out, the North is the realm of the earth, but it's also the apex of the spirit and magical worlds. Everything is wilder and stronger here, but magic rules. In other words, we can't use a shortcut to circumvent the trap. We have to figure this out for ourselves."

Jessie looked out over the meadow deep in thought.

"What gives a dimensional rift its power?" she asked, watching the herd of reindeer placidly munch on grass.

"Awareness," Caliste said.

"Right. So how are the reindeer able to move around the meadow?"

"They're not aware that they're not supposed to be there!" Greta exclaimed.

"But a rock wouldn't be either, and it came back," Caliste argued.

"Yes, but that's because we threw it. If it could somehow move on its own, it probably wouldn't come back to us," Jessie pointed out.

"So how do we make ourselves unaware?" Greta asked.

"We take away the one thing that's making us aware. We close our eyes," Jessie said, reaching once more for their hands.

"This is lovely. I am so happy we're doing this. Words cannot express my excitement at agreeing to come along with you on this journey," Caliste muttered as they began making their way across the meadow in a chain, Greta leading the way with one hand outstretched.

"Your sarcasm is a joy in my life," Jessie retorted. "Don't open your eyes, no matter what happens."

"I know I'm not. I don't want to see what I just stepped in," Greta said in disgust.

After what seemed like hours, Greta felt her fingertips brush against tree bark.

"Stop, I think we're at the woods on the other side."

"How can we be sure we didn't just go around in a circle?" Jessie's voice sounded doubtful.

"I don't suppose anyone can verify that we made it?" Caliste called out.

"You did, indeed, make it!" Ingrid's voice came from right next to Jessie's head, making her shriek, Greta jump, and Caliste swear for the second time that day.

"If everyone could stop sneaking up on us, that would be lovely," Greta snapped.

They opened their eyes and looked around. The reindeer continued to graze behind them unperturbed. Greta looked down at her shoes and sighed.

"Aren't you glad you weren't barefoot?" Jessie asked. Greta glared at her.

"What's the third trap?" Caliste asked Olav who had appeared by them once again.

"You must be able to pass the peikko who is a prisoner in these woods," he said somberly.

"Any advice?" Greta asked.

"We're running out of time," Jessie said looking up at the sky, worried.

"We'll make it," Caliste placed a comforting hand on Jessie's shoulder.

"To defeat a peikko, you must work together. He cannot be overcome by one alone."

"Wait, the first time you said we had to be able to pass him. Not defeat him," Jessie objected. He gave her a knowing smile, tapped the side of his nose, and vanished.

The three witches looked at each other.

"What do we know about peikko?" Caliste asked.

"Well, the hill peikko lives in the forests. They're not as bad as people make them out to be," Greta told her. "They're more grumpy than anything and just want to be left alone. If you antagonize them, they will fight, but sometimes you can offer aid or food."

Jessie and Caliste exchanged a glance.

"Greta's an expert on this stuff," Jessie told her with a shrug. "Personally, I'm all for playing nice. I'm not a fan of hurting anything that just wants to be left alone."

"Sounds good to me," Caliste agreed.

They turned toward the trees. Greta sighed and squared her shoulders.

"Single file, watch where you're going, and be as quiet as possible. We don't want to sneak up on it, and we definitely don't want to piss it off any more than it's already going to be either," she instructed.

"Yes, ma'am," Jessie said as they started up the gentle slope that led into the forest's edge.

The path was narrow and lined with thick brambles that snagged their clothes. It took all of Jessie's willpower not to start swearing at the top of her lungs after the fourth time she had to stop to disengage her sweater from the thorns.

"If you ask me, the path is the real trap," Caliste grumbled, even her unflappable calm unraveling after she stumbled over a tree root that seemed to come out of nowhere.

"Then why don't you just go back where you came from?" a raspy voice growled from above them. The witches stopped and looked up as a tall, ugly man-like creature with long, tangled hair and a matching beard jumped out of a tree and landed in the path, blocking their way forward. His clothes looked like they were made out of tree bark.

"Hello," Jessie said. "We were hoping we could get by you please. We need to rescue our ghost friend whose soul is about to be sucked into the vortex of a spirit ball that Astrid used to trap him."

Whatever the peikko was expecting, that wasn't it. He stared at them stymied.

"I know you want verification, but seeing as how she tricked Gertrud into helping bring back necromancers and then tried to kill her, we can't give you anything but our word, although we could probably open a portal into Astrid's cell at the Witch Council so you can see for yourself. I understand she's not everyone's favorite around here," Greta piped up helpfully.

"The little bitch ensnared me, and now I am forced to stay here as her trap for trespassers," he snarled, his eyes glowing red in rage.

"Well, have we got a deal for you," Calista stepped forward. "How about instead of making us fight you, we set you free instead?"

"How do you know I won't try to destroy you once I am free?" he asked, saliva dripping into his beard. Jessie resisted the urge to gag.

"We'll take that chance," she said. "This isn't right, no matter what you choose to do with your freedom at the end."

He looked at each of them in turn.

"You might as well take the offer, Grubben," Olav said from a nearby tree branch. "They are honorable. The word of the Fae is behind them. They will set you free."

Grubben snarled.

"I accept. Free me."

Calista pulled a rose quartz bottle out of her pouch and poured a pinch of something pink on the ground in a circle that enclosed the two of them.

"Hold still. This will sting, but I swear on the Goddess that I mean no harm and am not trying to hurt you," she warned him before setting the circle on fire with a snap of her fingers. The flames sprang up bright blue, and Jessie saw the cords of binding that wrapped around his body glow in response. He looked down at his arms and legs and roared in fury, frustration, and a longing to be free.

Caliste pulled an obsidian dagger out of her pouch and passed the blade through the fire three times before walking around Grubben, slicing the bonds as she went. When the last one fell in pieces at his feet, the fire went out. She stood calmly before him.

"What is your decision?" she asked.

"I will not stop you. Go. The one you seek is at the top of this hill in the cave. Freeing him is the last trap for if you fail, you will join him, your soul devoured for all of eternity," he snarled before he took a great leap over the brambles which fell away to show the path stretched out before them.

"I wish he had shown up earlier," Greta complained as she pulled a briar out of her sock.

"Come on, we need to hurry," Jessie said, unable to keep the panic out of her voice. She broke out in a run.

The cottage appeared before them, but Jessie ignored it and kept running for the cave that yawned black and ominous in the side of the mountain behind the clearing. She didn't hesitate at the entrance, summoning a trio of fireballs to light their way and only pausing long enough for Greta and Caliste to catch up. The three of them moved into the pitch black together, the darkness so absolute that it was almost palpable. Jessie's fireballs barely made a dent in the smothering blackness; she was forced to use as little of her remaining power as possible.

"Hang on," Greta whispered, pausing long enough to take off her shoes. She crept barefoot, ignoring the damp autumn chill seeping up from the rock, and listened to the earth beneath her feet as it told her where to go. Beside her, Caliste tapped the butt of her cypress staff on the ground three times, and a pale blue light glowed from the top– the same shade of blue as the spirit bonds that Astrid had used to bind Grubben.

"Between your fire, Greta's link to the earth, and Astrid's magic signature that I captured, we have a better chance of finding them," Caliste whispered.

"Go this way," Greta hissed, leading them into the darkness and trusting the earth to tell her where to step. Jessie followed without question, her fireballs floating ahead of them to light the way.

The path wound steeply down into the cave, sometimes forcing them to squeeze between unforgiving rock walls slimy with moisture and sometimes leading them along treacherous drop offs into nothingness. Even Greta had no concept of how far down the bottom was.

"A long way. That's all the rock knows," she said when Caliste asked.

After what seemed like eons, the path leveled out onto a sandy floor, and there at the far side huddled a wan, pale figure wrapped around a glowing orb.

"Madame Blanche and Charlie!" Jessie gasped, starting to run forward.

"Jessie, wait! It's a trap!" Greta yelled, throwing up an earth barrier in front of her friend. Jessie howled in frustration, letting loose a sheet of fire that melted the sand to glass right as the ground rumbled and split open in front of them.

"What the fuck..." Caliste scrambled backward as the first skeletal hand reached from the chasm for her ankle.

"Oh, are you kidding me right now?" Greta snapped in exasperation. Why couldn't a search and rescue just end with the rescue instead of some ridiculous battle against the undead?

Five skeleton warriors climbed from the rift and faced the witches like silent statues, which was even more unnerving.

"Okay, we need a game plan, and why are you laughing?" Caliste asked Greta. Jessie was locked in on the orb in Madame Blanche's arms, unable to react to the skeletons that blocked their path.

"Because this is quite possibly the stupidest trap in the entire world. I'm starting to question how much Gertrud taught Astrid, because this is so simple that a child could get through it. Skeletons are literally mindless. All they can do is whatever they were resurrected to do, which I'm pretty sure is to stop us from reaching the other side. We just have to distract them long enough for Jessie to reach Charlie. Everyone ready?" Greta asked with a nod to Jessie.

"We distract and she rescues," Caliste agreed.

"Jessie, when I give the word, just go. Don't stop. Get them and get to the bar."

"Got it," Jessie forced out past the lump in her throat. She licked her dry lips and felt the kinetic energy from her fire pool in her gut, more potent than any shot of adrenaline.

"I'll make the bridges across the rift, and Jessie, keep creating glass. It's harder for them to take down. You and I don't have much power left, but we should be able to pull this off. Caliste, call the spirits to help us create a distraction. We have about five minutes to get Jessie to the other side of this cave, but this will only take one at the most," Greta projected into their minds just in case Astrid had the common sense to equip her skeleton army– such as it was– with the ability to hear. "Go!"

The skeletons were completely unprepared. They were more focused on destroying Greta's bridges than stopping Jessie, who simply melted a path of glass through the sand, sliding her way over a bridge and across the cave while adroitly dodging their grasp. Caliste's swarm of spirits harassed the skeletons, causing two of them to stumble into each other, resulting in a pile of bones that tried unsuccessfully to reattach itself at the wrong joints.

Barely a minute after the witches launched their attack, Jessie skidded to a halt on her knees in front of Madame Blanche, who flung herself into Jessie's arms with a strangled sob, clutching the orb like she would never let it go. Greta watched long enough to make sure Jessie's portal opened and her friend was through before grabbing Caliste by the wrist and activating her own portal to the library. She caught a glimpse of Olav's grinning face on the stairs as he waved good-bye, and then they were through.

2 2

"Jessie! Where are you?" Greta yelled as they burst through the Library portal into the hallway of the bar.

"We're in here! I need Caliste now!" Jessie's panicked voice came to them from the bar itself. They ran to meet her, a detached part of Greta's brain realizing that the bar was completely clean, as if the fight had never taken place.

"Give them to me," Caliste commanded, gently but firmly pushing Greta out of the way and moving forward with long strides.

"She won't let go," Jessie looked at them pleadingly.

Greta looked more closely at Madame Blanche and recoiled in shock. The once beautiful woman was now wraith-like, her hair hanging around a sunken husk of a face in a dull, gray veil. She looked like a mummy. Caliste drew in a sharp breath.

"Shit! She bound herself to the orb. She must be feeding him her essence to keep him alive. Jessie, we have to separate them and get Charlie out, and we have to do it fast or we're going to lose them both. This is going to be tricky. The timing has to be absolutely perfect. Do you understand?"

"What do I need to do?" Jessie asked, unquestioningly putting herself into Caliste's hands.

"When I tell you to, you and Greta spin your magic into a fire-earth cord and feed it into the orb like an umbilical cord. This will give Charlie something to cling to so he can follow it out. Jessie, you focus on rejuvenating energy, and Greta, focus on healing and creation. I'm going to drop into the spirit plane with Madame Blanche to break her bond to the orb," she told them, nodding to Madame Blanche. Madame Blanche shifted her grip from Jessie's hand to Caliste's without speaking. Her face became more gaunt by the second.

"Ready... now!" Caliste snapped, slamming her staff on the ground and blinking out of sight, taking Madame Blanche with her. Jessie spun a stream of pure fire that intertwined with a stream of pure earth coming from Greta, and together, they forced it around and through the membrane of the orb. Jessie remained hyperfocused on the cord until she felt the tentative pull from inside the orb.

"Got him," she yelled triumphantly.

"Be careful or we'll lose him," Greta warned. "We have to draw him out slowly. We don't have enough power left to do it a second time."

For what seemed like an eternity they painstakingly withdrew their cord bit by bit until ghostly hands, then arms, then shoulders, then Charlie's head, and then the rest of Charlie tumbled from the orb and floated over the floor between them. Jessie burst into tears.

"Charlie!"

"Don't touch me," he gasped. "I can't handle that right now."

She hovered over him, trying to think of anything she could do to help him. Greta shifted from foot to foot in the background. She knew Charlie of course, but not as well as Jessie. He buried his face in his hands, his incorporeal shoulders shaking.

They stayed this way for several long minutes before Greta cleared her throat, "I'm going to let Isabel know what happened and check on everyone else. Let me know if I can bring or do anything."

"Okay. Thank you," Jessie sniffled.

"Of course," Greta replied, hugging her little friend before heading down the hall to the Library.

"Jessie? Are you in here? *Charlie!*" Caroline and Jared burst through the front door with Cassie on their heels and fell in a heap together at the ghost's side. "Oh, Goddess! You're here! Are you okay?" They started talking at the same time.

"Charlie! I'm so sorry for every mean thing I ever said about the Suttons! I will never be ugly to them again! We thought we had lost you!" Cassie chimed in, wringing her hands as she tried to find some way to hug him.

Charlie drew himself up and blinked at them, his form tinged dark green and purple like an old bruise.

"I never thought I would be so happy to see all of you, and boy, if I could hug you, you better believe I would never let go," he said. "I thought I was never coming out of there. That was..." his voice trailed off as his face blanched.

"It's okay, Charlie," Jessie comforted him. "We're here, but you don't have to talk about it until you're ready."

"*Charlie!*" The earsplitting shriek nearly deafened them as Mary Jo ran through the door and skidded to a halt in front of her ghostly lover, somehow becoming slightly incorporeal herself and flinging her arms around him. The others stared in surprise.

"Well, that answers a few questions," Jared whistled.

"Come on, let's give them some space. She can probably do more for him than we can right now, and I want to find out what's going on with Madame Blanche," Jessie guided her apprentices and Cassie out the now repaired back door and into the garden with a gentle but very firm push.

"How did she do that?" Caroline asked Jessie.

"The succubi are actually a class of demons, so when you think about it, it makes sense that they would be able to link to the ghost world," Jessie replied, filing this new piece of information away for further study.

"Wait, they're demons? But I thought they were cryptids," Jared said, startled, probably thinking about his many encounters with Ruth Ann.

"No one knows where demons fall in the order of things," Jessie explained. "But before you jump to conclusions, you should learn more about them. They're creatures of chaos, but that doesn't mean they're all bad."

"You call Rupert chaotic neutral. Is he a demon too?" Cassie asked.

Jessie laughed.

"No, Matagots are spirits, and they're actually cryptids. No one really knows their true nature though. They're very reclusive and hard to get close to. Rupert is the first one I've ever met."

"Every time I think I'm making progress, you blow my

mind with a whole new bunch of information I never even thought of," Jared shook his head.

"You never stop learning, even when you're as old as I am. But you're stuck with me for a very long time, so get ready to learn more than you ever thought possible."

Jessie's smile faded as she thought about the witches, no older than her apprentices, who had been killed in the attack on her bar. Maybe they were as guilty as Astrid, but they had also been taken advantage of by older, unscrupulous witches who had no qualms about poisoning the minds of the innocent.

"Jessie? What's wrong?" Caroline asked.

Jessie sighed.

"Sit down. We need to have a serious conversation," she told them as she led them to the circle of benches in the garden they used for their classes. Cassie followed, and Jessie realized that she and Caroline were holding hands.

"Oh, did you finally get that out of the way?" Jessie grinned at them. Caroline blushed bright red.

"We'll talk about it later," she informed her mentor. "What were you saying?"

Jessie sobered.

"This was a very bad night. I don't know who cleaned up in here, but I assume you saw the carnage."

"We cleaned it up. It was the least we could do, but it was hard," Caroline told her.

"Yeah. Not gonna lie, I puked," Jared admitted.

"Oh, you probably weren't the only one. Believe me. Even Renard was shocked, and he's a Visigoth," Jessie told him. "The thing is that they were all children. They were your age, maybe even younger. And there were a lot of them. I don't know where they came from, but my guess is they were recruited from all around the world and transported here to attack us.

"The reason why I'm telling you this is because you were their targets too. They thought the doppelgängers were you, and they tried to take you. Whoever is behind this is trying to create an army of expendable, malleable, suggestible young witches that they can throw in the path of the Witch Council as cannon fodder and use in despicable ways for their own ends."

"A bit of an oversimplification, don't you think?" hissed a voice from behind her.

"Jessie!" Caroline and Cassie came off the bench, a saber in Cassie's hand.

"They're projecting," Jared squinted at the glowing figure. Jessie turned and looked the shape up and down.

"Okay, first of all, those robes are ridiculous," she said, crossing her arms. "I don't know if you saw what happened today, but I can guarantee your army could have done a lot more damage if they had been able to see where they were going and didn't keep tripping over the hems."

"Your input is as insightful as ever, Jennet" the voice snarled. "But I think that will hardly matter once the world discovers that you slaughtered dozens of innocent apprentices."

"Ha! Seriously? You're going to try to pin this on her? Have you not heard of social media? Because your girl Astrid sure has, and she had plenty to say all over the internet before she attacked us," Cassie sneered.

The figure grew very still, radiating anger.

"Ah, yes. Astrid," the voice said. "I must thank you for tying up that loose end for me, Jennet. You were always an obedient child. So helpful."

The corners of Jessie's mouth twitched.

"Are you really going to keep pretending that you're my superior right now?" she asked, not bothering to hide her amusement. "You tried to launch an attack on the Witch Council and stop the Alliance with a handful of children, one of whom did more damage to your cause with her ghouls and botched attempts to create necromancers than I ever could. If she hadn't decided to attack me personally, I would have been happy to just sit back and watch your little scheme implode from the sheer levels of incompetence that riddle your cabal or whatever this is supposed to be."

"Oh, you will regret that tone, child," the figure snarled furiously.

"Whatever. Go back to your mistress and let her know that the next time she wants to send me a message, she can talk to me herself and stop wasting my time," Jessie turned her back with a dismissive wave of her hand. The echoes of furious screams rang around the garden.

"What did you do?" Jared asked.

"Sent her back where she came from through a nasty part of the spirit world compliments of Caliste's circle that's still in the garden," Jessie gave a feral grin. "If she hadn't decided to project herself, then it wouldn't have been as much fun. But since she didn't have a body, she can't defend herself as easily on the spiritual plane."

"Why did she call you Jennet?" Cassie asked, perplexed.

"Because that was my birth name. She tried to intimidate

me by implying that she knew me or knew more about me than most, but she failed. Very few people know who I really am– or was. However, I now have a pretty good idea of who she is. In fact, I think I'll pay her and her mistress a visit of my own. I'll bring tea! Maybe some flowers. And a cake," Jessie added sweetly.

"You're scary," Cassie said in awe.

"Thank you!" Jessie beamed. "Look, I know that you know how to defend yourselves. But if you know anyone who is coming into their powers and doesn't have the luxury of studying under a witch like me or Isabel or Greta, then bring them by to talk to me. I won't force anyone into an apprenticeship, but I at least want them to know what they're up against."

Jared and Cassie nodded. Caroline looked at the ground but stayed silent. Jessie frowned as she looked at her apprentice, making a mental note to get to the bottom of whatever was bothering Caroline soon.

"Well, you certainly lead an interesting life, my dear," Caliste said as she came around the roses, leading Madame Blanche who looked more like her normal self.

"Oh, you're okay! I'm so glad!" Jessie exclaimed in relief, rushing forward with hands outstretched.

"*Oui*, I thank you for your part in my rescue. I do regret that I was so easily fooled and captured. There is no telling what damage the imposter wrought in my absence," Madame Blanche said stiffly, pulling away.

Jessie had to remind herself that the Madame Blanche she had gotten to know in the last week had been Brigitte the banshee and not the real White Lady. Apparently Greta's impressions of reservation were right.

"I'm sure you will have everything straightened out in no time," Jessie said in her most reassuring voice. Madame Blanche gave a reluctant smile.

"*Merci*," she said. "But now I must return home. I need to determine what of mine is really mine anymore and set things right."

"Will the talks continue?" Caroline spoke up.

"*Certainement!*" Madame Blanche snarled. "If these imposters think that I am so easily cowed then they are quite mistaken! We will see these peace talks through to the bitter end, come what may!"

She turned to Jessie with a small, shy smile.

"Perhaps I may return and try this visit again?" she asked.

"I would be delighted," The sincerity in Jessie's smile was genuine.

"Then I bid you *adieu*. I must find my companion and return to France. Caliste tells me he became an associate of yours as well. I wonder if perhaps he should remain here as my liaison since it seems that we are equally enmeshed in this conspiracy."

"I would be delighted," Jessie said, surprised and pleased. She had grown fond of Rupert in the past week and was not looking forward to saying good-bye.

"Excellent. Then it is decided. He can easily traverse the spiritual plane between our locations and keep me abreast of your activities and needs."

"Wait, if he can just jump through the spirit world then why does he fly?" Jared asked puzzled.

Madame Blanche raised an eyebrow.

"Are you suggesting that I dictate the whims of a cat?" she asked with a hint of dry humor. Jessie was going to enjoy getting to know the Queen of the White Ladies better.

"Although I was not certain he could fly at all," Madame Blanche continued. "He wisely does not share his secrets."

"Come, let's get you back," Caliste said, gently taking Madame Blanche by the elbow. "There is much to share with the Alliance."

"Until we meet again, Jessica," Madame Blanche stepped forward and to everyone's surprise, kissed Jessie on both cheeks. "Please let Rupert know where I am and that I wish to speak with him at his earliest convenience."

"Of course," Jessie replied. Then Caliste and Madame Blanche stepped into the air and were gone.

"Woo hoo! Rupert's staying!" Cassie crowed.

"Now what?" Caroline asked.

"Now I need to pay a little visit to a certain witch, and you two need to get ready to open," Jessie told them.

"Do we even have enough liquor and glassware left to open?" Caroline asked.

"Huh. I didn't think about that," Jessie paused. "I'm sure you can think of something. Convince everyone that they want beer instead."

Caroline rolled her eyes.

"Right. That's sure to work. Okay, boss. See you back here soon. Come on, guys, let's go get ready."

"Why do you get to be in charge?" Jared argued.

"Because I'm older. Besides, I was here first," Caroline pointed out.

Jessie smiled as she listened to their bickering, the smile fading as she squared her shoulders and twisted her portal ring, picturing Isabel's study and bracing herself for what came next.

23

"Are you sure you want to do this?" Isabel asked for the second time since Jessie had shown up in her office demanding to see Astrid as Greta followed them down the hallway toward Astrid's cell.

"Isabel, she has answers we need, and she's been cast out by her whole group. If I don't talk to her now, then there may not be another chance. You know as well as I do that there's probably a spy here who's going to try to make sure she disappears as soon as possible– or at least shuts her up."

Isabel sighed.

"I know. I just think you're too close is all. I mean, can you really talk to her without thinking about Charlie and your bar and everything she did?"

"It's me or Greta," Jessie grinned. "Which one of us do you want to question her?"

"Never mind," Isabel said hastily. "You do it."

Greta scowled.

"I'm not that mean," she objected.

Jessie snorted.

"You have no patience, the world's shortest temper, and she attacked me and our friends," she pointed out.

"Whatever. Fine," Greta sulked, leaning against the wall and pouting like a grounded child.

Jessie squared her shoulders as she faced the room holding Astrid's cell. It had been decided that Astrid should remain isolated for the duration of her imprisonment. To her surprise and delight, Olav opened the door.

"A pleasure to see you again," he bowed as he joined them in the hallway. "I hope my presence is not intrusive. As Gertrud's oldest companion, she requested that I stay with her."

"We're thrilled that you're here," Jessie told him with a warm smile as Greta nodded in agreement, pique momentarily forgotten.

"The cell is made out of wormwood," Isabel told them. "It's in the very middle of the room, and only the high council can get through the outer door. Since Olav is essentially Gertrud's seneschal, he and Gertrud are the only ones who can get within six feet of the cell itself."

"Gertrud?" Jessie was puzzled. "But how can that be if she doesn't have her magic?"

"Oh, I'm proud of this one," Isabel smirked. "We still have all of the talismans with her magic that she gave to Brigitte. We let her use one long enough to set up the spell of recognition and protection. It's brilliant. She came to me and asked if she could be the one to do it when she found out how we planned to imprison her daughter. As long as that spell is in place, only she and Olav can give Astrid food, bath water, clothes, and take away her chamber pot, and that's it."

"And the spell will be in place until her mother's power

returns because only her mother can take it down," Jessie realized with an extreme amount of delight.

"Exactly," Isabel's smirk turned into a grin.

"Oh, Isabel, that's amazing!" Greta marveled.

"Well, what are we waiting for?" Jessie cackled gleefully.

"Way to perpetuate a stereotype," Greta rolled her eyes.

"You're just mad because you can't come," Jessie sniffed.

"I only want to see her suffer! Is that so wrong?" Greta protested.

"Yes. Now stay here and behave," Jessie ordered.

"Hmph," Greta slid down the wall to sit on the floor and pout some more. Olav patted her on the shoulder.

"There, there. You can watch some other time," he consoled her.

Jessie followed Isabel into the room and suppressed the urge to shudder when she felt the chill from the wormwood, a natural magic dampener, as its bitter scent filled the air. Astrid had watched Jessie suffer enough. She didn't get to see it any more.

Astrid lay huddled on the cot in the center of the cell with her back to the door. There wasn't much else in the cell with her– a chamber pot, a tray with remnants from a meal close to the narrow slot at the base of the bars, some books, and a neatly folded stack of clothes in the corner.

"Astrid, you have company," Isabel barked in a no nonsense tone. Astrid didn't move. Jessie sighed and crossed her arms.

"Astrid, I want to fill you in on a few things, make the reality of your situation a little clearer to you," she began.

Astrid interrupted with a harsh laugh, finally turning to

meet her captors. Her skin was doughy. Her hair hung in lusterless hanks around her sallow face, and there were bags under her eyes.

"Reality? My only company is a Nisse who hates me, I tried to kill my own mother and ruined her life for who knows how long, and the only thing keeping me alive is a spell no one can get past. I never sleep because I can't stop listening for the sound of them coming to kill me, and I can't feel my power."

Jessie and Isabel looked at each other.

"Well, that was easier than I thought," Jessie said. She turned back to Astrid.

"Olav doesn't hate you. Really, really dislikes you... probably. And maybe one day your mom can forgive you and you can start trying to repair that relationship."

"She didn't ask to do the spell to watch you suffer," Isabel chimed in. "She did it so you would hopefully learn your lesson and also not die."

"We need to know everything you can tell us about the people behind these attacks," Jessie continued. "We know they're recruiting young witches. What exactly did they promise you?"

"They promised that we would head up the new world order. That we would be the superior race of beings we were always meant to be and that we would not be buried beneath the hubris of the Fae, cryptid, and human societies any longer," Astrid said in a dull voice.

"And it never occurred to you to talk to your mother about this?" Isabel asked. She didn't bother to hide her skepticism.

"She never talked to me about her past. She refused to

come down off of her mountain and acted like the rest of the world didn't even exist. I was always so angry. That's how they got me," Astrid gave a bitter laugh.

"I thought I was made for better things. I thought I was the next head of the Witch Council. I thought I was so great and powerful. I had no idea. This figure in a robe showed up one day when I had gone down the mountain and told me how my mother was afraid of my true potential because I was a stronger witch than she could ever be and that she was trying to stifle me and stop me from growing."

Jessie snorted, and Astrid flushed an ugly red.

"I know I'm a fuck up," she snapped. "You don't have to rub it in."

"You're right. I'm sorry. Go on," Jessie said.

Astrid looked taken aback. Jessie shrugged.

"Your mother did you no favors when she decided to hide you from the world without telling you why. You grew up lonely, confused, and angry. You do have potential. I don't know if you or anyone will ever be as powerful as your mother— she's very ancient and strong. At one point she was the Witch Queen back when we had courts instead of a Council. She was my teacher, you know, before things happened to make her a recluse."

"What happened?" Astrid asked, her curiosity getting the better of her.

"She needs to be the one to tell you that," Jessie told her. "She should have done it as soon as you started to come into your own powers. Maybe then it wouldn't have been so easy to fool you."

"If she was your teacher then are we sort of sisters?" Astrid asked. Jessie smiled a little.

"I suppose we are. Look, you're stuck here for a very long time. I'll come back and visit you if you want. But if you want to make your time here bearable, consider being nicer and think about repairing your relationships with people, starting with Olav. I met him when I freed Charlie, something you and I are going to have a very long conversation about, by the way."

Astrid looked at the floor, guilt written across her face.

"I know. They told me to get rid of him. The trap was my idea. I own that one. I didn't know what it would do to him until Madame Blanche asked how I thought I would defend myself when you took apart the earth to find the one who destroyed your beloved friend's soul. So I made Brigitte use my mother's magic to open the path to the cave, and I hid them both there. It didn't occur to me that the Fae on my mother's farm hated me so much that they would show you the way," she gave a bitter, mirthless laugh.

"You never play with things you don't understand," Isabel snapped, getting her anger in check. "That's lesson number one. There's no room for trial and error in magic when lives are involved."

"Yeah," Jessie said flatly, her blue eyes flaring in anger when she thought about Charlie whimpering on her floor.

"Anyway, what else can you tell us?"

"Just that we never saw anyone's face. There was only one person who talked to us who said they represented a consortium of powerful witches. I'm not sure if it was a man or woman, but they called me the lieutenant and told me I was in charge of the recruits. I was the first one they brought in. They told me I would be allowed to join the consortium once I passed the test by destroying you and recruiting your apprentices."

"Makes sense," Jessie shrugged. "Grab the young daughter of the most powerful *völva* who ever lived and start filling her head with flattery, empty promises, and half bits of magic and then let her take the fall. Honestly, I don't even know if they'll try to kill you. It sounds like they covered their tracks pretty well. They never gave you anything we can work with."

"Great. I'm not even worth killing," Astrid morosely stared off into space. Jessie rolled her eyes.

"Stop feeling sorry for yourself. You made a stupid mistake that cost dozens of lives, and your pride and misguided sense of self-worth are responsible. No, you're not worth killing. But you can fix what you did and become someone worth keeping alive."

Isabel looked at her watch, a pretty timepiece with an hourglass in the center. "Jessie, I need to wrap this up,"

"Yeah, I need to get back to the bar," Jessie said, turning toward the door.

"Will you really visit me?" Astrid asked, a pleading note creeping into her voice. Jessie hesitated for a moment.

"Yes, I will. I'll come back next week," she agreed.

"Thank you, Jessie. I know you don't have to, but I appreciate it. I think I could learn a lot from you," Astrid said humbly, looking at her hands.

Jessie just smiled as they left the room. She opened her portal and hugged Isabel before she and Greta stepped through.

"Don't trust her," she whispered into Isabel's ear.

"It hurts my feelings that you think I would," Isabel whispered back, and then Jessie stepped through into the warm glow of the bar and was gone.

24

Epilogue

Jessie looked around in contentment. The bar bustled with noise and laughter. Caroline poured out rounds of shots while Jared served foaming pints of beer, and Cassie sat at the top of the bar with a shocking green concoction in front of her, watching Caroline adoringly.

LaSalle and Matthias lounged at the front door next to Tug, passing Matthias' pipe and LaSalle's goblet back and forth. They had immediately bonded over their love of tobacco and beer and became friends overnight, something that made Jessie and Greta very happy after everything they had to go through to make Matthias believe that the invitation to visit Jessie's bar was really sincere.

When an exasperated Tam sent word that Matthias had decided they were just being nice and didn't really mean for him to visit, they camped out on his front steps for two days until he agreed to come to the bar just so he could stop tripping over them every time he tried to walk out the door. Camping on an Irish marsh in late September had been a very uncomfortable experience and one Jessie was not eager to repeat any time soon.

"How's it going with Astrid?" Nicky asked, walking up and slinging an arm around her shoulders.

"Great. She tells us absolutely nothing and asks me to come back and visit. She wants to make us believe that she's reformed and helpless. She's the world's worst manipulator though. She actually told me she thinks she could learn a lot from me," Jessie grimaced.

He shook his head.

"Babies," he agreed, taking a sip of wine.

"How are you doing?" she asked gently.

"I miss him. It's not getting better," he said, his voice sad. "I'm in this with you until these people are ripped apart. I hope you know that."

"I wouldn't want anyone else by my side when we go into battle. Except maybe Renard and Cassie. Can you believe her? I had no idea she could rally that many people on her own!"

"I hope Caroline knows what she got herself into. Charlie looks like he's doing okay," he added with a little nod to where Charlie and Mary Jo nestled in their usual corner.

"Yeah, I don't think she plans to let him out of her sight anytime soon," Jessie agreed. "I didn't know she could fight like that. Their clan made a huge difference for us."

"I was equally indispensable in that little skirmish," Rupert objected from behind them. Jessie turned to him, grinning in delight.

"I, for one, am extremely happy to have you here," she told

the big cat. "I hope Madame Blanche is recovering and that she can come back too."

"She will," he said, grooming his whiskers. "I believe you may have the rare ability to draw my companion out of her shell, something that is a joy to witness and rarely seen."

"Where's Mikael?" Jessie asked Nicky.

"He is with Madame Blanche and Robin at the Alliance Headquarters," Nicky told them. "They're testifying about what happened over the last few weeks. Renard is with them. He managed to convince that Belladonna girl to go and testify on behalf of Marshall."

Jessie winced.

"I hope he brings her back in one piece," she said.

"I'm sure he will, although I make no promises. Matthias looks like he's finally relaxed."

"I know," Jessie agreed. "Robin brought Matthias and Tam to the High Court to participate in the mourning rites there, which is a pretty significant step on behalf of fae like the Fir Darrig."

"Have you talked to John?" Nicky asked, watching her out of the corner of his eye. Something had changed between her and John, and he had a suspicion he knew what it was.

"He should be here tonight. They couldn't get him to change back without puncturing the lung, and he had to have surgery," she tried to keep the worried tone out of her voice. She had only left his side when the nurses explained in very kind but slightly exasperated voices that visiting hours were long since over, and he had to sleep. Or else.

"Here I am," John walked up behind them. "That was very unpleasant. One star, do not recommend."

"Aw, poor thing," Jessie cooed, standing on her toes to pat him on the head. He scowled.

"At least werewolves are fast healers," she pointed out as she wriggled under his arm and gently wrapped her arms around him. "Any of the rest of us would still be in the hospital."

"Yeah, that's true," he admitted, kissing her on top of her head which caused Nicky to choke on his wine.

"What?" Jessie asked with a challenging note in her voice.

"Nothing! Just glad to see you took my advice for once. So what now?" he asked, toasting John who grinned back.

"Well, now we need to regroup," Jessie said. "Greta and I have to present ourselves to the Witch Council with everything we learned and then see how many young witches are missing. We need to try to rescue anyone who's left. And we need to try to figure out how deep this thing goes. Is it just witches? Are there any fae, cryptids, or humans involved? How bad is the infiltration?"

"This seems daunting," Nicky said glumly.

"That's because it is," Jessie sighed.

"Jess, don't get mad at me, but I think it's time you sit down with Tug and get his story. I know you don't want to," John said as he saw anger flash through her eyes. "But we would have been dead if he hadn't shown up. What if there are more ogres out there somewhere who can help us, or worse, be used against us? We need to know what happened to them and why."

Jessie's anger faded as she considered his words.

"You're right," she admitted. "I'll talk to him. But for now let's just enjoy the rest of the night and see what tomorrow brings."

"Agreed," John said, bending his head to give her a real kiss, which resulted in cheers from the bar. She blushed bright red while smiling happily. Almost losing him in the fight had made her reprioritize some things in her life very quickly.

Nicky raised his glass in a toast, "I'll drink to that."

Jessie looked around at her tiny domain and sighed. They were in for a long fight, but at least, for now, she had peace.

Astrid huddled on the cot shivering. Why did it have to be so cold? The wormwood felt like it cut her to the core, fueling her anger and sense of injustice.

"Have I done well, mistress?" she whispered. A shadow detached itself from the wall.

"Well enough. Now sleep. You must have your wits about you for what is to come. Soon you will begin to work on the Nisse. Once you have his trust, your mother will be an easy target."

"I'll trick her. It will be easy," Astrid boasted.

"You are too vain and let pride and ego dictate your decisions. It is time to grow up. We must have the talismans! Do not fail me, Astrid. Your little wormwood cell will seem like a dream vacation compared to what I will do to you if you disappoint me again," the voice hissed coldly, and then the shadow melted back into the wall.

Astrid shivered as she fought down the doubt and regret that grew in the back of her mind. She was in too deep, and there was nothing Jessie or her mother could do to help her now.

"I will not fail, mistress. I will defeat them all. You'll see," she swore to the empty room.

About the Author

Eli Rainwater moved to Durham, NC from Atlanta where she lives with her three cats and drinks way too much coffee. When she's not playing in her garden, she can be found draped over furniture reading a book, throwing a temper tantrum when she plays video games, yelling at the television during football season, or sleeping through one of the many movies and TV series she keeps meaning to watch. You can follow her on Instagram or TikTok at @elirainwaterbooks.